Virginia Dale has had two other books published, *Never Marry in Morocco* (Fifthian Press, 1996) and *The Bushy Daughters Go to War and Find Rumi* (iUniverse, 2007). Both received good reviews in the *Santa Barbara Independent*, and she was scheduled for readings by them at the local book stores. They had several in 1996 and still have an excellent independent one named Chaucer's.

She lived abroad for seven years in Madrid, Spain and Rabat, Morocco, where she became well acquainted with the Spanish, French, and Moroccan cultures. She currently resides in Santa Barbara, California.

Dedicated to Robert and Doris Bywater, my parents.

Virginia Dale

RICH WHITE AMERICANS

AUSTIN MACAULEY PUBLISHERS™

LONDON • CAMBRIDGE • NEW YORK • SHARJAH

Ordering Information:
Quantity sales: special discounts are available on quantity purchases by corporations, associations, and others. For details, contact the publisher at the address below.

Publisher's Cataloguing-in-Publication data
Dale, Virginia
Rich White Americans

ISBN 9781641828390 (Paperback)
ISBN 9781641828406 (Hardback)
ISBN 9781645366225 (ePub e-book)

Library of Congress Control Number: 2019937089

The main category of the book — Fiction / Thrillers / General

www.austinmacauley.com/us

First Published (2019)
Austin Macauley Publishers LLC
40 Wall Street, 28th Floor
New York, NY 10005
USA

mail-usa@austinmacauley.com
+1 (646) 5125767

Chapter 1

A U.C. Berkeley buddy, Jack Smith, introduced me to Andronicus Wyland and a few of his other ultra-wealthy Montecito friends when I arrived, fresh from my junior year, in 1963, to spend the summer with my parents in their new home in Montecito. Everyone told me it was a swell place to live, with trees and spacious gardens everywhere. I was excited and happy to meet my friend's friends.

Andronicus was the stepson of State Senator Michael Dorland. Husky, redheaded with fleshy, ill-defined facial features, he didn't make much of an impression on me until I started losing at a game of strip poker, which I'd never played before. We were in the sumptuous room where his family vault gleamed. You couldn't miss it, even though it was a cavernous room. There was nothing more than a poker table and the vault in it. I had no qualms about the game, since Jack was such a good friend, and it never occurred to me that the boys would take it seriously. We were out for fun, nothing more. I loved my friends, for they were my mainstay, and I wanted to be a part of whatever party or gathering they concocted. Geoff Jones, whose father owned the expensive men's clothing stores called Tweeds and Deeds, and another couple of boys who'd been at the posh party Jack had invited me to, sat next to him. I was meeting people for the first time, finding them amiable and, of course, a bit drunk by now. Alcoholism was rampant in Montecito, I'd soon find out, along with even more devious elements.

My inexpensive bracelet and earrings lay on the poker table. We'd all had a few scotch and sodas, mostly straight scotch in their case, at a lavish party at another Montecito home, before we arrived.

All I had on was my pink party dress, pantyhose and high heels. "Take it off," said Andronicus. He curled his lip as he spoke. He narrowed his small, red-veined eyes and stared at me like a bird of prey. A vision of a white laboratory rat came to my mind, perhaps because I was a psychology major and had worked with lab rats.

"Take me home," I replied. I pushed my chair away from the table and stood up, putting my costume jewelry back on.

"You lost. You have to take off your dress."

Andronicus took another swig of straight scotch in one of his parents' fancy beveled glasses, leaned forward, leering at me. He couldn't take his eyes off my body.

"I said, take me home!"

"You're a bad loser," said Andronicus.

"I'm not going out with you next weekend either." I started walking toward the door.

"She's a Cal girl. I'll take her home," said Jack, backing me up.

I flashed him a warm smile. I figured I had lucked out because I went to Cal Berkeley. I wondered about other girls. I'd heard that the cards were stacked against us, but I didn't want to believe it.

God gave me a curvy wiggle of a butt and a cute face with a hint of mischief to top it off. People who didn't know me thought I wasn't what I really was: dead set on graduating from Berkeley and getting a job.

I got into Jack's shiny black sports car, and we thought nothing more about it. He'd dropped out of Berkeley and gone to USC, but we'd always maintained a good friendship. He was outgoing and fun, which was all I required of my friends in those heady days of the early sixties. He respected me, never pressing for a kiss or anything more than friendship.

During the week, I applied for sales clerk jobs and landed one at Bonnie Langley's Music Shop in downtown Santa Barbara. I'd worked summers to pay for my college clothes and make my mother happy. She was frugal, plus Daddy had had a rough go of it lately even though he was an engineer.

Andronicus called me the next day to apologize. I stayed mad at him and said I wouldn't go. He kept calling. He'd take me to the San Ysidro Ranch for dinner and dancing at the Coral Casino afterwards. We'd have a fine time. He wouldn't give up, and he suddenly was all charm. I finally agreed to go, because I liked eating in elegant places and dancing, too. He couldn't be that bad. A bit rude and slovenly, unkempt, but fun was fun.

I put on one of my favorite dresses, a white cotton pique sheath, since we were going to elegant places. Andronicus arrived on time. I introduced him to my staid parents, who shook hands with him, impressed that his father was a state senator. Then, we were off in his bright red Ferrari to the San Ysidro Ranch. I talked and laughed with him, our high spirits bubbling over. The eucalyptus trees that framed beautiful Montecito provided a lush, green background. The air was perfumed by honeysuckle and sweet-smelling flowers that grew in abundance in this lovely town.

I ordered lobster thermidor for dinner at the San Ysidro Ranch restaurant, which was delicious. The restaurant overlooked a lovely wooded area. It was famous because John and Jackie Kennedy had honeymooned there. The other diners ate lavish meals, dressed to the nines. Its elegant, rustic setting made it a popular place to dine, plus the food was reputed to be the best in Santa Barbara. Andronicus was attentive; he made sure I had plenty to drink. Bloody Marys. I loved a good Bloody Mary in the early sixties when I was twenty years old. Andronicus kept putting his fingers in the air to attract the attention of the waiter, saying, "More drinks, and make it snappy!"

By the time we arrived at the Coral Casino, an exclusive Montecito nightclub adjacent to the Biltmore Hotel, we'd gotten pretty drunk. I don't remember what he said, but it didn't matter. I was ready to dance, and dance I did – with half the men at the Casino, young and old. My Berkeley buddy, Jack, laughed at my shenanigans; he knew I loved to dance and cut up. Someone had told me not everyone found my antics amusing; they thought I was unladylike. I ignored prudes and looked down upon them for their lack of courage and ease of condemnation of others. At one point, I danced around a pole, laughing my head off. Andronicus kept buying me Bloody Marys. I was sobering up by the time he decided to take me home. Only, we never made it to my house. Instead, he parked his fire-engine-red Ferrari outside the Plow and Angel, an elegant bar owned by his stepfather, for another drink. As I downed it, he said, "Will you marry me?"

I looked at him. He was serious. At least, he seemed serious at the time.

"I don't even know you," I replied. I swished my long, dark blonde hair over my shoulders as I shook my head. "Take me home." I'd never marry anyone as slovenly as Andronicus. Never.

We got back in his fancy car. He drove to a large house I'd never seen before. This was my second week in Montecito, so I had no idea where we were.

"This isn't my house."

He got out, walked around to my door, opened it, and slung me over his shoulder like a sack of potatoes – a kicking and screaming sack of potatoes.

"Put me down! Take me HOME!"

He stormed up the stairs to the second story of the empty house and flung me onto a bed. I bent my knees back, preparing to stick my spike heels into his plump stomach. He landed on them, pulled my head back by my hair, and took them off. I fought like a demon, screaming and scratching his back with my long fingernails, drawing blood, but he was hefty and I slender. By the time he got my pantyhose off, I asked him if he planned to kill me. I'd heard of rape and murder, in that order. My breath was sporadic; I gasped for air.

He just laughed.

My life reeled before my eyes. I thought fast and said, "Look, Andronicus, I really like you. This is silly to put up such a fight. I want to do it with you." I had to distract him.

He let go of me to unzip his pants. I slithered out from under him, and fleet as a frightened doe, ran out of the house, taking the stairs three at a time, which split my white cotton pique sheath dress up the back. I ran like the devil himself were chasing me to the house next door, hallucinating a Methodist minister opening it, shaking his finger at me.

Instead, a boy my age opened it. He had a drink in his hand. He was tall with dark hair. I shrieked, "Andronicus Wyland tried to rape me!"

He looked surprised. I bolted inside, sobbing hysterically. He showed me to a bathroom, where I tried to calm myself.

I sobbed for a few more minutes. I looked in the mirror and saw a reddened face and watery blue eyes. I wanted to go home. I splashed cold water on my face and dried it. I opened the bathroom door, where two boys my age, Jim Hopman and Bruce Washly stood staring at me.

Jim shoved yet another Bloody Mary into my hand. "What happened?"

"Andronicus Wyland tried to rape me! My purse and pantyhose are still next door in that house."

The two boys exchanged looks. "Hasn't this ever happened to you before?"

"No!" I took a gulp of the Bloody Mary to try to steady my nerves.

"It's fairly common in Montecito."

"My parents just moved here."

"You'd better tell them," said Jim, nodding his head like a sage Buddha.

"I'll go get your things for you," said Bruce, also tall, but he made no impression on me, and walked out. I was still collecting my wits.

Jim offered me a chair, and I sat down. We both had drinks in our hands. Taking each other's measure, he drank some more of his Bloody Mary, and I drank some more of mine.

"He asked me to marry him at the Plow and Angel. I said, 'No, take me home.' He drove to that house and hauled me out of the car. He carried me up the stairs and flung me on a bed." I sniffed and rubbed my eyes.

"Andronicus has a reputation," said Jim.

"As a rapist?"

"He's being taken to court by the head of the Theta House at Amherst for raping her."

"Why didn't Jack tell me this?"

"You're a friend of Jack's?"

"We were friends in my freshman year at Berkeley."

"So you go to Cal?"

"Yes."

"I go to Harvard."

"I've got to go home."

"Where do your parents live?"

"On Cima Linda Lane."

Bruce opened the door, holding my pantyhose and chartreuse-green purse my grandmother had bought for me at Kann's in Arlington, Virginia, my hometown. She had giggled and told me I could buy anything on sale that day. My grandfather, Audus T. Davis, was head of the Washington, D.C., post office. He'd placed first in the civil service test after test and ended up in charge of the post office and two thousand employees, whose names, ages and salaries he knew by heart. That's how we did things in my family. Fair and square. Auntie had been president of the Daughters of the American Republic for thirty years. She and Uncle Emory Starke, the head of the math department at M.I.T. were teetotalers. I was a cork sniffer myself but loved letting loose once I'd had a drink. What people thought of me was of little import. I liked my wild side and my serious, bookish side. It was fun to be yourself, with a little let-the-devil-take-the-hindmost free-spiritedness. Of course, I kept my grades up at U.C. Berkeley with an eye on grad school.

Jim stared at me, wide-eyed. "Andronicus arranged to have the house next door left unlocked," said Bruce. "It's empty because the owners are getting a divorce."

"What!" Stunned, I could barely fathom such a thing as premeditated rape. I was also surprised to hear the word divorce. No one got divorced where I came from.

Jim stared at me. "You'd better tell your parents."

"They'll kill me!" I couldn't imagine telling my Puritanical parents I'd almost been raped.

"Stories like this get around Montecito pretty fast; everyone will know about it."

"Oh." I couldn't believe my ears.

"Why don't you finish your drink and I'll drive you home," said Jim. "Where do you live on Cima Linda?"

"239 Cima Linda Lane."

He nodded his head; Bruce tried to smile, and I finished what must have been my sixth Bloody Mary that evening. In those days, we didn't worry about sobriety. When we drank, it was to have fun. If you had too much, you had a bad hangover the next day. No emergency room visits.

Bruce handed me my handbag, pantyhose, and high heels. I went into the bathroom to put them back on. When I came out, Jim smiled and ushered me out of the house to his car, which turned out to be a new Chevrolet convertible, which it turned out Bruce's father had sold him from his car dealership. I was getting used to ultra-rich kids at this point.

Although my parents had bought a home in Montecito, they weren't wealthy. My paternal grandparents lent them three thousand dollars for the down payment. My dad had a job in Santa Barbara working for AMF as an engineer. He'd been having trouble finding a steady job since he'd retired from the Navy, prompted by having been passed over for captain, crushing his hopes for a career in the U.S. Navy, which he adored. It was a huge blow, as he'd attended Annapolis and all the grads made captain as a rule. He was a WWII veteran, to boot.

I got into Jim's car; he drove toward my house; the wind rushed through my bedraggled hair, reviving my spirits somewhat. I had no idea where I was, but the shapes of shaggy pines and eucalyptus trees reassured me. Nature had always been my solace.

Within five minutes, we arrived at Cima Linda Lane. I saw my parents' home with its spacious driveway and breeze-through carport and said, "That's my house." Jim stopped, opened the car door for me and I thanked him.

He waited while I opened the locked front door to my house. Then, he took off.

I tiptoed to my parents' room. Their door was shut; the house was quiet as a tomb. I knocked at the door. No response. I waited a minute. Then, I cautiously opened it an inch or so and said, "Mother?"

I heard my parents stir in their twin beds, waking from a dead sleep. "Huh? What?" I heard my mother's muffled voice from within the bedroom.

"I have something to tell you," I said.

"Innocence, it's late." She used my full name, Innocence.

"I was almost raped tonight."

A long silence ensued. I felt like I was in a sarcophagus. Finally, my mother said, "Oh, Innocence, how could you!"

I lowered my head at her disapproval.

"Here. You can have a Valium."

"What's a Valium?"

"It'll make you sleep."

Too stunned by my narrow escape earlier in the evening to protest, I said okay. My mother got out of her twin bed next to my father, who seemed to still be sleeping, and put on her bathrobe. I waited behind her as she shuffled through a drawer full of scarves, gloves, and pill boxes and caught the glint of a revolver. I knew they kept a gun because they were always sure someone was about to harm them. I'd never met stranger people than my parents. Their paranoia contributed to my love of wild, devil-take-the-hindmost times. Mother found the Valium and gave it to me. I withdrew from the room, pill in hand.

I found a glass in the kitchen, looked at the pinkish pill in the palm of my hand, hesitated for a second, and swallowed it. I knew my parents wouldn't discuss this with me, nor I with them. We never talked about anything personal, such as our feelings. Then, I went to my bedroom and slept a long time, determined never to date a rich, cocksure ass again. I'd double down on my studies in the Psychology Department at the University of California at Berkeley and accomplish things I'd be proud of, not that I wasn't proud of using my wits and fists to escape rape.

Chapter 2

The next day dawned sparkling bright, a typical day in the woodsy area called Montecito, in Santa Barbara. I got up and had breakfast. I didn't see my parents, but I did feel unusually happy, except when I tried to brush my long hair. I felt like I'd almost been scalped from all that hair-pulling last night. That pill my mother gave me had had an agreeable effect on my brain, plus I had outwitted a violent young man. I felt happy as I looked up at my little sister, who ran about.

"Let's play badminton!" She larked about, full of teenage energy, plus her own natural verve.

"Later on," I replied.

"Oh, all right, party pooper." We laughed and looked into one another's eyes. I adored my little sister.

She was seven years younger and knew nothing of the events of the night before. I wouldn't tell her until she was older. Nonetheless, I felt proud that I'd fought off Andronicus. What a horrible brute. How did men get that way? I'd learn more about wealth and entitlement as the summer progressed.

My mother came into the kitchen, a striking natural brunette beauty worshipped by my father. She still looked youthful with her unwrinkled porcelain-white skin. I waited for her to say something. She glanced at me without seeming to see me. She'd always appraised my outward appearance with a frown on her normally smooth brow; she'd criticize me if I didn't meet her standards.

She'd made it clear that she didn't approve of showing emotions and made fun of people who cried at relatives' funerals. Early on, I'd learned to ignore her as best I could and make lots of nice friends. Often, they had mothers who sensed I needed mothering, who took me under their maternal wings.

It was Grandma, my maternal grandmother, who loved me without reserve. Born into her house with my father fighting in the Pacific, in World War II, she helped my mother raise me until the end of the war in 1945. She was the one who got up at 5 a.m. to build a fire in the fireplace of her spacious home in Arlington, Virginia, so I wouldn't cry and awaken my mother. She rocked and cradled me. My mother married my father right after the bombing of Pearl Harbor in 1941. She didn't expect to become a mother in nine months, but she did. Known for her striking beauty, as well as my grandfather's substantial wealth, her maternal instincts… I don't know if she had any because mothering must not have come easy to her, but my grandmother stretched out her arms to take up the slack. She was my soul mother. Today, my mother directed her attention to the woman who helped clean our house once a month. I knew we'd never talk about what happened to me last night.

"Make sure you polish my silver this time," she said to Rosa, who nodded. She looked up at my mother almost as if expecting a blow. "If you don't do a better job, I'll have to hire someone else."

"You might be a bit kinder to someone who works so hard," I interjected. My mother's imperious lack of tact, which amounted to cruelty at times, had become unbearable over the years. I always took the side of the underdog. I knew my parents were wrong. I'd especially hated their racist views since I was eleven, which is unusual, but I'd told our whole neighborhood. Eleven-year-olds don't lie. My girlfriends' mothers started treating me with extra kindness because they felt sorry for me.

"Inny, I'm paying her. Valerie Hasting's silver always sparkles."

I gave her a furious look and started to say something. I couldn't stand the way she treated Rosa, who worked hard and took my mother's cruel remarks without comment. I wondered if she always received this rude treatment.

"I'll help Rosa!" I jumped up and grabbed the silver service tray. Rosa tried to take it back.

"No, no…" she said. We grappled over it until I started to laugh. It was comical, in a sad way. I saw Rosa's confusion. I'd bet she never dared complain for fear of losing a job. I yanked the silver tray harder.

"Inny, stop that! You're insolent." My mother glared at me, her eyes pierced my soul.

"I was almost raped last night. I could've been murdered!" The words flew out of my mouth like a hawk, guarding my right to be indignant.

My mother raised her hand to slap me. I dodged and ran to my bedroom to calm down. I started to write a letter to my best friend to alleviate the trauma and tell her of my ordeal. I had fought that devil off. I had escaped intact. The words riveted themselves to the page. I couldn't stop my flow of thoughts. I was still reeling from Andronicus' attempt to violate me, to have his way with me, no matter what.

Before I could finish the letter to Karen, the doorbell rang. It was nearly 11 a.m. I walked out of my room to see my younger sister run to open it. To my surprise, there stood Jim, asking if I was all right.

"Inny's fine!" said my sister. My mother swished by and Jim introduced himself. She peered outside; after spotting his new convertible, she smiled her best company smile. "It's always nice to meet Inny's friends," she said, suddenly all charm.

"It's nice to meet you, Mrs. Johnson," said Jim.

I put my pen down and bounded toward him, happy to see my gallant ride home, someone who sympathized with me and who knew I wasn't 'just fine.'

"I just woke up."

"You had a late night."

"It was a memorable evening." We started to laugh.

"Are you going to press charges?"

"What?"

My mother turned and walked onto the patio, where a burst of hydrangeas lit up the scenery.

"He's already being sued by the president of the Theta House at Amherst for rape."

"Yes, you told me last night. I don't think my parents would…" Jim smiled at me. "Would what?"

My sister walked by, looking at Jim with curiosity. I wondered when I could tell her what had happened last night. Kendra and I might discuss intimate events and feelings, but my parents never would. It was all about rank and status, which I'd begun to abhor. My poor father suffered miserably from the humiliation of having been passed over for captain by his superiors in the Navy. They'd announced the names of the twenty percent of his class who hadn't made captain, the equivalent to colonel in the Army. Yet, he'd fought in the Pacific in World War II and was an Annapolis graduate. He and my mother considered him a failure for not making captain, but he still had us. My sister adored him without reservation.

"Aren't your parents upset?" Jim smiled a deep crinkly smile of encouragement. He was tall and, trite but true, quite handsome. And, I'd later learn, rich.

"They gave me a Valium last night after I told them."

"That was all?"

"They're afraid to talk about… um… you know." I smiled, thinking everyone must have parents like mine. "Would you like some orange juice?"

Jim chuckled. He said no to my offer of orange juice. He had a warm demeanor that I liked. We talked about last night and Andronicus a bit more. He stood about six feet tall. I just looked up into his warm brown eyes and accepted his kind words with gratitude. Not everyone was so nice.

"Do you want to go to a party tomorrow night?" he asked as my mother opened the patio door and swished by in one of her prettier below-the-knee dresses. She smiled at him.

"I'd love to!" I loved parties, after all, and he was nice-looking and sweet. I'd soon learn that he was the last child of the three marriages of John Hopman, the Pullman Freight Train heir. Jack Smith's family owned mansions in Montecito and Ojai, where they cultivated vast tracts of lemon orchards. All of these people came from families with fabled fortunes, and many of them were from the second or third or fourth wife and had already developed an unhealthy attachment to alcohol. I gathered that divorce and alcohol were related.

I drank at parties, but never elsewhere, plus my father had a tough time supporting us after he got passed over for captain. We weren't rolling in dough. I always worked whenever I could and kept my grades up. I loved Berkeley and planned to graduate in psychology. I liked to party, but Berkeley had changed me. I had developed a love of ideas and original thinking. I loved just walking through its lush grounds, full of trees and lovely green grass. I often lolled in the grass for the sheer pleasure of it. And I studied hard.

As the daughter of a naval officer, I'd moved with my family every time Daddy got new orders. Arlington, Virginia, remained our home base until I was thirteen when I left my best friends, and worst of all, my grandmother and cousins pretty much forever.

West Point brats and Navy juniors, as people called us, suffered the trauma of constant relocation, which usually resulted in our becoming either insecure or tough, sometimes radical. I had developed a tough independent streak, plus I was impetuous. Nothing much impressed me other than genuinely nice people, like the relatives I'd left behind in Arlington, Virginia. I found that these wealthy families made an interesting story, but that was all.

Hadn't I just turned down Rock Hudson's producer's offer to be in the movies at a party at his house in Laguna Beach a couple of months ago? A fellow had poured a drink all over my raw silk dress because I wouldn't dance with him, and I'd slugged him. Rock Hudson's producer, who was infatuated with my handsome, straight boyfriend, saw the scuffle and ran over with a kaftan and a movie offer. I told him I just wanted to be happy, not a movie star. The idea had never crossed my mind. Stacey Lord intervened and said, "She has no voice." The producer nodded sagely and respected my decision. I knew being in the movie business was glamorous, but I was more interested in psychology and literature. I wanted to live my life on my own terms. I was a budding egghead disguised as a glamour girl, through no fault of my own. It was hereditary. My boyfriend and Stacey wanted to be in the movies, not me.

My boyfriend Robin left the United States to work on a trawler in the waterways of Europe that summer. I never saw him again. I never saw any of them again or gave the episode much thought. Now, I was in Montecito with my family and a nice boy who'd solaced me after a very close call.

Jim and I began to go out together. He impressed my parents with his good manners and expensive convertible. The party he'd invited me to was held in a spacious home in Montecito with a lot of people who'd gone to school together. I loved meeting new people and dancing, so Jim and I had a grand time. Someone remarked that he was more popular on the West Coast than the East, indicating that West Coast women fancied him more. I smirked at the girl who made the remark. There was a lot to eat and drink, small talk, dancing, and there was a spectacular view of the Channel Islands.

"My father lives in a house that Frank Lloyd Wright built especially for him," said Jim.

"Frank Lloyd Wright? It must be spectacular!"

"I'll have you over for dinner sometime and introduce you, if you like," he said as we admired the view from the terrace.

"I'd love to meet your father!" Jim was so sweet. Perhaps Andronicus Wyland's opposite, if that were possible.

When I told my parents I was having dinner with Jim's father, John Hopman, my own father threw one of his fits. He rarely spoke to me unless angered. "That man's a Communist!" he said.

"He owns the Pullman Freight fortune. He lives in a house Frank Lloyd Wright designed especially for him," I replied. "He's no Communist."

Daddy turned bright red, his blue eyes sparkling with pique. "He's a Communist! I've read about him! He champions the poor! He contributes to the NAACP and… he's a Socialist!"

"That sounds very generous to me. I don't think it makes him a Communist. Why do you think everyone is a Communist, Daddy?"

My father continued to rant and rave about John Hopman's unorthodox beliefs, which only increased my interest in this worldly elderly gentleman. I looked forward to meeting him.

Daddy was a midshipman at Annapolis when the Japanese bombed Pearl Harbor. My mother stayed with my grandmother, a singing lark of a woman who adored children and hadn't an inhibited bone in her body. This embarrassed my mother, but nonetheless, we stayed at Grandma's house until my father returned when the war ended in 1945.

It was my grandmother who got up at five in the morning to stoke the fire and rock my cradle so I wouldn't waken my mother. It was with my grandmother that I fed the magnificent, giant gold fish in the stone aquarium in the sunroom. A room full of tropical plants and sun and light and magic to a tot. She even took me to the movies in Clarendon when I was not yet three, sang lullabies to me and mothered me a lot more than my biological mother, her daughter, who was a bit chagrined to have a child instead of being the belle of the ball in the fancy Washington, D.C. office where she'd worked and dated several of the men. Grandma loved me unconditionally, lavishly, without reserve, and taught me to love life as she did. And, Grandma never spanked me.

When my father finally came back from the war and met me for the first time, we looked at one another like two strangers. He took me to an amusement park and I cried on one of the rides, embarrassing him in front of the onlookers, especially as he was in his naval uniform. Me, all of three years old. We failed to bond, although he tried a couple of times. So, when Jim invited me to meet his father, I was impressed that he had a father who invited his friends to dinner. My father always had his head buried in *The Scientific American* or a newspaper. He rarely spoke to my friends. In his defense, I must admit that he was a sweet-tempered, witty man who would do anything for his family.

He and my mother tried hard for a second child, and seven years later, my younger sister was delivered right into his waiting arms. She became the apple of his eye, 'Daddy's Little Helper,' as he called her, or his little angel. I was branded the devil. Why? I'll never know, but I began to hate my parents for giving me such a nasty image to live up to. Of course, I did my best. Grandma noticed that my sister was the preferred one, and she did her level best to make up for it, making chicken sandwiches for me and my girlfriends when we visited and lavishing attention on me. I loved her all the more dearly.

I put on my favorite Lanz magenta dress, sleeveless, with eyelets tracing a lovely neckline, which wasn't of the plunging variety. Dressing for myself, rather than for others, had been my natural choice, plus I didn't care to show off my breasts. Most women dressed conservatively in the early sixties.

I glanced at my face in the mirror as I brushed my long, dark blonde hair, wondering what the movie producer had seen that made him offer to put me in his films. My cheekbones were more prominent; I had less of a baby face now that I was almost twenty-one. An oval shape with deep blue eyes gazed back at me, and I had to laugh for being so vain. Looks were so superficial. It was your brains that counted, in my opinion.

Jim picked me up for dinner in his convertible. After he made polite conversation with my parents, he whisked me out to his convertible, which was parked in our semi-circular driveway, banked by large ferns and Eucalyptus trees. The rest of our street curved towards a bluff above a large field of wildflowers and untended grass. As Jim pulled out of the driveway, I saw a red sports car out of the corner of my eye. It sped away. A shiver went down my spine.

Putting my shock at seeing a sports car that resembled Andronicus' aside, I asked Jim how his father came to live in a house designed by such a famous architect.

"They were friends," said Jim.

"Oh," I replied, nonplussed. It occurred to me that I had distinguished relatives, too, only in academia or in the government, like my maternal grandfather, who had been president of the post office in Washington, D.C with a handsome salary. He was thought to be next in line for postmaster general; however, he quit at age fifty, saying, "If you haven't made it by fifty, you never will." He turned down the social security benefits he had coming, too. A. T. Davis was a tough old bird.

Grandma put up with him and raised me, along with my mother, until we left Arlington. A.T., as he was called, had given my Uncle Jimmy a job as mailman for the post office back east. Married to my mother's only sibling, Aunt Edna, he'd delivered mail with a handsome smile that belied his Irish heritage. Uncle Jimmy was as genial as he was handsome, and so were my two cousins, Jimmy and Billy.

They'd moved to California to further my cousin's aptitude in kayaking, as he hoped to participate in the Olympics. High expectations were the name of the game for us kids, and we were trying hard to fulfill them.

Jim's Frank Lloyd Wright house was hard to distinguish, as it was behind a very high wall of concrete with a high, handsome redwood gate. It bespoke the privacy that John Hopman, no doubt, cherished. Most of it was on several levels, each lower than the last, although I wouldn't see Jim's sunken bedroom until much later. I was much more interested in meeting Jim's father than in the house's architecture.

The dinner went well. As it turned out, John Hopman had a profound interest in psychology, which I'd receive a bachelor's in next year. I later learned he had a doctorate in the subject and had written many books about Freud. I treated him with great admiration and respect. He had about a thousand books in bookshelves that he could display with the flick of a switch, something Frank Lloyd Wright had, no doubt, done especially for the heir of such a vast fortune. The books were hidden by a crenelated wooden covering, which folded onto itself when he pressed the switch, revealing more books than I'd ever seen in one man's library. I noticed a copy of Marcel Proust's *Remembrance of Things Past*, my favorite book to date. Jim's mother was not visible; I assumed she had obtained a divorce like the others. I wondered if Jim missed her and if she drank, too. I'd never met a family like this.

"They are trying to establish psychology as a science at Berkeley," I said. "They experiment on rats. It's called experimental psychology."

"That's such a shame when Freud has already contributed so much to the study of the human psyche." John Hopman smiled at me. I smiled back.

"It's cruel to the rats," I commiserated. "I'm a Freudian."

"You're a fine young lady," John Hopman smiled again. So did I. *He must be a connoisseur of women after marrying so many times*, I thought. I wondered why his knowledge of psychology hadn't helped his marriages. Little did I know that everyone has their blind spot, which often goes completely sightless when the opposite sex is involved.

"Thank you." We kept smiling at each other, and I kept talking. No one could ever shut me up. I was just like my grandmother: talkative and outgoing. "I think Freud's discovery of the ego, superego, and the id is the most important discovery of the nineteenth century, don't you?"

"Yes. And I disagree with Jung."

"So do I! I don't like all of his Christian symbolism, the cross and everything…"

"You're not an…?"

"I stopped believing in God when I was seventeen."

I looked at Jim, who was grinning at me. Or was it a smirk? Perhaps I'd gone too far. I knew atheism wasn't acceptable to many people. The ultimate trauma of Daddy moving us from Hawaii to Los Angeles pushed me into the abyss of depression, something I'd never experienced. I felt like I'd gone to hell, with pimples sprouting like mushrooms on my face and no friends. Not one for six whole months, plus I missed everyone in Hawaii. I was still close to Kathy Stimson, whose own father had driven across the United States with mine in the late thirties while they were both still midshipmen. When they stopped at my grandparents' house in Salt Lake City, he'd dated Barbara, one of my father's four sisters, the one who'd been crowned Miss Salt Lake City.

"I hope I'm not shocking you. It's just that, as a Navy junior, I had some unusual experiences… I made so many wonderful friends, and then my father would get orders and we'd have to move. I'd have to change schools. When he was passed over for captain, we were in Hawaii; I had fallen in love with a captain's son… at least I missed him horribly when we left… and had so many good girlfriends there. Plus, there was Punahou, the wonderful school I loved. I used to pray every night that I'd be able to graduate from Punahou… That's when my father retired from the Navy and accepted a job in Los Angeles as an engineer." I began to feel embarrassed. I wasn't used to revealing so much about myself.

"Don't worry, Inny. You're among friends," said Jim to reassure me.

"Most people who study psychology become… shall we say, disenchanted with the pat ideas offered by religions," said John Hopman.

"I threw the Bible through the window!" We all laughed while the maid came and cleared the table. I was certain a Communist wouldn't have a maid. As usual, I decided my parents were wrong. I had no idea what the difference between a Communist and a Socialist was at the time, but it was huge.

"I noticed that you have a copy of Proust's famous tome," I said with an appreciative smile.

"It's his memoir; a book that made him almost instantly famous," remarked John Hopman.

"I loved its intimate tone, the humor, and, of course, the famous scene he makes to get his mother to give him his bedtime kiss goodnight during the course of a dinner party with Monsieur Swann."

"You're a remarkably well-read young lady," said John Hopman, "Where are you going to graduate school?"

I looked down at my white linen napkin in my lap on my raw silk dress. I knew I had to get a job after I graduated from Berkeley and then go to graduate school at a state college.

"I hope to get a Master's in psychology." I was flattered that he'd taken such an interest in my studies. No one asked me what I planned to do after college, because very few women graduated in the early sixties. Most married. I had no marriage plans, but I thought I could get a Master's and work as a high school counselor. I knew I'd have to work, because my parents said they couldn't afford to pay for any more of my education.

Jim was duly impressed. So, he invited me to get drunk with him and Bruce, his friend at the house I'd run to the night of the attempted rape, at a bar called the Ofice. It was misspelled on purpose; we loved it, especially after several gin and tonics. Life was such a giggle in those days. Kennedy had successfully foiled the Russians' attempt to install nuclear weapons on Cuba with a daring standoff. America reveled in JFK and Jackie's elegance and style. Andronicus' attempted rape receded into the recesses of my mind as I went to party after party with Jim. That his friends were all business majors didn't faze me. I was used to being the only psychology major among my friends. It never occurred to me to study anything else after reading Freud's works.

We climbed into our neighbor's tree house, behind her immense garden, one warm summer day. The sun was warm and delicious, and so were Jim's love-struck brown eyes. He leaned forward and I did, too. We shared a slow, passionate kiss. I was smitten. He kept kissing me. I opened my eyes and looked down at the hard earth beneath us. Regaining my senses, I tickled him under his armpit and we almost fell out of the tree house, laughing the whole time. I thought of my beloved grandmother in Arlington and how I wished I could introduce Jim to her. I loved her more than anyone. Boys came and went, but my maternal grandmother was my first and best love.

Summer's end approached. Jim took me to Montecito's beautiful Butterfly Beach. We were lying on beach towels, listening to the soft lapping of the waves, our arms entwined, when Jim asked me if I'd like to spend a week with him, Susie Brecken, and Bruce Washly at Susie's cottage in Berkeley. We would return to our respective schools afterwards for our senior years. I lunged at him, wrapping my arms around him. He knew that meant yes. I knew that spending a week with him would entail lovemaking. Still practically a virgin, Jim's sweetness reassured me, always the optimist, that all would go well.

Mother and Daddy decided I should take the Amtrak train up to Berkeley that year to save money. They rarely spoke to me, unless it was about a decision they'd made, a hauteur I was used to. I told them I had to go early to find a place to stay, which was also true.

Little did I know it would be with Ed Morales' girlfriend, Janey Komanaroff, who'd have an illegal abortion in my bed while I spent the night elsewhere. Most of my Berkeley pals looked upon pregnancy as a curse, especially if it was unintended. Graduation was our goal, not motherhood. We had a reputation. They called us the faction in action. That suited me just fine.

Before I left, my mother took me aside. She sat down in my bedroom with me, something she had never done before. But, she wanted to impart some important information. I knew she'd be blunt; she always was. Sometimes, her words stung like wasps.

"Inny, why don't you marry Jim?" We made eye contact with some difficulty. We weren't used to such intimate conversations together. Her hair was its usual permed perfection, but it framed a deep frown. I could tell she was not happy with her oldest daughter, me.

I shifted my weight on my bed, feeling uncomfortable. "I'm not sure, I... I don't think we know each other well enough."

"You don't have to know him that well."

"Just because he's from a rich family... doesn't mean I should marry him." I groped for words.

"I doubt if he'd ask you." She stared at me, trying to think of a more stinging insult. I'd rebuked her request.

"I haven't thought about marriage yet, Mother. I don't think Jim has either. But when I marry, it'll be to someone I love."

"Love," she scoffed. "If you don't marry soon, you'll be an old maid." Her voice hit a high C when she said old maid. The stigma of the term dug into my psyche; she'd made a direct hit. I flinched. Then, I looked her in the eye and said, "I don't think being an old maid is the end of the world."

"Inny! You must marry someone! Otherwise, you'll be an oddball, a loner. No one will play bridge with you. You must move up in the world."

"Oh, Mother. I want to graduate from Berkeley before I think about marriage. Besides, I'm not in love with anyone."

She uncrossed her legs and moved closer to me. "What kind of fool are you? Asking for love…"

I stared at this woman whom I'd called Mother my entire life. "Do you want me to marry just anyone?" I stood up and turned away from her in the small enclosure of my bedroom, really more of a den than a bedroom. My younger sister always got the larger, more nicely furnished bedroom, it suddenly occurred to me.

"You're not getting any younger."

"You don't care about my feelings!" I felt my heart beating faster.

Quick as a whip, she pounced on me, taking me by the shoulders and shaking me. "You fool! If you don't marry well, people will talk behind your back. You'll be an embarrassment."

"An embarrassment?" I looked at her as if she'd just dropped a brick on my head. "I want to live my own life. Leave me alone." I took her hands off my shoulders and glared at her. Deeply hurt that she'd called me a fool, I was on the verge of tears. When she smacked me, I recoiled. Stunned, I watched her walk to the door of my bedroom.

"Thanks a lot, Mother!" I yelled.

She slammed the door shut. Stung by her insults, not to mention the slap in the face, yet relieved that she had left, I started packing my suitcases for my senior year, my last year at my beloved Berkeley, where no one called me an old maid or a fool. And no one hit me.

Yet, deep down, I was shaken. I realized that I was ill-prepared for, not only matrimony, but love, for no one had ever told me they loved me in my entire life. They'd given me instructions, told me what I must do, which exams I must take, and which college I should go to, which skirts were too short, and how unladylike my behavior was. I'd been disapproved of and deemed unworthy of their deeper emotions, if they existed. My grandmother had loved me without saying so; she had held me and given me everything she could. Her love had seeped into me like warm chamomile tea. But not my mother's.

Chapter 3

I waved goodbye to my parents, who didn't speak to me during the drive to the train station. I was relieved that my mother hadn't scolded me for being a less-than-desirable daughter. I looked at my father, driving his daughter for her last year in college without much thought. My mother looked grim and unforgiving.

I couldn't help but think of the time Daddy had gotten into the car to drive us across the country to San Diego, in California, for one of his last tours of duty. A slightly built man, he'd climbed in behind the steering wheel with a wave to the cluster of friends and relatives that had come to see us off, for we were leaving our comfortable Colonial-style house in Arlington, Virginia, for the last time. We'd never return, except for a short visit.

Lined up across from our sloping driveway were my eight girlfriends whom I'd played with before, during, and after school for the past three years. Like me, they were thirteen years old. Some of them wore the latest style – blue jeans turned up at the cuff. Anne Young was dressed to the nines in a nice suit her mother had bought at Best & Company, a store known for its expensive apparel. She, Sheila Barton, and I had been inseparable for most of the last three years, including going away to Girl Scout camp in the Appalachian Mountains. Anne missed her parents so much she'd cried. I thrilled at my newfound freedom. All their mothers had treated me like one of their own, especially after I had shown them the red mark my father left on my thigh, right below my buttock, when he'd lost his temper and hit me. We wore shorts in the hot Virginia summers, so the mark showed beneath mine. My parent found me too loud and obstreperous one night and punished me for not acting like a lady. Acting like a lady was what my mother insisted on. I never knew what she was talking about, but when they started calling my six-year-old sister the little angel and me the little devil, I got their drift. I began to hate them. The seeds of rebellion were planted and would soon sprout.

We had left my naturally platinum blonde, vivacious Aunt Edna, who had been valedictorian of her high school class and married her grade school sweetheart, Uncle Jimmy, whose dark curly hair was carefully combed back as he beamed his warm-hearted, sincere smile, making my heart glad. My cousin, known as little Jimmy, two years younger than me and like a brother, smiled a big grin and tried to mimic his father, whom we adored. Then, there was Grandma, dressed in a cotton dress a bit big and blousy, one that she'd no doubt found in a bargain basement sale, even though my grandfather, Audus T. Davis, earned a princely sum for being the head of the Washington, D.C. post office and its two thousand or so employees, whose names and salaries he knew by heart. Grandpa had the brains, but not the heart, to even accompany my grandmother to say goodbye to us. Grandma always joked about his parsimony but accepted it as her lot in life. She sang on the bus and at children's funerals and loved every soul she met without reserve, a woman whose generosity knew no limits. She was universally loved. Over the thirteen years we'd spent off and on in Arlington, she'd become my soul mother. She was also the source of my mother's disapproval, knowing that I loved Grandma more than her. She also attended White House dinners without her anti-social husband, where she sat in a love seat and chatted up President Harding's wife. Grandma loved every minute of it. My mother grew up quite the opposite: reserved and introverted.

I'd been taught to be stoic, so I stood there and stared at everyone, not quite grasping that we were leaving forever. That couldn't be possible, because they meant the world to me. My mother hustled my little sister into our nineteen fifties Studebaker and waved good-bye.

"Hurry up, Inny!" she said. "We have to go!"

Just then, Sheila and Anne walked up to me with a gift-wrapped box. They handed it to me. I looked at them in delighted surprise as I unwrapped a small, gray radio.

"Inny, you can't take that!" said my mother, who didn't allow music in the house, not to mention that she didn't approve of me accepting gifts.

"But, Mother…" I turned to see her glowering at me. I turned and saw the panorama of my friends, my aunt, uncle, cousin, and beloved grandmother waving at me.

I heaved a sob and burst into tears. Uncontrollable, heartfelt sobs. I blubbered a tearful thank you to Sheila and Anne as my mother pushed me into the backseat of the car, holding the radio in my arms. My father started the engine and backed out of our driveway with me bawling my head off. It was the last time I would see them. My thirteen-year-old heart had just broken in two.

Jerking myself back to the reality of taking leave of my parents to go to Berkeley where I'd meet Jim, sobered me. Glimpsing the stately palms that lined the walkway next to the Amtrak station for the last time that summer, I marveled at their beauty and boarded the train. I found a seat next to a conventionally dressed, nice-seeming lady. I began to talk, which I always did when I had a case of the nerves, and the thought of Jim picking me up at the station and what was to follow had me tied up in knots. So I talked – for ten straight hours. My grandmother and I had this in common: talking was our panacea. Fortunately, the lady sitting next to me and I got along quite well. She found my thousand and one stories entertaining. We were fast friends by the time the train pulled into the San Francisco station.

I also had time to reread one of grandma's many letters. 'Keep your eyes wide open before marriage and half-shut afterwards,' she wrote, along with other wise and witty advice. She quoted the Bible and told me to 'give thanks for another day, to accept the beauty of God's way.' Grandma was very religious.

Jim paced back and forth at the San Francisco train depot. When I arrived with four suitcases, running madly about trying to organize them, he laughed out loud. "Why are you so nervous?"

"I'm not nervous; I'm excited!" My voice was shrill, because I was nervous. I knew we'd spend our first night together. I'd only had one other lover, and we'd broken up in my junior year. I kept running around, trying to organize my luggage, but Jim's tall frame and broad smile beckoned me like a lighthouse. He kissed me hard. I kissed him back. I looked into his eyes and laughed. We were going to spend the night together, and I was almost a virgin.

We had to contend with Annie Brecken and Bruce Washly, who were truly just friends and would share the ivy-covered cottage with us that week. The minute we got out of Jim's car, Bruce started cracking jokes about how close I had sat to him. I put up with his immaturity and laughed it off. Jim squeezed my hand. I smiled into his face and felt my heart beating fast. It was young love.

We went to Spengler's and dined on seafood, downing the usual Bloody Marys along with delicious prawns and lobster thermidor. Gaiety, salted with booze, prevailed. Bruce must have been jealous of Jim for making a conquest, for he and Annie were just old friends from Montecito. She laughed, making jokes of which she was often the butt. She was a good sport, a very likeable person.

At about nine o'clock, Jim said, "Let's go back."

A bit soused, we opened the door to our cute Berkeley cottage; it had plenty of ivy climbing its exterior; the perfect weeklong getaway before college.

Jim and I undressed in our sparsely furnished bedroom, rather chastely, our backs to one another. His long, lean body hulked over me as I put on a nightgown.

"I, um…" I was tongue-tied for once. I thought of my grandmother's letter and felt ashamed. He reached for me as we stood next to the bed, and we embraced, exchanging a long, passionate kiss. He said I love you. Down we went and made love, or should I say almost made love. He couldn't get a full erection. The Pullman Freight heir might have trouble producing heirs! I'd imagined every scenario but this. Not quite twenty-one and fairly clueless about sex, we kissed goodnight and slept. At least he slept. I laid awake and wondered how messed up he might be with a famous, brilliant father whom he told me had had three wives. His mother was the last. My parents were the opposite; I think they had both been virgins, or nearly so, when they married right after the attack on Pearl Harbor and Daddy had to join the fleets on the Pacific Front. Yet, they treated me like an outsider, not to mention that my mother thought nothing of smacking me from time to time. I had remained a virgin until my sophomore year, thanks to her constant reminders that 'men only want one thing from a woman.' At least Jim seemed proud of his father and close enough to invite a girlfriend to dinner. Envy seeped into my veins.

The week passed with more unsuccessful attempts at love making. I tried to figure him out; perhaps it was the alcohol, but what had led to that? Too much money and alcohol; an absentee mother didn't help, I concluded. I tried to make up for embarrassing moments with long kisses that I hoped would tell him I cared about him.

Annie and I got along well; we enjoyed playing practical jokes on Bruce to pay him back for his immature pranks. One time, we put his cut-off jeans in the oven to dry. We returned to a smoking house; the pants had caught fire. We developed a good-natured raillery with him and Jim. It was sort of like boys against girls, back in grammar school.

"Liar, liar, pants on fire," I chanted. Annie took up the refrain. We were undeterred. What's a little fire when your parents are on the Forbes richest people list?

Meanwhile, I looked for a place to stay and found an apartment with Janey, a stunning blonde, Ed Morales' pregnant girlfriend. I'd met Ed at a party the year before; he was majoring in criminology. We were all seniors at Berkeley.

Janey told me she was going to terminate the pregnancy, which was not far advanced, with shots that a doctor interested in keeping the unwanted children's population down agreed to give. I'd have to spend the night at Sally Zimmerman's, another sorority sister who'd dropped out, flunked out of Berkeley, to be exact, and was living with an older man; he must have been twenty-nine, which seemed much older to us. He was also a horse's ass and chose Sally for her vulnerability. Sally was a bit homely with short cropped hair and features that didn't quite fit her longish face, so she was deemed homely, but no woman should allow herself to be judged by her looks.

I packed my suitcase back at Jim's and our so-called love nest. He watched me, shifting his weight from one foot to the other. We both felt awkward; our attempt at an affair hadn't gone as well as we'd hoped. I looked up and mentioned that I should pick up the keys at the flat I'd sublet to four girls over the summer. Mary Jane, Lynne, and I had signed a year-long lease, so we'd found summer renters to pay for the months we were back home. Actually, Mary Lou had flunked out and Lynne had gotten engaged to a handsome fellow from South Africa. Jim pricked up his ears. "Are the girls you sublet to still there?"

"Yes, but they said I could pick up the keys and return them to the landlady. They're about to leave."

"Can I come with you?" He gave me a petulant puppy-dog look that made me smile. What a sweet boy. My mother was probably right. He'd even invited me to tour Europe with him the next summer. I didn't want to, so I just said a polite 'sure' and figured I'd tell him I couldn't go later in the year. Off we drove to Parker Avenue, to the upstairs flat my friends and I had had shared in my junior year. They'd hosted quite a few memorable parties. Someone had even given Mary Jane an entire case of Chivas Regal Scotch, which I was told was the best. We had to leave at the end of the school year. As we'd signed a contract for a year, we were lucky to have found three other girls who wanted to rent it for the summer.

When Jim and I arrived, no one was home, so I was left to search for the keys on my own. Jim followed me, staring at the interior of the flat.

"What a nice ashtray," he said, admiring a rather attractive receptacle for cigarette ashes.

"Yes," I mumbled while looking for the keys. Jim pocketed the ashtray. Flabbergasted, I watched as he started taking vitamins and other various items from the apartment. "Those belong to the girls who sublet this apartment," I protested, turning and facing him with my arms folded across my chest.

He smiled a huge, ingratiating smile. "I don't think they'll miss them."

"Put them back!"

"Oh, come on, it's just a few vitamins and little things." He pouted, sitting down on the living room sofa. I couldn't believe my ears. Here, was one of the richest young men in the world committing petty theft, stuffing everything in sight into his bulging pockets.

"Put them back this instant or I'll do it myself!" I stepped closer to him.

He stepped back. "Inny, this is just sport. We do it at stores in Santa Barbara all the time."

29

"Why? You've got enough money to buy ten times those things."

"Oh, people who didn't grow up in Montecito don't understand," moped Jim.

"No, we don't. It's called stealing. Have you ever read the Bible? 'Thou shalt not steal?'"

"I thought you weren't religious." Jim's face reddened as he spoke. I guess I'd hit a nerve.

"There's a big difference between believing in a big, whey-faced god up in the sky and having decent morals. Now, give everything back." I held out my hands so he could put them in them. Out came the ashtray. The vitamins followed, along with the other small things he'd stolen. I put them back as best I could.

"Say, Inny," said Jim.

"What?"

"You know that trip to Europe I was talking about?" He turned his back to me.

"What about it?"

"Do you think it's such a swell idea after all?"

"No."

"Some kind of tramp you turned out to be!" He turned around; his face was beet red.

"Just call me Charlie Chaplin," I smiled slyly.

"You think you're funny."

"I know I'm honest. I like to help poor people, just like your father, who would be ashamed to call you his son, if he knew."

He raised his hand. I stared him down and said, "Hit me and I'll call the police." I took a step or two backwards, just in case.

"It says, 'Thou shalt not steal' in the Ten Commandments!" I repeated myself out of shock.

"You're a fine one to preach. You don't even believe in God." Jim's face kept getting redder as he spoke. That insult had gotten his blood flowing at last.

"I believe in morality. I don't steal or lie or cheat! You're the son of one of the world's richest men, and you thank him by guzzling so much booze you can hardly make love and you steal!"

"Wha... what do you mean... I can hardly make... love?"

I tried to conjure some sympathy for him, even though he'd almost hit me. After all, we'd just spent a week together.

"Jim, you're a sweet guy, but let's face it, you're all mixed up. You haven't been able to make love to me once because of all that vodka you drink every night."

"That's…" His face contorted from its normally placid, happy-go-lucky expression to a puckered baby face. He turned away from me.

"I'm sorry. I didn't mean to hurt your feelings, but… you almost hit me in the face! Any man who hits a woman is… is not exactly a gentleman." I felt my heart racing in my chest. I didn't know how he'd take my outburst, but he had it coming. Thoughts raced through my confused mind.

He put his face in his hands and started to cry. "I didn't mean to hurt you."

"We had a good time, but you have to admit…" I ran my fingers though his hair to try to solace him.

"Admit what?" he blubbered.

I pulled him to his feet. "That you drink way too much. Come on, let's get in the car. It's time to go back. We've got a big day tomorrow."

I steered him down the stairway to the street, and we got in the car. I drove as he started to cry harder. "I've never had a mother," he sobbed. "She left because… I don't know why she left, but I missed her."

"Don't you ever see her?"

"Not since she remarried. I mean, I only see her on certain holidays; it's not like she cares."

"I care. I care enough to tell you the truth after you all but whammed me in the face."

That did it. He became inconsolable. He was a puddle of tears by the time I pulled up to our former love nest. I felt like a wrung-out dishrag after what he'd put me through.

When I finally got back into our bedroom in the cottage, I found my suitcases and called a taxi. I picked them up and started lugging them to the sidewalk. Annie appeared out of nowhere. "Jim seems upset. What happened?" she asked.

I sniffled a little bit. "We had a fight." I turned my head so she wouldn't see how upset I was.

"Do you need a ride?" She had some car keys in her hand.

"As a matter of fact…"

We walked to Jim's car; he'd given her his car keys. She drove me to Janey's and my new apartment in silence.

"He seemed like such a nice boy," I sniffed and wiped my nose. There were tears in my eyes. I felt sad that my knight in shining armor had dissolved into a puddle of tears. He'd even raised his hand against me. I couldn't believe he was the one who had opened the door to a sanctuary the night Andronicus tried to rape me.

"Don't they all," replied Annie with an air of sophistication that astonished me. She was from an ultra-wealthy family, too.

"Why does he drink so much?" I ventured.

Annie sighed, "It seems like they all do in Montecito."

I looked into her eyes, trying to see the depths of her knowledge. "He tried to steal some vitamins and stuff at my old apartment – from girls he'd never met. Why would the heir to such a huge fortune do that?"

"Jim is especially insecure, because his mother was the third wife," explained Annie. She gave me a knowing look. "It's his way of paying his father back for divorcing her, or vice-versa."

My eyes widened. I couldn't believe my ears. "Do you mean, they drink and steal BECAUSE they're rich?"

"Not exactly," continued Annie. "They may seem rich to you, but they compete with each other in weird ways."

"I'll say!"

"They might be practicing for future theft on a bigger scale." She winked at me. "They don't want to feel guilty about it." My mind reeled at the implications of what she'd just said.

She pulled up to my new place of residence, helped me with my suitcase, and murmured something to the effect that she was sorry things hadn't turned out better. I agreed. I was still stunned from Jim's complete breakdown.

Later on, I reflected. My ardor for Jim had cooled; no, it had vanished with our last unsuccessful coitus, followed by a cigarette and cocktail and the petty theft in my sublet apartment. I wasn't in love with him. I never planned on seeing him again, and I'm sure he felt the same. I was sorry about his rich-boy complex, but that didn't make up for the stealing. Meanwhile, I unpacked my suitcase at lovely, blond Janey's apartment while packing a smaller overnight bag, preparing to spend a night away so she could have the shot that would start her menstrual period.

"I'll call you tomorrow," she said as I wished her luck. Her parents weren't rich. This was the poor-but-ambitious woman's way out of having a child she couldn't afford.

"I hope you'll be okay," I said with an air of sympathy. I smiled warmly into her eyes. Feeling sorry for her and her predicament, I breathed a sigh of relief that I'd started taking the pill after I lost my virginity last year.

Off to Sally's I went. She had rented a charming studio apartment across the hallway from her boyfriend, Jerry. He was there when I arrived.

Sally introduced us. Instead of smiling and offering his hand, he took a short glance at me and turned away. Sally was used to his rudeness, so she thought nothing of it.

"Ahem," I said. "You could at least say hello."

He stood up, not a very tall man, a bit stout with a rough complexion, and said a reluctant hello. I hunched my shoulders in bewilderment. Why couldn't he act friendly?

"Inny's just here for one night," Sally said.

"Sure. You usually sleep at my place anyway."

Sally nodded and started to get her pajamas and bed things together. "I hoped we could talk for a while," I said.

"Tomorrow, after Jerry goes to work," murmured Sally.

Just then, I heard someone coming down the brick pathway that led to the four studio apartments behind the large Berkeley house; it turned out to be the very popular Albert Curtis, the first African-American English professor at Berkeley, one of my favorite people. He loved to throw parties and wear lavender wigs; he made fun of his skin color, as the TV ads promised, 'Softer, whiter, more beautiful hands' to sell hand lotion. He made everyone laugh and love him. Did I say he was gay? Everyone told me he was. It was such a shame, because he possessed the kind of beauty you couldn't take your eyes off of, with his chiseled features and brilliant smile. Albert was wonderful in so many ways, and after Sally and I celebrated our twenty-first birthdays on September 15, he would end up my neighbor as my living situation was going to change. His nattily dressed, slender silhouette and fun-loving attitude had made him a popular and well-known figure on campus.

I ran out to greet him as Jerry and Sally made their bedtime arrangements. Jerry glared at Albert as he walked by.

"He's a friendly sort," I said to Albert with a wry smile.

"It takes all kinds," said Albert. I realized he must receive the cold shoulder from jerks just like Jerry altogether too often. Once was too much.

"What's Sally doing with him?"

"There's no accounting for taste," said Albert. "I've got papers to correct, or I'd stop and talk."

"I'll take a rain check!"

He smiled his warm, broad smile and I felt cleansed from Jerry's bad treatment. I slept soundly in Sally's bed that night.

Janey had her drug-induced abortion and we were settling in. It was time to celebrate my twenty-first birthday, a big one in Berkeley, where the bartenders offered you free drinks. Ed, a handsome, muscular Latino who was a criminology major, offered to drive us around while Janey went to the opera, something I hadn't yet grown to love. Sally came with me for the free drinks. Jerry was out of town, so she was free.

We were pretty tipsy by the time Ed decided to drive us home. The lovely trees formed a leafy canopy as he drove across campus. He encountered a roadblock consisting of metal posts stuck in the ground to block the road for a Peter, Paul, and Mary concert. Ed dutifully pulled a couple of them up as the trio sang, "If I had a hammer, I'd hammer for justice…"

Ed got back in the car just as the police came up and asked to see his driver's license. He showed it to them.

"Get out of the car," said a burly Berkeley policeman.

"I don't have to," replied Ed. "It's my constitutional right to remain in the car. I've done nothing wrong."

The police officer opened the door and pulled Ed out. The Berkeley policemen had a reputation for brutality in 1963. Before Sally and I could say stop it, there were six Berkeley policemen beating Ed to a pulp. Ed was a wrestler; he put up a fight, slipping in and out of their blows like a fish on a hook. But they were six against one U.C. Berkeley senior. He couldn't win.

Sally and I exchanged stunned looks as they continued to pummel Ed. "Let's call the police!" I said.

We ran to a nearby kiosk and called the local police. "Six Berkeley policemen are beating our friend. They ripped him out of the car…"

A thick-set policeman grabbed the phone from me and hung up.

"You can't do that!"

"Why not? It's the truth!"

"Get back in the car, young lady!"

Sally and I exchanged looks. We saw he didn't have much of a choice, so we got back in. They'd already cuffed Ed. Stone sober, I drove home.

We visited Ed in jail the next day; he was black and blue from the beating. "But he didn't do anything wrong!" Sally and I protested. "One of the policemen yanked him out of the car…"

The sergeant gave me a stern look. "It's time for you to go."

"It's the truth!"

"Do as you're told!"

Tail between our legs, Sally and I left the jail.

Ed got out of jail the next day and decided to move in with Janey, his girlfriend and my roommate. I jumped at the chance to share the rent with Sally for the studio next to Jerry's and downstairs from Albert Curtis.' I loved the authentic woodwork on the walls and ceilings, plus I'd have a place of my own for just half price, as Sally would pay half the rent and leave most of her clothes in the closet, so it wouldn't look like she was living with Jerry when her parents came to visit.

A charmed year was off and running, except that Sally and I soon received telegrams from Dean McGruder, telling us to meet him in his office at separate times.

"It's about Ed," Sally told me as she changed clothes.

"He didn't do anything!" I replied. "Removing a post to drive us home isn't a crime. They could've given him a ticket, but instead they beat him to a pulp!"

"What should we say?"

"Just tell them exactly what happened."

Sally agreed.

I put on a nice dress with low heels for the appointment, applied some lipstick, and walked to Sproul Hall, where Dean McGruder's office was.

"Come in, Miss Johnson," he said, smiling.

"Thank you," I said, and walked into a nice office decorated with Cal banners. He motioned to a well-upholstered chair. I sat down in it. I peered into a round-faced individual without distinction.

"Tell me what happened on the night of September 15," he said. "Ed Morales was driving me and Sally Zimmerman around the campus on our twenty-first birthdays so we could celebrate. On the way home, we encountered a road block by the Peter, Paul, and Mary concert. Ed got out of the car to remove two of the metal poles that were blocking the road, so he could take us home. When he got back in the car, six Berkeley policemen came up and asked him for his driver's license. He showed it to them. They asked him to get out of the car; he refused, because they had no right to ask him to do so. The next thing I knew, they were piled on top of him, beating him..."

"Just a minute, young lady," said the dean.

I stopped midsentence.

"Do you realize what you just said?"

"You asked me to tell you what happened."

"That's perjury."

"What's perjury?"

"You can go to jail for it. It's your word against six Berkeley policemen."

"You asked me what happened."

"Are you sure that's all that happened?"

"Do you want me to analyze every detail? They beat him black and blue!"

"Just think about what you say before you go before the court."

"What court?"

35

"Ed Morales is on trial for resisting arrest. There will be a trial with a few of the deans and perhaps the President of Berkeley, Clark Kerr."

I must have looked dumbfounded, because he showed me the door and I was soon standing in the brilliant sunshine in Berkeley's spacious open space, next to Sather Gate, Dwinelle Plaza. The contrast of the threats in his dark office left my head spinning. I had to talk to Sally. Ed had been brutally beaten before our eyes. We had to defend him.

I ran the ten blocks to my studio apartment and waited for Sally to arrive. She and her boyfriend Jerry often spent time out of town, so I hoped she'd get home soon.

While waiting, I saw Albert Curtis walk up to his studio, so I stuck my head out and said hello. Albert was tall and slender, with a somewhat beaked nose. He was Berkeley's first Black English professor.

He waved. "Do you want to come up later? I'm showing some experimental films to a couple of friends."

"I'd love to!"

I was thrilled Albert had invited me. Experimental films? I'd never seen any, so my curiosity was piqued, plus Albert looked so handsome and dapper in his Brooks Brothers jacket and slacks. Just then, Sally and Jerry walked by.

"Sally!"

"Hi!"

"Have you talked to Dean McGruder yet?"

She shook her head. "My appointment's tomorrow."

"Make sure you stick to the truth when he tries to rattle you."

"Rattle me?"

"Yeah, he accused me of perjury, whatever that is, if I told the truth."

Jerry grimaced at me and pretty much shoved Sally into his apartment. I'd never liked Jerry. I found him unsocial and wondered why Sally put up with his rude behavior. She was shy and unprepossessing, not a beauty like my other friends from the sorority, but nicer. Too nice for her own good, it turned out.

"We'll see you later."

"Fine."

I decided to go watch experimental films at Albert's. As clips of an octopus eating a glass rolled before my eyes, along with a scene from the Holocaust – fictional, I assumed – of German soldiers eating sausage, slobbering, and chomping their jaws in front of famished Jewish captives, my mind began to reel.

They finished eating, let the Jews run into the forest, and took off after them, belching and laughing.

"Did that really happen?"

"Everything happened in the Holocaust. The Nazis were infamous for their cruelty," said Albert.

I'd read about the Holocaust, but not enough to know about the endless atrocities. After seeing Ed get beaten for removing a metal post from the road, my faith in humanity took a stumble.

"Why do people do such hateful things?"

"No one really knows, but it's usually because they themselves have been hurt or because they're afraid," said Albert.

"But no one had hurt the Germans. What did they have to fear?"

"They didn't come out of World War I unscathed… And then, Hitler rose to power… on anti-Semitism. It was uncanny, but it worked. He bullied the Germans into submission. He said he'd make Germany great again, and they believed him."

"But that was before World War II." I gave him a guileless smile. "Why didn't they stand up to him?

"How could a tiny little man with a silly mustache be so… so scary? There's got to be a psychological reason. What would Freud say?"

Albert could see I was not terribly hip to world history, and psychology wasn't his field. He changed his tack. "Many of them regretted it later. Most of them claimed they had no choice."

"Especially after they lost the war."

"Especially," said Albert with a wry smile.

We were starting to become good friends. I told him about my encounter with Dean McGruder, as well as the threat of perjury and jail. He advised me to stick to the truth.

"I always tell the truth."

He smiled at me in approbation. Maybe he thought I was nice. Nice was my specialty, unless someone put their hand on my knee.

The next day dawned bright and clear. I received another telegram telling me to be at Sproul Hall at four o'clock the next afternoon. I wondered about Sally.

I dressed in a conservative shirt dress, popular in 1963, and low heels to impress the jury favorably. After a quick brush of my long dark blonde hair and a dab of lipstick, I headed for Sproul Hall, which was only a few blocks from Sally's and my studio apartment.

I loved walking along Telegraph Avenue and passing through Sather Gate, Berkeley's famed campus entrance of wrought-iron artistry. How many times had I passed under it carrying a couple of books and laughing with friends? No one wore backpacks. We just carried our books in our arms.

This time, I looked skyward as I passed under the famed archway and hoped for the best. I walked up the marble stairs to stately Sproul Hall and found the room where the trial would take place. Dean McGruder and other stern-looking men were already there. He motioned for me to sit down. I took a seat and waited.

The men looked at their watches. It was time to begin, but Sally hadn't arrived yet. They started without her. They ushered me into a rectangular room with about seven men seated around a mahogany oval table and Ed seated next to Dean McGruder. We exchanged looks; I nodded. I'd never been in a courtroom before, but there was no judge or jury, not even a secretary to take notes. It seemed rigged.

There was no formal swearing in; they simply started questioning me immediately.

"What were you doing at 12:30 a.m. on September 15, Miss Johnson?"

"I was driving across campus with Sally Zimmerman and Ed Morales, our driver."

"What happened at 12:30 a.m., Miss Johnson? Innocence Ann Johnson, correct?"

"That's correct." I smiled at him and started to tell the story.

"The road was blocked with metal posts. We couldn't get through, so Ed got out of the car and removed two of them so he could take us home. When he got back in the car, several policemen approached us and asked for his driver's license, which he showed them. They asked him to get out of the car, which he said he didn't have to do under constitutional law. Then, they pulled him out and beat him…"

"Do you realize what you're saying?" asked Dean McGruder.

"Yes, I'm aware of what I'm saying."

"Had you been drinking?"

"Sally and I were celebrating my birthday, but Ed had had nothing to drink!"

"Answer the question."

I stared at the older man in a rumpled tweed suit. "We'd had a few drinks. He tried to fight them off, but there were six of them, so it was six to one."

"That will be enough, Miss Johnson."

"We ran to the kiosk…"

"So, you were absent during part of the event."

"We…"

"You may go now. Thank you for your testimony."

I looked at them. "I haven't told the entire story," I protested.

"That's quite enough, Miss Johnson. You may go. Innocence, indeed!"

Anger coursed through my veins like molten lava. I had no idea what to do. I left the room, chagrined. I felt I hadn't defended Ed well enough, although I'd done my best.

I passed Sally, white-faced, as I left.

"What happened?" She looked terrified.

"They just asked me what happened."

"Did you tell them?"

"Yes. Now it's your turn."

"I'm so nervous, Inny," she stammered. She slumped against me and grabbed my arm.

I steadied her and hissed, "Just tell the truth, Sally!"

She went in and I waited in the hallway. A few minutes later, she staggered out, white as a sheet.

"How did it go?"

"I tried to tell the story, but I got mixed up."

"About what?"

"About when we were in the kiosk and why the police started beating Ed."

"What?" I had a sinking feeling that Sally had screwed up.

"Well, that dean threatened us with perjury and I was scared."

"For Christ's sake, Sally, they beat Ed brutally right before our eyes!"

"Yes, but I was a bit drunk…"

I knew Ed was in trouble. Sally had gotten the facts mixed up plus it wasn't a fair trial. They hadn't let me finish testifying and there was no one to take notes.

"I have to meet Jerry now. He wants me to take a flying lesson."

I knew Jerry was trying to make Sally learn to fly, to conquer her greatest fear: her fear of flying. I shook my head in dismay. Sally ran to meet her tormenter.

I waited for the court to decide Ed's fate. He came out about ten minutes later with an ashen face and downcast eyes. He'd been expelled from Cal Berkeley in his senior year.

"What are you going to do? I asked, panicked. I couldn't believe this had transpired. And, it was partially Sally's and my fault for asking him to drive us, though we hadn't encouraged him to remove the roadblock. Still, he was beaten black and blue by six Berkeley policemen, a police force with a reputation for violence.

Janey came around the corner, her lovely oval face and shimmering blonde hair catching everyone's eye.

"Ed's been expelled!" I told her.

We sat down on a bench. Ed and Janey hugged for a long time.

"I told them the straight truth."

"Your story was fine. Sally wobbled all over the place; she didn't tell it straight."

"Sally always screws up," I said, shaking my head. "She has no confidence in herself." I put my hand on Ed's arm. "I'm so sorry. I feel like it's partly my fault."

Ed shook his head. "You did fine. I'll try to make an appeal."

I breathed a sigh of relief. "I hope they reconsider your case. I'll be willing to testify anytime you need me to."

Ed smiled through his pain. "Thanks, Inny. Let's just make sure Sally tells it straight."

"I'll grill her next time!"

Since Ed couldn't afford an attorney, the appeal disappeared like so many foggy, alcohol-soaked Berkeley nights. He finished his college degree at a university in Florida, far from Berkeley and Janey.

I didn't know how to help him, though I made an appointment with Chancellor Glenn Seaborg to set the story straight. A towering figure of a man tut-tutted me after I told him what had happened.

"Surely you're mistaken, young lady." He showed me the door in less than five minutes.

I left in confusion, wondering why he hadn't taken me seriously. It never occurred to me that the University's reputation might come ahead of a silly girl's story about police brutality on the sacred Berkeley campus. My studies and blossoming friendship with Albert Curtis kept my mind absorbed. I had been ignored before, for unknown reasons, and had yet to develop a sense of outrage over such acts. I wanted to help Ed, but I didn't know how. He seemed to be taking this unfair turn of events in stride.

I walked into my cozy little studio apartment and put my books down on the kitchen table. It was actually part of the living room, which had room for a double bed. I sat down and paged through my behavioral psychology textbook when I heard a ruckus next door at Sally and Jerry's apartment. He pushed her outside and wouldn't let her back in. I opened my door to find her sobbing like a lost puppy on her master's doorstep.

"Sally! What happened?"

"Jerry… Jerry gets upset with me sometimes," she faltered, sobbing.

"And locks you out in the cold hallway, crying your eyes out?" I was shocked. I helped her stand up and led her into the studio we supposedly shared.

"Could I spend the night with you here tonight?"

"Yes, of course! But I think you need to stand up to Jerry!"

"I'm afraid to."

I put my arm around her shoulders. "Sally, he's not for you. Let's face it." I looked deep into her eyes. She looked at me and then averted her face with a look full of shame.

"Why don't you come to the Monkey Inn with me tonight? All our friends will be there! We can have some beer and some fun!"

"Jerry doesn't like me to go to bars."

"Well, isn't that too bad? He pushes you into the cold hallway and wants to make you suffer. No friend of mine is going to be humiliated like that! Come on!"

Sally dried her eyes and tried to smile though her tears. Her bangs got in the way, so she pushed them aside. "I can't go. I look awful."

I brushed her bangs aside. "Sally, just comb your hair and you'll look fine. There's nothing wrong with the way you look."

Sally shook her head. No one could convince her she looked okay. I took her into my studio… our studio, considering she paid half the rent. I suggested she take a shower and change clothes. I couldn't understand why she allowed Jerry to treat her badly. My father always treated my mother like a queen. I'd never seen anyone accept such demeaning behavior.

Once she was refreshed from her shower and dressed, I fixed her some tea. We sat down at the kitchen table to drink our tea. I delved into her relationship with Jerry. "Sally, no one should have to spend the night in a hallway. Why does he do that to you?"

"He says he's important, and that I'm lucky to have him. I know I'm not very pretty…"

"Every woman has her own special beauty." I took a sip of tea and looked at her with encouragement.

Her eyes opened wide. "Not me!"

"Do you mean to say that, because you're not Marilyn Monroe, you have to accept horrible treatment? What else does he do to you?"

Sally cleared her throat. "When he had a job as an engineer in India, he used to make me fly with him in a private plane. I almost got sick."

I remembered flying from Berkeley to Los Angeles with Sally. She clenched her hands the entire way and hid her head in her plaid skirt. She was waiting for the plane to crash. I laughed and tried to get her to shape up, but to no avail. She had a fear of flying; a terrified phobic reaction. Psych major that I was, I could see she was afraid of dying… a phobic fear. She needed to see a therapist. That Jerry would take pleasure in her terror made him a sadist.

"You've got to ditch Jerry!" I said.

41

plans were to rape and kill me. Crutches' hand on my thigh had convinced me, and my nervous system had imploded.

"Well, if they're coming, I guess we'll be leaving," said Crutches.

It was almost mathematic: enter two healthy men, exit two psychopaths. I could hardly believe my luck. Things had been different with Andronicus. I had to fight him off, so I didn't have enough advance warning to freeze up and have paranoia set in. I'd been lucky twice and made a run for it the other time. My brain was taking everything in so fast I could barely breathe.

The two creatures stood up hastily, too hastily, I noted. I was sure they would have raped me. Why they chose me, I had no idea. One thing I knew was that rapists were usually men who felt they were entitled to do what they wanted to a woman. Anxious to leave, they were halfway out the door.

"Good night," said Ira.

"Don't you want to stay to say hello to Fred and Chuck?" I asked, stifling a laugh.

"Those two big guys? No thanks. We'll be going now."

They left, Crutches scraping a fast getaway down the brick walkway. I've never heard a more welcome noise. Taking your anger at your disability out on women. That's real manly.

A red sports car awaited them, parked about a block from the entrance to our studio enclave. Crutches got into it and it sped away.

Sally opened the bathroom door and peeked out, her hair still in curlers, her face white like the belly of a dead fish.

"Fine friend you turned out to be!" I glowered at her, more relieved than angry.

She sank back onto the bed. "Who were they?"

"The guy I told you about earlier and a tough-looking friend named Ira."

I couldn't believe Sally's cowardice. Her disloyalty. No wonder she chose men who brutalized her. Maybe they chose her.

"Why did you let them in?"

"I didn't think it was really Crutches. I thought it was Ed getting his bicycle."

My anger mixed with fright flowed around and through my friend until there was another knock on the door, this time belonging to Fred and Chuck, to whom I owed – I felt they'd saved my life.

"You saved our lives!" I beamed at them. Freddie's bright blue eyes lit up. He laughed and shook his flaxen-blond hair. Sexy boy, almost a man.

"We do this all the time," he said.

I looked up into his handsome face; it was a minor miracle that I wasn't raped and strangled with my own nightie. I felt like I was looking at an angel.

"Crutches was here with a friend!" I said. I tried to have an imploring look on my face. I knew these were good-time guys, but I'd almost been raped. His hand was on my thigh. Of course, they didn't see his hand on my thigh.

"Let's get going before the bars close!" said Chuck.

Sally and I bolted to the closet, grabbed dresses, took the rollers out of our hair.

"Sally, those guys were going to rape me!" I hissed as I slid a sleeveless dress over my shoulders. She gave me her blank stare. *No wonder her boyfriend beats her*, I thought, somewhat surprised at myself. I ran a comb through my hair.

"Inny, they were just visiting." Sally combed her bangs.

"They were going to rape me!" I screamed as loud as I could.

She put her fingers to her lips and said, "Shhhhh! Don't tell anyone."

Who could I talk to? Just as we left, I saw a light go on in Albert Curtis' studio. He opened the door. I waved frantically at him. He waved back as the boys hustled down the brick pathway to their car. He shouted something, but we were moving too fast for me to understand what it was.

Before we knew it, we were in another bar, meeting more of Fast Freddie's friends. Everyone called him Fast Freddie and Chuck, Chunky Charles, because he was a bit short and stout. The friends had nicknames, too, like Tapioca Terry and Ornery O'Brien. It was drinks on the house, with Sally and me clinking beer out of bottles with the fellas', thanking our lucky stars for our change in fortune. I knew she knew but wouldn't say a thing, because she never did. She was a weak link in my chain of friends.

Pretty soon, we were engaged in beer drinking contests, which consisted of Fast Freddie challenging a perfect stranger to a beer-drinking contest with his friends standing around, barely able to keep from laughing. Freddie would throw his beer over his shoulder, onto the floor, while the other guy resolutely tried to chug his down. He'd lose, and Freddie would get a free beer, which, sometimes, he gave to me. When a pretty girl went by, he'd drop to his knees and say, "Will you marry me?" She'd walk away fast, sometimes turning her head to give Freddie a quick stare, while I stifled my laughter. Freddie was unpredictable and a character, and I loved characters!

It was a crazy, drunken evening, the crowning event for having to stare down a disabled, mentally disturbed psychopath. What would Sigmund Freud have attributed it to? Sublimation? What turns men and women into creatures so mean and depraved that they must hurt others? Especially those who are least able to defend themselves? I called it cowardice and a heart long turned into a vile, rotten substance that only loved pain and misery, especially when experienced by others. Nonetheless, I'd had another close call and was beginning to wonder how many of my nine lives I'd used up.

We winded our tipsy way down the brick pathway with Freddie and Chuck, laughing our heads off. As we approached the hallway between Sally's and my studio and what had been hers and Jerry's, I saw an ominous shadow. I almost walked into Jerry. He made a beeline for Sally, who cowered in front of him.

"Hey, what's going on?" I practically shouted.

"You tell me!" said Jerry.

Freddie and Chuck exchanged amused looks, too drunk to understand what was going on.

"These are friends of ours," said Sally, giving Jerry a look that begged for mercy.

"Get in there!" said Jerry. He pushed Sally into his studio.

"Who's that guy?" growled Chuck. He scowled at Jerry.

"He's Sally's, um, ex-boyfriend; at least, I think he's her ex."

"Why's he so rough with her?"

"I've been trying to figure that out for a while. I guess because she lets him," I said. "I think she needs help."

"Well, we're not father confessors! Chuck was starting to like her!"

"Yeah, I didn't know she had a boyfriend."

Chuck's happy-go-lucky countenance changed into confusion, and Freddie frowned at me, waiting for an explanation.

"They've been fighting lately," I said.

Freddie laughed. Chuck tossed his head and said, "Fine by me. We had a good time tonight." He kicked a stone in the hallway, onto the brick walkway. "Girls."

"I don't know what to say. I thought she'd never go back to him. He's going to give her a hard time." I leaned against the wooden railing of the stairway that led to Albert's studio.

Chuck leaned on Freddie. He laughed and said, "Look, Miss Inny, don't you worry. We'll find another young lady to have some good times with."

"The main thing is the good times!" I agreed.

Freddie gave me a big smooch, and they walked away, laughing and making wisecracks.

"Thanks for the beers… And for saving me from that monster!" I said with a smile full of gratitude.

"Anytime," said Freddie as they turned the corner and disappeared into the empty street that led to Berkeley's campus. "We specialize in saving girls from bad guys." They laughed. "Although your friend needs to be saved from herself!" Freddie said.

Still reeling from the earlier events, plus Sally jumping back into her tormenter's arms, I took a shower and tried to calm down. I put on my favorite Victorian nightgown, given to me by my beloved grandmother last Christmas. She'd broken down and cried when we called her. I'd only see her two more times before she died.

Before going to sleep, I said a prayer to my grandmother, who loved me unconditionally. I imagined her sweet voice saying, 'There, there, Little Inny, don't fret.' As she had when I was a toddler, growing up in her big, welcoming house, as big and welcoming as her heart.

Chapter 4

The next day dawned unusually sunny and clear for late September in Berkeley. It seemed surreal. I had psychology and American history classes in the morning. I had to take American history to graduate, just like I had to take this rat psychology class. I had no interest in either, but I was determined to get my degree.

Rat psychology was what students called this class because the course material dealt with experiments performed on rats. The professor had a bit of a reputation for eccentricity. Two days ago, he imitated a rat on a hot iron grid, jumping up and down and squeaking on the platform in an amphitheater, in front of two hundred and fifty students. I was beginning to think that my psychology professors could use some couch-time themselves.

I thought of Crutches and shook my head, thinking there might never be enough clinical psychiatrists, especially good ones.

Most of my classes consisted of large amounts of information being stuffed into students' heads. The classrooms were huge, to keep the cost of mass education down. The professor also assigned a book called *Men and Beasts.* I couldn't agree more. I wished I could talk to John Hopman, but he was in Santa Barbara and Jim at Harvard. He called from time to time, but we didn't have much to say. I couldn't tell him about my latest near-rape. Then, I remembered Albert. I could talk to him. He was kind and highly intelligent. He knew men were beasts; after all, he was gay. I wondered why men became gay. Why did so many mistreat women? And vice-versa. What would Freud have said? A Mommy complex? An over-active id? Childhood trauma? I knew it came from being spoiled rotten and thinking they were entitled to do as they pleased with a woman, much like some nasty people mistreat their pets.

Later in the morning, Adrianne Koch finished her lecture on American history with a flourish, her lavishly ringed fingers and magenta satin robe added to her place as a unique woman on the U.C. Berkeley faculty. Widely respected for her research and writings on Cotton Mather and other old Puritans who had given the United States its unique take on sexuality, she'd quote them, '*Dyed in the blood of the Lamb,*' for example, and make them come alive for her class of two hundred students. History took on a new life for me; I began to love it and especially Adrianne Koch. Little did I know I'd be in her office when she would receive a phone call saying that President John Fitzgerald Kennedy had been assassinated. I had other things on my mind today as I left the classroom with Mel Levine and others who were finishing up their required classes so they could graduate in June of 1964.

A pleasant breeze riffled my long, dark blonde hair as I walked towards my studio on Parker Avenue. Dwinelle Plaza's fountain burbled and sparkled. Despite my close call with mortality last night, I enjoyed the brisk fall weather that was fast setting in. It reminded me of the first day of fall in Arlington, Virginia, where I'd grown up. I could smell the autumn air when it turned from warm to cool; it invigorated me. I was a happy soul.

As I turned into the brick pathway that led to the studio apartments, I noticed Maria Dolores, the cleaning woman, smiling stout and resolute – waving at me. I waved back.

"Albert's there!"

"Good!"

I knew Maria Dolores had a hopeless crush on Albert, because she proclaimed it every time she had a chance. Pathetic described her best, I'm afraid. He couldn't stand her.

I saw the windowpanes that made up almost an entire wall of my lower level studio. As I walked in, I noticed that Albert's door was open upstairs. I decided to say hello.

He was jovial and hospitable, his usual self. He offered me a seat, and I took it.

"I hope we didn't disturb you last night," I said.

"You had quite a few visitors." His grin revealed teeth that were straight and even; he had a large, genial smile. He was handsome. That, coupled with his generosity of spirit, attracted me. Here was a man who wouldn't diminish me in any way. He was kind.

"Not all of whom were invited."

Albert flounced his shoulders and grinned. "You just never know who might drop by." He giggled.

"Crutches and his friend Ira dropped by."

A frown corrugated Albert's smooth forehead. "Crutches has a nasty reputation."

"I can vouch for that." I rubbed the spot where he'd clutched my thigh.

"Did he... do anything?"

I put my thumb and index finger about an inch apart. "He came that close."

Albert inhaled sharply. "How did you get mixed up with someone like him?"

"I don't even know how he got my address. He said some of our friends gave it to him, but I think he followed Sally and me home from the Monkey Inn. I told her not to let him in."

"Did she?"

"She thought it was Ed coming to get his bicycle." My voice had a sarcastic ring to it.

"Of course she helped you get rid of him."

"She suddenly found reason to lock herself in the bathroom. If Fast Freddie and Chuck Buchman hadn't called, I might not be here talking to you."

Albert leaned forward. "You need protection. The next time that happens, scream as loud as you can."

"What if you're not home?"

"A scream usually scares thugs like that off. You could also keep a handy pair of scissors or a small knife near your bed."

"Why do men hurt women?"

Albert paused. He cleared his throat and said, "I think it's about asserting manhood by force. Showing women who's the boss by punishing them. It happens to men, too." He lowered his head.

"Oh, Albert!" I unburdened my fears. "I think they wanted to kill me." My pent-up emotions flowed over and around his kind, sympathetic, understanding heart.

"You poor thing!" He put his arms around me. I had a good cry.

"Those boys can be such brutes." I looked at him through teary eyes. I figured he knew what he was talking about. The Berkeley football team called him the African Queen. It wasn't easy to be gay in 1963. I hugged him back. Slowly, my pain ebbed away, absorbed by his kind soul. We rocked back and forth for a few minutes. Then, we let go of one another.

"Would you like some din dins?"

"I'd love some din dins!"

"Come on up at about six o'clock and Mama Albert will have some chitlins ready for you, poor child."

I stood up awkwardly, wiping away a stray tear.

"Thank you so much, Albert. I can't tell you how much I appreciate your kindness."

"It's my pleasure…"

"*A bientôt…*" I sang out in the only French I could speak, my minor subject. I walked towards the doorway and down the stairs to my apartment, waving goodbye. No wonder Maria Dolores loved him. Why were some people so wonderful and others so horrible? I'd soon realize that it had to do with cowardice. It takes courage to be kind.

When I opened the door to my studio, I saw Sally packing a suitcase. "I'm so glad you're leaving Jerry!"

She looked up and smiled blandly. "He just got another job in India. He's taking me with him."

"Sally, that man hurts you!" I felt like shaking her to try to shape her up, but I knew better.

"He's apologized. He says it won't happen again."

"You told me he terrorized you in India. Why are you going back?"

She continued to stare at me through opaque, bland, if not blind, eyes. "I won't have to do any housework. He says we can hire maids for next to nothing." Her straight bangs hung over an eye that looked bruised.

"And you'll take advantage of the poor women in India." I put my hands on my hips. She wasn't fooling me. Sally would always try to take the easy way out, which would backfire.

"I'll be nice to them," she said, continuing to fold and pack her shirt-maker dresses, so popular and practical.

"That's not the point! Unpack your bags! I'm going to talk to your parents."

"You can't do that!"

"If you don't start sticking up for yourself, I'll never speak to you... Come on, Sally. You're afraid of Jerry."

"He takes care of me."

"I'll say. He makes you pay a steep price for the so-called care. And you're doing stuff for him, too."

Sally wiped her eyes. "We have good sex together."

Just then, Jerry walked into the studio.

"Come on, Sally! It's time to go!" He gave her a steely-eyed look like a red-eyed rat.

"She's not going!"

Jerry took one look at me and started to laugh. "What? You skinny excuse for a chick thinks she can tell Sally what to do?"

"Yeah!" I stood between them with my arms crossed over my skinny self. Others called me slender; I wasn't skinny, and I knew it. "Look, Jerry, you've been hurting her and I know it."

Sally slammed her suitcase shut. She gave me a puppy-dog pleading look. "Don't worry, Inny! It's going to be different this time, isn't it, Jerry?"

"You betcha!"

Jerry grabbed her suitcase and out the door they went. Sally gave me a backwards glance; I could see fear in her eyes. "I'm going to call the police the next time!" I yelled.

Albert peeked out of his door upstairs. "What's all the noise?"

"Jerry's making Sally go to India again!"

Albert shook his head. "I know. I can hear them talking and packing. I can hear him smack her, too."

"She always makes decisions that... hurt her... and others." Sally's decisions hurt me, because I cared about her and kept hoping she'd gain enough confidence to free herself of such a contemptible man.

Jerry hoisted her suitcase onto his shoulder, grabbing Sally with his free hand. They ran down the brick pathway, headed for another disaster, I was sure.

Albert motioned for me to come up to his studio. I walked up the wooden stairs and sat down on his sofa.

"It's nice of you to try to help your friend, and I know he's cruel to her, but she's got to learn on her own."

"I don't think she ever will." I looked down at his Persian carpet, with its lovely, intricate design. *Just like abstract art, only lovelier,* I thought. "I've been trying to help her for years now."

Albert got up to stir something in a frying pan on the stove. "It's the male dominance thingy."

"What?" I sat bolt upright. "Outright male dominance? I thought those days were over!"

Albert stirred the omelet and chitlins some more, giving me a wry smile. "Some things are never over. Women can be cruel, too." He winked at me. "And men can be cruel to each other."

"Oh." I felt deflated. "Well, dominating Sally would be like dominating a kitten... or a flea... or..."

"I've heard him slapping her around more than once."

"No!"

"I live directly above them. I thought you knew."

"I've seen him kick her out into the hallway, but I didn't think... I've never heard of men slapping women around." I hesitated and thought about Jim almost slapping me. "I mean, I saw it in a movie once..."

"Not at home." Albert gave me a penetrating look. I started to laugh. "My father's terrified of my mother! She's the queen. He's her humble servant; he adores her. If anyone is bossy, it's my mother."

"Is your dad hen-pecked?"

"He adores my mother. If there's a draft in the room, she yells, 'Craig, there's a draft!' He jumps up and starts shutting all the windows. If he'd hit her, she'd have divorced him the next day."

"Your mom sounds like quite a woman."

"She is... Let's say nothing gets by her."

"So, how about some scrambled eggs and chitlins?" He smiled at me.

"How can I resist?" I smiled back. "Besides, enough about men and women."

"It's all about love."

I nodded my agreement. We sat down, ate breakfast, and gave up on humanity for the time being. I knew I was lucky to have a friend like Albert.

"I'm working on a screenplay about a relationship," he said while chewing on chitlins.

"Oh? You mean for a movie?"

"A movie starring Alexia Roma." Albert looked up from his plate and gave me a big, toothy grin.

"She's a lollapalooza! I'll bet she'd know what to do with a guy like Jerry."

"What would she do if he hit her?"

I slurped down some of the omelet and put my fork in the chitlins. Albert poured some orange juice; I had some, too.

"She'd be all over him screaming, kicking, biting; she'd be so indignant, he'd be sorry he ever touched her. Alexia Roma can be ferocious! She's a great actress! You're writing a screenplay for her?"

"I'm supposed to meet her and Alessandro Rossi in Los Angeles to discuss the script." Albert finished his breakfast. He looked at me.

I was almost through. "This is delicious, Albert!"

"I love to cook," he said with a sly smile.

It crossed my mind that gay men liked to cook; maybe that's why he was smiling. I didn't care; I liked to eat.

"Isn't it hard to write something like that?" I was mildly curious, having next to no interest in the film industry.

"You have to develop an ear for dialogue and an eye for scenes; it's not easy, but I love writing – good writing," said Albert.

"Well, if you want a tough woman's advice on how another tough woman would react to a slap in the face, I can help you." I smiled and tossed my head with confidence. "I've been in some challenging situations and come out on top, so far."

"I don't think of you as tough."

"Just try me," I laughed. "No, really. A guy tried to rape me this summer, I mean a caveman-style rape, and I got away. He had quite a few scratches on his back, I'm sure."

Albert pushed his chair away from the kitchen table. "Inny! How terrible!"

"No! How wonderful that I escaped! That's what just went on with Crutches and his buddy Ira. That guy had his hand on my thigh. I was watching my life pass before my eyes when Freddie and Charles called. Brave Sally had locked herself in the bathroom. I was cornered and nearly died of fright."

Sheer disgust crossed Albert's normally benign countenance. "Men can be such brutes."

Albert and I exchanged looks that took the sting out of my recent encounter. He sympathized. He cared. He KNEW.

"I guess some men think I'm easy." I pushed my chair away, breathing harder at the thought of what I'd been through. "I get pretty crazy when I drink. They call me a cheap heat." I laughed. "I get high on a can of beer."

"I'm glad you didn't get hurt." Albert sympathized with such sincerity that I felt like hugging him. "And your drinking shouldn't affect the way they treat you." His voice became resonant with indignation when he said that. He understood so well.

"I probably did what she would've done, only she's bigger than me," I smiled. "What a body!"

"She is well-endowed." A gleam came into Albert's eye. "I love her almond-shaped eyes... and her playful, yet gutsy, way of...

She's got Neapolitan blood."

"I'm sure she does. If you need any help with a scene, you'll discover I'm part Italian. I'll be your gal Friday."

"Are you really part Italian?"

"My grandfather told me there was a Reynaldo in the family tree, so who knows? Who cares? We all came from Luci, you know, the carbon-dated skeleton Leakey found in Africa where Homo sapiens evolved."

"That's right," Albert chuckled. "You're a highly intelligent woman... Next thing I know, you'll tell me all about chitlins."

We wiped our mouths with checkered napkins and stood up. A deal had been struck. It was love. Hetero-homosexual love or something on that order. I didn't care; I lived for the precious moment. I was in love with life.

Chapter 5

Fast Freddie called me while I was fixing my usual calves' liver dinner.

"Hey, Inny! We're going to San Francisco tonight! Me and Charles, the one and only, and a few friends. Wanna tag along?"

I thought of his long, lean, muscular body and sexy, almost slanting, big blue eyes, usually laughing at some hijinks he and Chuck had pulled off. My kinda guy. Fun and good-looking! Plus, he was on the basketball team. In the back of my mind, I was thinking of asking him if he knew anything about Crutches' whereabouts, since his brother Ned played on the same team. I'd like that guy out of Berkeley; I'd at least like to know if he was still after me.

"Sure! Where are we going?"

"Oh, no place in particular. We just thought we'd have some fun."

More beer drinking games, I imagined.

"Okay. When will you pick me up?"

"In about a half an hour."

"That's pretty short notice. Do you mind if I wear a leotard?"

He laughed. "You can wear your birthday suit if you want. We're not fussy."

"Okay." I laughed and put the receiver down. It sounded like my kind of fun, spontaneous, with no strings attached.

When Freddie knocked on my door, I had my favorite party dress on. I opened the door and Freddie nodded his approval. Chuck was with him.

"Are you ready to board the Good Ship Lollipop, Miss Inny?" asked Chuck with a chortle.

"The Good Ship Lollipop? Where's the candy canes shop? Let's go!" These guys were characters, and we'd have a good time. What more could I ask for?

I'd put on my favorite magenta, above-the-knee-length Lanz dress, which meant I'd act as hot as my dress. That dress always enhanced my mood, which was ecstatic.

Fred jammed in to hustle me out to his funky car, which practically ran on three wheels, especially the way Freddie drove. Chunky Charles got in the backseat with another friend of mine, Lynne, whom he called Miss Lynny. Charles had a name for everyone.

Before I could say chugalug a beer, Freddie spotted an ambulance, siren blaring. He took off after it. "Here we go!" he yelled.

Chunky Charles, Lynn, and I shrieked and squealed in delight as he followed the ambulance through every red light on Shattuck Avenue, clear into Oakland. I had to gasp for air to recover from that antic.

"I thought you said we were going to San Francisco," I said, breathing hard.

Freddie turned the car around, heading back for the hills of Berkeley, namely, for the Sigma Epsilon Alpha fraternity house, where a tub of rum and who-knows-what mixed with soda candy sweet sugar drinks awaited. Several of my former sorority sisters were drinking with some of their fraternity brothers. We joined them. There was a party at their fraternity house that night, even though they no longer lived there, but who cared? Booze is booze. This was what they called a pre-party. It was at a small, unpretentious house next door to the SAE fraternity house, which was pretentious, with Greek columns and a large, lush lawn in front.

The four of us started downing the sugary brew with the best of them, laughing and joking. As I downed a glass of the brew, one of the fellas told an off-color joke. That was my cue.

"Do you know the difference between a staple and a screw?" I widened my eyes to look as virginal as possible.

"No," said the boy who'd told the joke.

"Neither do I. I've never been stapled."

Everyone laughed on cue. I started reeling out my repertoire of dirty jokes just in case they thought I might have been intimidated by theirs.

Chunky Charles clicked glasses with me. "Miss Inny, you've got quite a mouth on you!"

"No one can shut me up!" I laughed.

Fast Freddie looked down my dress to see if I was worth the trouble. We kept on drinking until the punch bowl was empty.

"Let's dance!" I yelled.

"Let's go to the party!" said Freddie.

We walked next door to the SAE house, noting that a girl had already passed out on the lawn.

"Guess she had a bit too much to drink," said Charles.

We all laughed. Passing out was not unusual in those heady days.

Once there, we entered a sumptuous room decorated with palm tree fronds and branches, an island in the middle, and about a hundred students doing the twist in sarongs and other appropriate Hawaiian get up. So much for my magenta dress.

We started dancing to Chubby Checkers, "Let's do the twist like we did last summer, twist and twist and twist again…" rang out his melodious voice. Everyone twisted. Freddie and I twisted so long and hard that I began to feel like I had a stomachache, but it was transitory… like life. Freddie smiled into my deep blue eyes and I smiled back into his lighter blue eyes. Drunk as skunks, we made for the island in the middle. It had a moat around it with a wooden plank for crossing.

Lynn walked gingerly over and beckoned for us to join her. I jumped on the board and swoosh, Freddie pulled the board up and down I went into the moat, not without cutting my leg, a superficial cut, it turned out. I still had some of my nine lives left.

"Hey!" I yelled. "You pulled that board out from under me!"

I looked up to see everyone laughing. Practical jokers.

"My leg is bleeding!"

Freddie, Charles and I looked at the minor injury and decided to dance some more. It was just a superficial cut. The throbbing beat of the twist had us in its thrall. Freddie and I twisted till we gasped. Then, Freddie took me by the hand. We ran up the stairs to the second floor, and before you could say Sigma Alpha Epsilon, he was on top of me. "Hey, wait!"

"Wait?" He said. "What for? Come on, baby, let's do the twist!" He put his hand on my breast; I felt a distinct tingle of pleasure, but this was premature.

I screamed. He grabbed me again, but this time to get away from some voices headed in our direction. I sprinted to keep up with his long-legged, six-foot-two-inch frame, becoming less amused by his antics every time my foot hit a board and the slight gash in my leg throbbed.

Every now and then, a girl comes to her senses.

"Let's go home," I said. "I've had enough for one night."

"But you haven't seen our apartment yet!" He gave me a frustrated look.

He probably still wants to have sex, I thought.

He pulled me through what seemed like a hundred college kids gyrating to Chubby Checkers' twist music trying to find Charles and Lynn, who had also disappeared.

"Just drop me at my place and you can find Charles and Lynn later," I said.

"What's wrong with you?"

"It's just a slight cut, that's all."

"Not the cut!"

"What did you expect, Freddie?" I paused. "Maybe I'm just frigid." I smiled to myself.

"Do you need to see a doctor?"

"I probably should get a tetanus shot."

"For your fucking frigidity!"

"I'm not frigid! I'm just not fast! Just because I drink like a fish doesn't mean I'm easy. Take me home!"

Freddie scowled at me and mumbled something to the effect that I was a penis tease. Then, he ushered me out the entrance to the fraternity house and to his funky car. We drove home in silence. We did not, however, encounter silence when we arrived at my studio apartment. There sat Sally, wailing in the hallway, with Jerry about to hit her. I saw Albert open his door and peek out. I ran up to Jerry, who was holding a suitcase. Sally held another one.

"I thought you'd gone to India!"

"The job got postponed at the last minute," said Sally.

Jerry shoved her into the doorway. "Shut up!"

"What are you doing to Sally?"

"It's none of your business!"

Albert descended the stairs and said, "When it wakes me up, it's my business! Treat the little lady with some respect!"

"Shut up, nigger!" yelled Jerry.

I slugged him as hard as I could, right in his bulbous nose. Blood trickled from it.

He tried to hit me back, but Freddie interfered by slugging him again. Jerry fell back against the wall. Sally sniveled in the background. He got up and tried to run back into his studio, but Freddie and I grabbed him. Freddie towered over this cowering excuse for a man, who put his arms in front of his face and said, "Don't hurt me!"

"When *are* you going to stop hurting Sally?" said Albert.

"Shut up, nigger!"

I kicked Jerry in the leg closest to me. Albert grinned.

"Apologize to Albert and Sally!" I said.

"Fuck you!"

Freddie grabbed him by the shirt collar and hauled him to his feet. "Fuck you!" he said.

"I don't have to apologize to anybody! I'm an engineer!"

I grabbed him by his short, sand-colored hair. I pulled it as hard as I could. "Apologize or move out!" He started to snivel. "Only cowards hurt women and animals!" I yelled. I gave him another kick for good measure.

Albert motioned for me to follow him upstairs to his studio. I nodded goodnight to Freddie and followed Albert.

"Hey, where are you going?" said Freddie.

Jerry slunk back into his studio; Sally followed him, probably to try to patch things up.

"Come back here!" I said.

Sally cast me a sorrowful look. "Jerry's hurt. I have to help him."

"When has he helped you? He beats you and we know it," I continued.

Sally started to snivel. She was a lost cause. I turned towards Albert.

"I'm going with Albert! We have a lot to talk about." I looked at Freddie. I felt sorry for him. "I'm sorry about... I mean, I think you were brave to hit Jerry!"

Freddie nodded, turned tail, and walked down the brick path. I liked him for hitting Jerry, but I didn't want to sleep with him.

Albert was waiting for me with a huge smile. He always emanated warmth around me. Did I have a magic elixir? No, Albert was naturally warm. "Where have you been all my life!" He practically yelled it.

"We may have more in common than meets the eye," I said as a warm sensation invaded my body. I started grinning with embarrassment, and so did he. He hugged me. He put on some soft romantic music. "Let's dance."

We danced, forgetting about the crazy scene down below. I examined the nape of his manly neck. I couldn't resist kissing it. Before I knew it, we wound our arms around each other, kissing each other on the face, neck, chest... Then, I took a step backwards.

"Albert, I'm a woman!"

"An amazing woman!"

"You mean..."

"Don't listen to people. They say all kinds of nonsense about me." He hesitated. "I might have tried alternative scenes." He arched a brow. "I was young and impressionable. Would you care for some champagne?"

Delighted by the turn of events, I hugged him. His muscles were hard. A shiver of excitement ran through my small frame. I could feel his hard pectorals.

Albert went to his small refrigerator, and next to the milk was a bottle of pink champagne. He opened it and poured two glasses. He handed me one. I couldn't stop smiling. We clicked glasses. "Here's looking at you!" he said, mimicking the famous Bogart/Bacall line. I winked at him, trying to imitate Lauren Bacall.

We drank and danced some slow, sexy numbers by Ray Charles. Entranced, I stared into his eyes, but I felt shy. Albert picked up on my pulchritude and said, "Would you like to take a bath?"

"Together?"

"Unless you prefer to bathe alone." He smiled at my virginal attitude.

"Cleanliness is next to godliness."

I slid my dress off one of my shoulders. Albert kissed my shoulder, then my neck. I took a deep breath, feeling giddy, and kissed him on the lips. We couldn't stop kissing. He put a finger under my bra strap and ran it down to my breast. I pulled him over to the sofa. That he was older than me made no difference. I wasn't jail bait. I was a woman.

By the morning, I had a new black boyfriend who wasn't gay after all. He was also a Berkeley English professor, and I was twenty-one, an adult who made her own decisions.

Albert got up first and started making eggs Benedict.

"Are they named after Benedict Arnold?"

Albert turned around. In a shrill voice, he said. "How can an egg be a traitor?"

"Is it an illegitimate egg?" I ventured, running my hand down my bare body. I shivered from last night's excitement. I think I'd had what they call an orgasm. Or an orgy!

Albert stroked his chiseled, square-cut chin slowly with his hand. I admired his handsome, classic profile as I bantered with him.

"Do chickens get married?"

"I think they can if their parents give them permission."

We laughed. Then, he continued fixing breakfast. With his back turned to me, only the beautiful paisley print on his bathrobe showing, he said, "Would you like to co-author the screenplay I'm writing for Alexia?"

"Co-author a screenplay?" I pulled back the covers and jumped out of bed. "I barely passed freshman English," I said, grabbing my underwear.

Albert turned around, spatula in hand, and went to his closet. He took out another bathrobe. "Here. Try this on for size." As I put the large bathrobe on, he chattered on, "You could help me with her dialogue and some of her reactions…"

"She adores Alessandro Rossi… She has a wonderful sense of irony, combined with humor and earthiness… I'd love to try. But I'd just be helping you; I wouldn't qualify as a co-author."

"You never know," said Albert with a ring of amusement in his voice.

I hugged Albert as he served the eggs with champagne. Albert never did anything halfway. "Where's the caviar?" I asked.

He laughed and turned his profile for me to examine. He had a high brow, a long, rather beaked nose, and a good jawline. "Do I look Egyptian?"

I grinned at him. "I haven't met too many Egyptians; but if you want to look Egyptian, I'd say you resembled King Tut."

He laughed so hard he spilled his champagne. I tossed some of mine at him. We slurped the rest down and had some more. Soon, we piled back into his unmade bed. His black hand on my white breast excited me. His brilliance excited me. His black penis was more than I'd ever bargained for. Shit. I was in love.

I felt like Gabriel had just opened the gates to heaven. I was smiling from ear to ear. Albert tried to be more serious, but we both, ended up getting out of bed and wolfing down our remaining eggs Benedict breakfast. The empty champagne bottle sparkled in the morning sunshine.

I stood up and walked around to Albert's chair. I began toying with his ear. The bed wasn't far away. By afternoon, we were working on the screenplay and I'd talked to Alexia over the phone in Italy. Buon giorno, fabulous woman! I was in heaven! And not one angel – well, perhaps yes, there was a black angel sitting right next to me. Maybe I wasn't such an atheist after all. Kick Freud in the balls!

We heard some noise from Jerry's studio. We exchanged looks.

"They're at it again," Albert said.

I jumped up and walked to Albert's front door and opened it. From his landing, I could see them leaving for India again, vintage suitcases in hand. "Good luck!" I yelled, pen in hand.

Sally waved. Jerry stared at me with a small, beady-eyed squint.

"I'll get you, you… you, nigger lover!"

Albert stepped out just then. I put my arms around him and kissed him. "Thank God you're not white, Albert!" I said.

Jerry started to run up the stairs, but his suitcase opened and half his grungy underwear spilled out.

"The taxi's waiting, Jerry," said Sally.

They shoved the undies back in the suitcase, closed it, and ran off.

Good riddance, I thought.

"Shall we go for a stroll?" Albert was still holding a glass of champagne, debonair in his silk paisley bathrobe.

"Where to?"

"The UCEN? For coffee?"

"I'll run and get my things. Are you coming as you are?"

"Oh, I forgot my lavender wig. I don't want to frighten anyone." Albert assumed his high-pitched voice full of irony. Laughing my head off, I ran downstairs to my studio, mine alone at this point. I grabbed a bright shirt-maker dress I'd concocted out of some material I bought in the drapery department. There were huge flowers on it. No one had anything nearly that bright in 1963, even at U.C. Berkeley. I felt like the belle of the ball. Not quite Scarlett O'Hara, but joyous and fulfilled in a way I'd never felt.

Yet, violence had lifted its repellent head once again and taken a bite out of my *joie de vivre*. I determined to enjoy the magic of the moment as much as possible, but with an awareness that life wasn't always perfect. I wondered why Albert had been with men. So much was happening all at once. I could hardly think straight.

Chapter 6

While daubing some Revlon Cool Coral lipstick on, the only makeup I ever wore, it occurred to me that Albert wasn't my age. He must be older, even though he didn't act old or stodgy in the least, but he had to have a doctorate to teach at Berkeley, which can take years to get, I'd heard. I put that thought in the back of my mind, hearing his footsteps descending the wooden staircase that led to his studio. He rapped lightly on my door, and I ran to greet him with a wraparound smile, my specialty. Despite an occasional quirk of fate or crazed state senator's son, I had a happy disposition, just like my grandmother. The one who loved to sing on the bus and at children's funerals, anywhere. The one who was my mother's opposite. The one who loved me.

Albert had something in his hand. He gave it to me.

I looked at the cover with brads punched through it. "*Venus's Delight.* What a terrific title," I said.

"I thought you might like to peruse it while we are having coffee at the UCEN," said Albert. He was wearing khakis and a Brooks Brothers shirt; Albert had always been a snappy dresser. I smiled proudly at everyone as we walked towards Sather Gate, the gateway to the Berkeley campus. The new UCEN, or student cafeteria, was immediately to the left of it, so we didn't have far to go.

When we arrived at the modernistic UCEN, I saw Freddie and some of his friends sitting at a table. I waved as we walked past them.

"There's Fred and Chuck, my friends from last night."

"He has a strong right arm," Albert observed.

Freddie stood up and walked over to us. "You abandoned the Good Ship Lollipop last night," he said.

"Oh, I think I took a couple of trips to the candy shop," I said, picking up on the refrain of the once popular Shirley Temple song.

"Inny's helping me write something," said Albert.

"More dusting articles for *Good Housekeeping*?"

I put my chin up and said, "It's a screenplay that Albert's been commissioned to write for Alexia Roma."

Freddie scratched his head. "I don't know any Alexias."

Albert and I exchanged amused looks.

"Alexia Roma won an Oscar," I said.

Albert grinned to try to lighten things up.

"Well! Is she from Africa? Is she a queen?" said Freddie.

"She's the queen of Italian cinema and fast becoming one here!" I said. Freddie's remark annoyed me… Freddie suddenly looked very small and sounded petty. "And don't be so sarcastic!"

"Now, now, Miss Inny," Chuck stood up and injected a conciliatory tone. "We're just harmless SAE frat rats."

"Your moat wasn't so harmless," I said, pointing to the long scratch the board had left on my leg.

"How did that happen?" said Albert.

"At the SAE fraternity party last night," I laughed. "Was that just last night? So much has happened!"

Freddie arched an eyebrow.

"Would you care to join us?" asked Albert.

"I'm not into threesomes," said Freddie.

I gulped and tugged Albert by the arm. "Let's just have some coffee."

"Yes, let's."

We sat down, a bit ruffled by Freddie's remarks.

"Is he crazy?" I couldn't believe Freddie could be so mean.

"Oh, people say the silliest things when I'm around. It's just because of my pigmentation." Albert smiled a big, toothy Albert smile.

"He's jealous!" I insisted.

Albert beamed at me. "Who wouldn't be?"

I blushed. "I'm not Alexia Roma…"

"You're beautiful!" He squeezed my hand; my heart skipped a beat. It felt so wonderful to have someone care about me.

"I'll make amends," said Albert.

He stood up and walked over to where Freddie was sitting with Chuck and some other friends.

"I'm having an open bar party tonight, if you'd care to indulge." He gave them his best, huge, infectious Albert Curtis grin.

Freddie and Chuck exchanged looks with the rest of them. "A party? With free booze? Can we bring girls?"

"It's *carte blanche*… of course you can bring girls! What's a party without girls?"

"We'll be there!"

I blanched when I realized I'd be partying with Freddie and Charles AND Albert tonight.

"Anyway, let's look at *Venus's Delight*." I decided to change the subject, to get down to business.

Here I was, with the most popular teacher on campus, whom I'd just *turned*, for heaven's sake, and we had to bump into my date from last night. I guess I'd had several dates last night, come to think of it.

Albert and I put our heads together over coffee and the script, talking and laughing our heads off. We were ON! Plus, there was another party in the offing. Life is a giggle, we said in those days. Berkeley's tuition was seventy-five dollars a semester, there were twice as many boys as girls enrolled and President John F. Kennedy, Jr. had just invited Martin Luther King Jr. to the White House. Life was good; unless you were a member of the Bush family, which considered the Kennedys their rivals.

I made a few suggestions about Alexia's reactions in a scene or two, Albert took note of them, finished his coffee, and tucked the screenplay under his arm. He offered me his other arm, which I took. We headed back to our respective studio apartments, drawing the occasional stare. A middle-aged woman made a remark. "Haven't you heard of miscegenation?"

Albert and I ignored her, but she reminded me of my mother, whose racism loomed like an enemy ship in one of Lord Nelson's battles which suddenly seemed to glare at me. My mother. I shuddered.

I yelled at her, "Chagacious chagrin!"

Albert looked at me as if he'd just seen me for the first time.

"You're a riot! Chagacious? What a word!"

"I always yell chagacious chagrin at… certain people."

Albert laughed. "Chagacious chagrin? Why not? Have some more champagne."

"I just adore you."

He took my hand and kissed it. A familiar tingle coursed through my body. We held hands the rest of the way home.

When we arrived at the brick pathway that led to our studio apartments, I looked up at him. He was taller than me by several inches. He smiled. Maria Dolores saw us.

"Albert! I need to clean your studio!"

"Not today, Maria Dolores," he said. He looked back into my eyes, sparking with joy. "Would you like some more of the bubbly?"

I grabbed him by both hands and started to whirl him around. "Yes, yes, yes!" He laughed with delight and swung me under his arm. We ran to the staircase and up into his studio. Champagne, ardor, screenplays, and Albert's

My eyes teared up. "She insults me. She… she doesn't seem to care about me except as someone to marry off. I feel like she doesn't love me. I loved my grandmother." My eyes misted over.

"You still have to love your mother. You have to forgive her." Albert stared directly into my teary eyes.

"How?"

He put his strong arm around my shoulders. "Just love her. We have to love our parents, no matter how bad they may seem or be, so we can grow up. We have to forgive them for being less than perfect."

I stared back at him in shock. What he said made sense. It made perfect sense. I had to release myself from my anger at my mother. No matter what.

"How can I do this?" I looked at him as if he were a deity of some sort.

Albert chuckled, "That's for you to figure out, Inny. You will. It just takes time."

I laughed, "Like an eternity?"

He ran his hand under the back of my blouse. I opened the top buttons on his Brooks Brothers shirt, felt his hard chest muscles, and inhaled sharply. He looked deep into my eyes as if asking permission. I nodded. He undid my bra and slid his hand gently over my breasts. Off came the clothes. Down we went, ending up on his sofa, squirming and slithering like a couple of lovesick Anacondas. Laughing, managing to drink more champagne, and then again, and again. My breath came in spurts, as well as laughter. Albert never let up.

"Freddie and Chuck…" I gasped.

"Let them eat cake, darlin'," said Albert. "Now you've got a real man." He grinned his infectious grin. I inhaled sharply.

We slid off the sofa, landing on a carpet on the floor, laughing and holding each other. We couldn't stop. There was a noise at the door.

"What's that noise?" I asked.

"I hope it's not Maria Dolores," said Albert, feigning fright.

We started laughing again. Oh, too much champagne, and yes, too much love making, and… what was that knocking?

Albert staggered to the closet and took out a robe; he made it to the door and opened it a crack.

"Adrianne Koch!" He threw open the door. "Welcome to the party!"

I slithered under the carpet, trying to estimate the distance between my clothes and the doorway. They came flying through the air. Albert tossed them to me. He stood in the doorway while I madly tried to put my skirt and blouse, not to mention bra and panties, back on. I heard Adrianne laugh. She was my history professor. The room started to spin just as Albert refilled my champagne glass and offered her some.

No one seemed to have noticed that I was still buttoning my magenta dress.

"Oh, Albert, how splendid of you," she said, taking the glass. "What a lovely robe you have on. Is it from Morocco?"

"It's a kaftan," said Albert, "that I bought in Morocco on my way home from the Cannes Film Festival last year." He took a sip of champagne and motioned her to a seat, whereupon my presence became obvious. "This is Inny. She's helping me with the screenplay I'm working on for Alessandro Rossi and Alexia Roma."

"I'm so glad you asked a woman to help you; we have a slightly different point of view, you know." She gave me a knowing look. I turned bright red as I dressed under the rug. Too much champagne. Nonetheless, I forged ahead because she'd brought the old Puritans to life for me in her lectures. She was my American history teacher, who always arrived wearing a magenta-colored taffeta coat, her arms covered with silver and turquoise Mexican jewelry. She was flamboyant and known for having the largest vocabulary of any of the professors on campus.

"I keep wondering why they burned women at the stake in Salam, drowned them, all that religious nonsense. What do you think their real reasons might have been?" I looked at Adrianne, knowing she'd help me understand.

Adrianne's middle-aged, wrinkled, wizened face broke into a smile. "Powerful women have often been persecuted. Joan of Arc was burned at the stake for kicking the British out of France."

I looked into her deep blue eyes. We connected. "They called her crazy, just like Zelda Fitzgerald, or eccentric like Emily Dickenson… what about Cleopatra?"

Albert's eyes lit up at the mention of an Egyptian.

"Men have to maintain their dominance," said Adrianne, glancing in Albert's direction.

"They wouldn't have burned a man at the stake who saved France for hearing messages from god. Half of those kings were drunk with power and a bit nutty, weren't they?" I said.

Albert interrupted. "George Orwell said that some of us are more equal than others. So that may include…"

"That's why the civil rights law that Kennedy talked about in June is crucial to justice," said Adrianne. "I think we're on the right path, at last. He'll sign it if Congress will present it to him."

"I think Kennedy's call for justice, not to mention Martin Luther King's marches, had something to do with my being added to the Berkeley faculty," said Albert.

Adrianne and I stared at Albert in rapt admiration. He was a living symbol of racial progress.

"Real progress will be made when they hire your sister," I said.

Albert broke out laughing. "I can't wait for you to meet her. Would you like some champagne? Adrianne? We're having a teeny bit of a pre-party…"

Adrianne stood up. "I have so much work to do, but this has been a lovely respite. It's always a rare delight to meet one of my students, especially such an inquisitive one." Her voice was deep and throaty, like one might expect from an English noblewoman. Perhaps I was just thinking of Dame Mae Whitty, my favorite British actress, who also was stout and sure of herself like Adrianne.

I stood up; I thanked her for the compliment.

"Try to finish up in time for my little soiree this evening," said Albert.

Adrianne smiled graciously, bussed him on the cheek like the French do, and said it would be impossible. I briefly wondered how close they were.

"Women have to be smart and…" Suddenly, my stomach gave a heave in the wrong direction. "Ummph," I said. I ran to the bathroom and threw up. That was not the impression I wanted to make on my history professor. Too much alcohol.

I heard her chat with Albert and then leave. I splashed water on my face. I came out to find Albert with a worried look. "I have a weak stomach," I said.

He grinned at me. "We'll have to stop at one bottle next time."

"You mean at the party tonight?"

"Oh, I *always* lose count at my parties."

I kissed him and ran down the staircase to my studio where I threw myself on my bed and fell into a deep sleep.

I didn't wake up until the party was in full sway. The sound of footsteps running up and down Albert's staircase finally woke me out of my stupor. I could hear his high, shrill voice and laughter coming from his studio. I had to get up. And I had a paper due on Monday. *Oh, drat*, I thought. *I'll write it on Sunday. And what about my resolve to double down on my studies? I'm learning more from Albert than any teacher ever taught me.*

After a quick shower and a change of clothes, I darted up the stairs to Albert's studio, which was lit up like a Christmas tree and just as enticing. Charging in full tilt, I saw Fast Freddie with a new date, Chuck with one of my old friends, and Albert with his arm around Kathy, the voluptuous blonde violinist who lived above me and across from him. The familiar feeling of a shaft running through my body kept me from lunging at them. Instead, I turned my back and introduced myself to someone named Jay Jay, another tall blond fellow whose smile lit up the already brightly lit room. The background music got faster; pretty soon, we were doing the twist or something resembling it. He told me he was a member of the Zeta fraternity house, the one reserved for ultra-rich boys, but lived in a closet he'd rented because he was a Communist. I began to smile just like him. To hell with monogamy, I'd try them all.

Jay Jay asked me to dance; with my wild wiggle and Jay Jay's blond good looks, we attracted attention, something I was practically immune to. I loved dancing; I didn't care if anyone was watching me. People started clapping in time to the music and other couples joined in.

Then, Albert and Kathy stepped onto the floor. He gave her a spin under his arm.

Kathy's hourglass figure and wild jitterbug with Albert expertly partnering her made people practically drop their champagne glasses. Even Marilyn Monroe might look frumpy next to her. She was a natural blonde bombshell. Fast Freddie cut in. Albert smiled and let them dance. Although Freddie wanted to dance close, Kathy pushed him back a bit with her left arm. "Ah, come on," said Freddie. I smiled; I knew Freddie too well.

Jay Jay and I danced till the Cole Porter album was over. "Even educated fleas do it… let's fall in love." Albert had terrific taste in music, especially old tunes. Jay Jay gave me a last spin, and then we stopped. He kept his arm around my waist, which felt warm and, yes, I had to admit that he was sexy.

"I've got a special cave," he said.

"Really?"

"I could take you there sometime." His smile swallowed my heart and my common sense.

At first, I didn't notice Albert standing behind me. I thought he might chide me for some reason. Instead, he yelled, "Conga line!" The music changed to a conga; everyone followed suit, soon we had a line of people dancing the conga, trying to stick their legs out in time to the music. I turned my head to look for Albert; he grinned at me from under his lavender wig. I started to laugh but had to keep dancing. Soon, we'd gone down his stairs and up the brick pathway to the street. We didn't stop dancing. Fast Freddie had Kathy by the waist and yelled, "Conga!"

I forgot about everything, except the pulsating moment.

Everyone yelled conga in unison. Cars had to stop. People leaned out of their windows. Some of them joined in. We kept going. We were a centipede of protruding legs yelling, "Conga!" I saw Sather Gate loom ahead of us. "Conga, conga!" I gasped for air. Albert was holding onto me for all he was worth. "Conga forever," yelled Albert.

Jay Jay had vanished, like so much blond smoke. There must have been almost a hundred people writhing in the conga line when the police arrived.

Passersby kept joining in; everyone wanted to be part of the fun.

Albert's hands dropped from my waist. He put them in the air.

"Albert, you don't have to do that."

I saw tension come into his face. "It's just a reaction." He tried to laugh, but the police were already out of their cars approaching us. The others scattered. Only Kathy, Jay Jay, and I stayed. And Albert.

"I can explain everything, Officer," said Albert as a police officer began to frisk him. His lavender wig hung at an angle over his face.

"You can explain everything at headquarters." The officer glared at him. "What is that on your head?"

"It's a wig," I said. "Albert wears it to make people laugh."

The officers started frisking all of us. I felt their hands run over my body. "How dare you!" I shouted, nearly knocking one of them off balance.

"I'd be quiet if I were you, miss," he said. He frowned at me. "What are you doing participating in this... this orgy? Let me see your driver's license. You look underage."

"I'm twenty-one," I asserted, looking him squarely in the eye.

"I'm a member of the Berkeley faculty," squawked Albert, his voice high and nervous.

"Straight out of Finocchio's," said a police officer.

"I'm not cross dressing," squealed Albert. His face contorted at the mere idea. I wondered what cross dressing was. I'd never been to Finocchio's, though I'd heard about it as San Francisco's most colorful bar.

"Disturbing the peace," said another officer. "Take him in."

"What about us?"

"Go home and mind your manners!" was the curt reply.

"But Albert hasn't done anything," I pleaded. I looked at the officer with a plea for reason in my eyes.

He laughed. "Disrupting traffic and leading a... a group of unruly protesters down Telegraph Avenue..."

"We were having a party!" I insisted.

"Call Adrianne," hissed Albert with a note of desperation in his voice.

"Okay, buster, into the patrol car," said the burly policeman as they cuffed Albert. His wig fell off. I darted over and picked it up.

"Gimme that!" said another one of the officers.

"Touch me and I'll call my attorney," I stiffened my spine and spoke with authority.

"Leave her alone!" said another officer. "She's got an attorney." I'd said the magic word – attorney.

I didn't have one, but I had a feeling I might need one soon.

The patrol car took off with Albert turning his head to mouth indiscernible words. "We've got to help him!" I turned to the others with an imploring look.

"My father has an attorney," said Jay Jay.

"He said to call Adrianne," said Kathy.

"Let's do everything we can to get him out tonight!" I put on the wig and started running for the studio. Suddenly, most of the conga line reappeared. "Let's free Albert!" I yelled.

"Free Albert!" They took up the chant.

"Wear purple wigs!"

"Wear purple wigs!"

"Go to the police station and free Albert!" I shouted.

"Go to the police station and free Albert," they repeated. I almost laughed, in spite of myself.

Jay Jay, Kathy, and I streaked down Telegraph Avenue to my apartment, where I immediately looked up Adrianne Koch's number in my telephone book. I found it and called her.

Kathy and Jay Jay ran upstairs to her studio. The other partygoers put a record on in Albert's apartment and started dancing again. It was mayhem incorporated, but I was determined to get Albert out of jail.

A drowsy Adrianne answered the phone. "Hullo?"

"Adrianne, the police arrested Albert Curtis and have put him in jail!"

"What!"

"Could you help us get him out?"

"Of course! Why did they put him in jail? This is outrageous!" Adrianne was fully awake and fuming. She'd save Albert.

"We were dancing in a conga line down Telegraph Avenue; Albert was wearing a purple wig; the police came and arrested him for disorderly conduct or some made-up charge."

"I'll meet you at the Berkeley Jail," she said.

I already knew where it was, from Ed's overnight visit. I headed down there, yelling for everyone to follow me and FREE ALBERT!

We arrived at midnight, yelling in unison, "Free Albert, free Albert!" This was turning into more than I'd bargained for, but I'd fight for my friends, no matter what.

As many of us that could fit in entered the police station. The desk sergeant furrowed his thick brow. "What do you want?"

"You've got to let Albert Curtis out of jail," I said, the lavender wig blocking my vision somewhat. I adjusted it.

"Take off that silly wig!" he said.

"You sound just like my father," I retorted, giving him my best rebellious daughter look.

"We should book you, too."

"For wearing a wig?" I started laughing. When I laughed, I howled, a long, sustained high-pitched sound that drove even dogs crazy. The others mimicked me. The sergeant stood up and put his hand on his holster.

"I wouldn't do that if I were you," said Adrianne. She'd already been talking to Albert. "Albert Curtis is an English professor at Berkeley. How dare you arrest him."

"He was disturbing the peace," replied the sergeant.

"You'll have to do better than that," said Adrianne. She looked magnificent in her wild pink taffeta coat and mounds of Mexican jewelry.

"And you're the queen of Siam?"

"I'm a history professor at Berkeley, and I protest this arrest."

She gave him a peremptory look that brooked no quarter.

"Better make some calls," said another officer.

"Free Albert, free Albert," chanted about twenty-five of the partygoers outside.

The desk sergeant picked up the phone. He dialed a number. "Excuse me for calling so late, sir, but we have a lot of confusion at the police station tonight, on account of two people claiming to be Berkeley professors. Their names? Um…"

"Let me talk to him," said Adrianne. "Hello, this is Adrianne Koch. Oh, hello, Clark. I hope we didn't wake you up."

"Give me that phone!" The sergeant grabbed it out of her hands. "I'm so sorry, Mr. Kerr, but this woman in a crazy getup… She always dresses like that…? She's a personal friend and history professor…? Please forgive me, sir. I'll make sure everything's all right. Don't worry. Not a word to the press."

At that moment, a newspaper reporter with a flash bulb camera burst in. I'd just run into the cell portion of the jail, where I found Albert. He got our picture, wig and all.

Between Adrianne Koch and Berkeley's president, Clark Kerr, Albert left jail at approximately two in the morning. He walked between me and Adrianne. The others had already gone home.

"I hope that picture doesn't hit the papers," remarked Adrianne. I pricked up my ears.

"She's wearing the wig," said Albert, quite jovial for having undergone an arrest, but I guessed he was happy to be free. "Of course, I wear the mask."

"What mask?" I asked.

"The mask of the happy black man."

76

"Aren't you happy, Albert? Even though you were arrested, you're loved, you have a screenplay contract with Alexia Roma..." I looked into his narrowing eyes, eyes that might hide secret pain, to see if he was listening.

"How old are you?" Adrianne turned and addressed me, her mature face crinkled with wrinkles and a reassuring smile.

"Twenty-one," I said.

Both Adrianne and Albert let out sighs of relief. I felt left out. I began to wonder if they hadn't had some of the bubbly with the accompanying fling, before I came on the scene. I wondered if I'd interrupted an affair when I hit that guy in the nose, winning Albert's admiration but not his heart... my mind wandered in several directions. I was more than confused; I was overwhelmed.

When we got home, they went up his staircase together; I stayed behind to catch up on my sleep; at least, that's the excuse I made up. I felt like the proverbial third wheel.

"Come on, Inny," entreated Albert. "We can celebrate my freedom with..."

"I need to have some time to myself," I insisted with exhaustion creeping over me.

Adrianne gave me one of those knowing smiles and whisked Albert up the stairway.

I opened my door and took off the wig and threw it on the floor. Then, I threw myself on my bed. What had I gotten into?

Chapter 7

I had an early morning rat psychology lecture the next morning. The phone rang before I could get out of bed.

"Hullo," I said, half-asleep.

"Inny, this is your mother," rang shrilly in my ear. I moved the receiver an inch or so away.

"Um, hi, Mother."

"Your Aunt Beth called. She said you're in the *San Francisco Chronicle* in a purple wig with a black man. You must come home immediately!" My mother gave orders and brooked no quarter.

"What? Albert and I were in the newspapers?"

"I've already bought you a plane ticket to LAX. I'll pick you up at five o'clock. Then, you can find a job."

"I'm not leaving Berkeley, Mother. I happen to love it here. I wouldn't care if my picture were in the paper with a serial murderer; I still wouldn't leave. Albert Curtis is a famous English professor here. He is so far superior to your world that you wouldn't understand."

"Your father will draw up papers to disown you."

"Fine. We hadn't much in common to begin with."

"I told you to get married! How dare you embarrass us like this! Black people are not English teachers! They're inferior and only know how to shine shoes."

I listened to her rattle off her list of prejudices against the black race. Then, I hung up on her. I couldn't take it anymore. I'd heard this all my life, and Berkeley had freed me. I intended to remain a free woman, a free soul, a happy soul! I started to laugh. Albert and I were famous! I decided I would throw on a dress and run upstairs to tell him before going to class.

"Hullo," I said as best I could manage. I hadn't gotten enough sleep; my mind wasn't clear. "Oh, good morning, Albert. How are you...? You're in the *San Francisco Chronicle*. We're in the *San Francisco Chronicle*. And me in the lavender wig." Somehow, it seemed silly; I started to giggle. "No, I haven't been drinking; it's just so crazy; I can't believe it. What should I do? Come talk to you? I have classes today… But I'll come up anyway."

I threw the covers off and ran to the bathroom, where I washed my face with cold water. Then, I ran to the closet and put on the first skirt and blouse I came across.

The phone rang again. I answered it.

"Inny," sniffed my mother, "how dare you hang up on your mother? I'm just trying to protect you!"

"Mom, I'm twenty-one; I can take care of myself. You don't have to worry about me. I'm sorry I hung up on you. I have to run now!"

She was so controlling. I ran upstairs to see Albert. The door was already wide open; he was dressed for school, too, natty in his Brooks Brothers shirt and tie.

"Just tell them it was innocent fun," he said with a grin.

"Who? My parents? They're in Montecito and don't believe in fun."

"Tell the press it was innocent fun." Albert grinned at me.

"The press? Why don't I just hide from them? I've never been interviewed; it'll come out all wrong."

Albert frowned. I'd never seen him so serious. From Alexia Roma to jail and back; it was too much for my young brain. I knew I didn't want to talk to the press.

"Maybe you can avoid them; Adrianne and I may be able to handle this."

"You and Adrianne?" I put my hands on my hips in indignation. "Have you been sleeping with her, too, Albert?"

He drew me to him and kissed me. "You're the only woman I love," he said with a touch of melodrama.

"Then don't make me late to my rat psychology class! It's at 9!"

I gave him a quick kiss and ran down the stairs, toward campus. Once in my classroom, which had over two hundred students, plus the professor, who mimicked a rat on a hot iron grid that day, confirming my suspicion that he was crazy. More than a few students stared at me. I avoided their stares. When class was over, I ran to my next class, Adrianne Koch's American history class. I wondered if she'd be there.

Adrianne walked into the amphitheater-sized classroom with her usual flair and the magenta coat she'd worn last night. She hadn't had time to change clothes. That didn't stop her from breathing life into those old Puritans – Cotton Mather and Jonathon Edwards – quoting some of their favorite sayings, such as, 'Dyed in the blood of the Lamb.' She was superb; everyone loved her, including me. After class was over, I winked in her direction, turned my head, and ran for the exit. Not fast enough.

Michael Schwartz, an old buddy from my freshman year, accosted me. "Your picture was in the papers today!" he said, grinning his head off.

"So I've been told," I answered, trying to outdistance him. No such luck.

"I didn't know you were an activist."

"Neither did I," I replied, looking at him out of the corner of my eye, hoping no one else would notice me.

"You and Adrianne Koch got Albert Curtis out of jail last night!" Michael raised an eyebrow; he acted as if he were impressed.

"I just wanted to get my wig," I tried to laugh it off.

"Your wig… Oh, yes, you were wearing a purple wig!"

"Lavender."

"Okay. Lavender. But you still sprung him with a bunch of other activists."

"What's an activist?" I'd never heard the term in my heady years at Berkeley.

"Someone who fights for other people's rights."

"Oh. Of course. Well, yes, I guess I'm an activist, but it was inadvertent… I mean… Oh, Michael, they'd thrown Albert Curtis in jail for leading a conga line down Telegraph Avenue. I wanted to get him out."

Michael started to laugh at me. "A conga line?"

Practically running, I replied, "You should've been there. Midterms start next week. I've got to study."

"Yeah. I've got to study for mine, too."

"Sorry to rush off, but this picture in the papers business has blindsided me."

"Good luck!"

"Thanks!" I kept running until I got to the brick pathway that led to my studio. I unlocked the door and ran into my kitchen, fixed a ham sandwich, and opened my psychology book to Skinner's rat experiment. I almost knew it by heart, but I was sure it would be on the exam, so I started memorizing it. I always memorized as much as I could for exams. My near-total-recall memory got me through exams at Berkeley. Meanwhile, I could hear Albert playing music upstairs.

I crammed until 10. I heard Albert put on a Barbara Streisand album, 'People Who Love People,' one of his favorites.

My phone rang. "Hey, Miss Inny, come on up and have some din dins," said Albert. "I've made something just for you."

"I'll be right up, but I have a mid-term tomorrow morning."

Albert laughed. "Do you want me to quiz you on it?"

"You can't."

"Why not? I'm a teacher."

"But you're not a rat. This is on rat psychology."

We bantered back and forth about the psychology of rats and people. Then, I skimmed into a sleek sheath dress and ran upstairs to his place.

He wore a sheer jersey that showed his muscular chest. I inhaled sharply. We smiled at each other; his perfect teeth highlighted his chiseled features. Albert shouldn't wear a wig anymore, I decided. A hat would be perfect.

"You'd look really good in a hat and coat over that jersey," I said.

"Do you think it would suit me?" he grinned.

"Almost better than the wig, although I'll have to think it over," I smiled slyly into his beautiful, deep-set brown eyes. "What should I wear?"

"Anything."

"Anything?"

"Everything you wear suits you."

My heart beat faster. I wasn't used to compliments. Getting them from Albert made me feel a bit faint after the events of last night. He went to the stove and stir fried some shrimp in a pan, like the most gourmet French chef. "I've fixed a little something to say thank you. You were my guardian angel last night."

"I love shrimp! I'll always be your guardian angel if you'll cook for me!"

"Deal! And here's some of the bubbly..." He popped a champagne cork. It arced high and hit the ceiling, making us laugh. After a few glasses, we were laughing even harder and I'd all but forgotten my exam.

I slid my hand behind his neck. He leaned down to kiss me. Then I remembered.

"Albert! I have a mid-term tomorrow! "

He froze in mid-kiss, not quite reaching my lips. We were so close...

"Oh, you tease! Go to bed and get an A! We can have our real celebration tomorrow night. Besides, I have something to tell you."

"Tell me now or I won't be able to sleep!"

"And you think I will be?" he motioned downward and I laughed. "It's a surprise." His smile dazzled me.

"So we're both teases. Can you save it for tomorrow night?" Albert rolled his eyes and acted like I was driving him crazy. "Whatever you say, Dahlink. You'd better get an A on your test."

I ran down the stairs wondering what he wanted to tell me. As I went into my studio, I glanced at Jerry's empty one. I wondered how they were doing in India. After I got in bed, I tossed and turned. I couldn't sleep with so much on my mind. I started mentally reviewing the Skinner rat experiment and fell asleep with rats jumping at pieces of cheese from their stands in experiment boxes, instead of counting sheep.

I woke up at 7, jolted down some scrambled eggs with toast and jam, pulled on a sweater and skirt, and bolted to campus.

The test attendants were passing out the questions when I arrived with my blue book, the infamous blank pamphlet that we'd soon pour our knowledge onto as best we could. I didn't recognize anyone; none of my friends were majoring in psychology. Berkeley's classes were so large that you had to enroll with a friend to find a familiar face, as a rule. Two hundred perfect strangers bent over and started reading the exam questions, then answering them. This was an upper-division class, so most of us were seniors. We wrote for three hours. When the attendants signaled that the time was up, we stood up, stretched, and handed them our booklets.

Bright noon sunshine hit me in the face as I wandered back to my studio. Some of the students went to the UCEN, the student cafeteria, but I was on a strict budget. My mother had already suggested that I marry, because they couldn't afford to send me to college anymore. Marry? Marry whom? Berkeley cost one hundred and fifty dollars a year; it was almost free and I'd taken a part-time job selling records at the Robert E. Lee record store. It was hard to believe that someone would choose such a name, but that was the owner's actual name. I didn't have to work until the next day, so I inhaled and enjoyed the walk home. I wondered what Albert had in mind when he promised me a surprise. I'd already had a few of those.

I fixed a ham sandwich for lunch and started studying for Adrianne's history mid-term, which was on Friday. Cotton Mather, Jonathan Edwards, 'Dyed in the blood of the Lamb' kept repeating themselves, as well as scenes of men trying to 'build a city on a hill,' a perfect world, with no female input unless their wives managed to influence them. What strange forebears we had. Had it changed that much?

After reading two chapters about Puritan history, I began to wonder what Albert had in store for me. Ours was not the usual love relationship; but love in any form is unique. I experienced a level of love and caring with Albert that gave me more self-confidence; he appreciated my intellectual acumen, and we were writing for Alexia Roma. That, thrown in with the rowdy party and resultant jailing of Albert, made for... what I hoped would be a fulfilling, even transformative, experience.

My phone rang. It was Sally. She sounded like she was having a transformative experience; Jerry was forcing her to fly with him, even though she had a phobic fear of flying. Especially because she had a phobic fear of flying.

"Why don't you come back here, Sally?"

"He won't let me," she sniffled.

"You've got to do what is best for you and to hell with him!"

"I'm afraid of him."

"What can he do to you?"

"I'll tell you when we get back," she sounded nervous.

"When are you coming back?" I was concerned. I twisted the phone cord. India was so far away.

"I don't know. I have to go now." She hung up the phone.

I held an inert phone in the air, expecting Sally's voice to come through it, for some reason. What on earth was he doing to her?

I was in a pensive mood when Albert got back from campus.

He whistled as he came down the brick walkway. I opened the slatted wooden blinds that covered my front window and waved. He waved back and motioned for me to come see him.

Now he'll tell me, I thought as I ran up to his studio.

He stood at a cocky angle, grinning ear to ear. "Are you ready for the news?"

"Yes!" I nearly shouted. What did he have in store for me?

"You're going to meet Alexia Roma!"

It was really happening. I was really in the movie business. I put my arms in the air and started yelling, "Yay! I can't wait! When? Will I have to miss any classes?"

Albert extended his arm, gently wrapping it around my waist. "During Easter break, Silly! I can't miss classes either. I have to teach them!" He kissed me on the forehead. "I've been invited to the Cannes Film Festival. You can attend as my assistant."

"Cannes? On the French Riviera?" I hardly knew what to think. "What should I wear? Will we go to nightclubs? Do I need party dresses? What's she going to think of me?" It all came pouring out; I couldn't contain my almost-exalted state of excitement.

Albert started laughing and almost did a cartwheel then and there. He grabbed me and we hugged and kissed out of pure joy.

"But first, we must meet them while they're in Hollywood. It's the chance of a lifetime!"

"Are you going to drive or shall we fly? Do you want to stop by my parents' house in Montecito…" An image of my mother chasing one of my dates out of the house flashed before my eyes. Albert was black; she'd have ten shit fits. I couldn't inflict her on him.

"I'd love to stop by your parents' house in Montecito," trilled Albert.

That did it. I'd have to subject him to the Ku Klux Klan of Montecito: my parents. I slumped a bit at the thought, and he detected it. "What are your parents like? They wouldn't object to…" he held his hand up, "…my beautiful pigmentation, would they?"

"They're racists, Albert! They're awful! I can't subject you to their petty cruelty."

"Jim Crowers, eh? Well, maybe we'll bypass Montecito, though I hear it is lovely."

"It might be good for them to meet you. Put on your lavender wig and let's have some laughs!"

"Get out the bubbly! Let's celebrate Alexia, a real woman!"

"We're going to have a real screenplay for her, too!"

Albert ran to the refrigerator and got out some pink champagne. My racist parents seemed like paper tigers after the third glass. Running my hands over those beautiful chest muscles, his chiseled features, his warm love flowed over and over me until I woke up the next morning, still high as a kite. I had to run to my studio apartment for a quick shower and change of clothes. Maybe a pleated skirt and blouse today…

As I ran into Adrianne Koch's history class, Jay Jay appeared out of nowhere.

"Hi!" he said.

"I'm late to class," I said.

"Could I sit in with you?"

"Sure. She's a fantastic lecturer. She makes the crusty old Puritans come alive," I grinned.

Jay Jay grinned his dazzling smile; something in me melted. Albert ran weakly through an obscure corner of my mind and disappeared into the present, which consisted of me and Jay Jay finding seats in the large auditorium, not as large as some at Berkeley, but big enough for a hundred students. We enjoyed the anonymity of it, leaning towards one another so that our shoulders almost touched. As Adrianne brought Cotton Mather chasing Jonathon Edwards out of Massachusetts back to life, I found my mind wandering.

Albert, run-ins with the police, the screenplay, Alexia Roma, and now Jay Jay. I was overwhelmed. "Would you like to stop for a coffee?" asked Jay Jay as we sauntered back to Sather Gate, Berkeley's entrance from Bancroft Avenue and Telegraph Road.

"Um, I have to study, but coffee might speed up the process," I said. Jay Jay smiled as if the sun had just risen. He was so good-looking that I felt intimidated. I girded up my loins as we found a semi-secluded place to drink coffee.

We chatted about our studies; Jay Jay was interested in physics and math; I loved psychology and the arts, but I loved the high of garnering new knowledge about almost any subject, so we discussed the Manhattan Project.

"Edmund Teller was my physics professor for Physics 101," I said. "He seemed like he was from another world. He just was like a big balloon-head, spouting words with a huge smile, but he didn't make sense."

"Maybe bombing Hiroshima had something to do with that," said Jay Jay.

I studied his pensive countenance. "Developing the atomic bomb that killed hundreds of thousands of innocent civilians might have something to do with that. I'd have gone crazy."

Jay Jay grinned his huge grin at me. "Would you like to go to a radio station with me tonight?"

"A radio station? I'd love to go; I've never been to one before, but I… I have to book for an exam." In reality, I needed a good night's sleep.

"We can do it another time."

"It's a date!" I smiled my own megawatt smile at Jay Jay. He seemed to appreciate it, because he took my hand and squeezed it.

"I'll give you a call later in the week."

"Don't forget!" I grinned at him, wondering how on earth I could start dating Jay Jay when I was involved with Albert and… Then again, who could say no to Jay Jay? Not many, I would find out.

When I got home, I could hear Albert listening to Barbara Streisand's 'People Who Need People' album again. Perhaps he's really lonely. *Maybe that's why he plays that song so often*, I thought, idly. I sat down and read some chapters Adrianne had assigned in my history book, taking notes on the ins and outs of Puritanism. I wondered what the Native Americans must have thought.

Then, I heard a knock on my door and Albert calling to me, "Say hey, Lady Day!" I ran to open the door and invite him in.

"So now you see my cozy den of inequity," I indicated my studio, which consisted of the kitchen and living room, with the bed tucked into a corner. It was smaller than Albert's, but everything fit and it wasn't too expensive, especially as Sally and I were still splitting the rent. Her clothes, those she hadn't taken to India, still hung in my closet.

"Fit for the Queen of Sheba," quipped Albert. "You're so… beautiful."

I blushed. "Oh, Albert. I look like any other girl on campus."

He grinned that contagious grin, and soon we romped up the stairs and were in his studio opening the bubbly. "How am I going to pass my exams if we keep this up?"

"Famous screenplay writers don't have to pass exams." He gave me a sly wink.

"So now I'm a famous screenplay writer? In that case, I want to make some suggestions."

"Such as?" Albert's eyes opened wider.

"She should have two men chasing after her, instead of a man and a woman."

"But that's been done before," Albert frowned. "I want something interesting, even shocking."

"It's been done before because it works. That's what people want to see. They're not interested in seeing Marilyn Monroe compete with Cary Grant for the charms of Alexia Roma." I crossed my arms over my chest.

Albert gave me a penetrating look, part surprise, part admiration. "Let me think about this." He poured me some more bubbly.

"Maybe in the next script, but this is your first attempt; don't get too adventurous."

"This is our first attempt," said Albert, suddenly dead serious.

"I've only made a few suggestions. How can you give me any writing credit?"

"Okay. Let's go get it, and I want you to go over it and rewrite anything that is dull or too *avant garde* for today's public."

Albert got the script. I took it, skimming over the first few pages. "I have to study for my exam, Al. Can't we do this tomorrow?"

"Won't you stay a bit longer?"

I sat down, realizing Albert was lonely.

"Do you need people, like in Barbara Streisand's song?"

He looked out the window, at the patio down below. A few moments passed.

"I was kind of a lonely kid, but that's all in the past." He stood up and went to the refrigerator.

"Bubbly time!" He started to grin. I grinned back, but a shadow fell over the thrall he usually held me in.

"Not tonight, Albert. I really have to study, plus read the script. That's a big order for me."

"Let's go to Hollywood and talk to some moguls!" He grinned from ear to ear. He was irresistible.

"That would be such fun! When will we have time?"

"During Thanksgiving break, if you don't have exams."

"Let me check my schedule. It should be fine." Jay Jay's bright smile flashed before my eyes. "Right now, I'm in over my head. And Thanksgiving is the day after tomorrow."

"You sweet thing, you," smiled Albert, grinning like nobody's business. "I just adore you."

"I… I love you, too, Albert." This felt a bit forced, but I did love him. At least, I thought I did.

"Are you sure?"

"Why do you ask?" I was teetering.

"Oh, sometimes I have bad luck with lovers."

I motioned toward myself. "But not me!" Then, I thought of Jay Jay and realized I couldn't make too many promises. I was only twenty-one. I was… confused.

"Not you!"

We hugged and kissed in the French fashion, bussing each other on the cheek instead of kissing on the mouth, in order to say goodbye rather than hello.

Chapter 8

That evening, I sat down to write a letter to my parents, telling them I'd be stopping by with a friend, *en route* to Hollywood. I knew they hated Hollywood for making sensual movies. I felt apprehensive, but I had to prepare the way. We had decided to leave on November 23, a Saturday, so we could spend at least a few days in Hollywood. I couldn't believe I'd be meeting someone as famous as Alexia Roma.

After studying and having some dinner, I tapped on Albert's door. He opened it and gave me a sly look. "Look what the cat dragged in."

I laughed at his sally. "I wanted to ask you about Alexia. I should know more about her if I'm going to help you form Alexia's character."

"Form Alexia's character! She's more likely to form yours. She's very assertive. She'll tell you what she wants."

"Still, I'm curious about her."

Albert and I sat on the sofa, facing each other. He began to tell me about Alexia and Alessandro. His demeanor was serious.

"Alexia grew up in… shall I say… not the best of circumstances."

I cocked an eyebrow. "Go on."

"Her father was a married man who wouldn't marry her mother or give her any money for the children. They were desperately poor."

"What a rat!"

"Yes, he was a rat. But Alexia was so hot that she entered a beauty contest at age fourteen… An Italian producer saw her and immediately asked her to start acting in his movies."

"No kidding!"

Albert grinned his wraparound grin, uncovering perfect teeth.

He could've been a model. "With her incredible figure…" Albert made an hourglass shape with his hands, "…she was almost an overnight hit. She has a fun-loving, down-to-earth sensuality that the Italians loved."

"What about Americans?"

"She's taken on gritty roles here… Remember I told you she won an Oscar. She's phenomenal. Some of the women have made nasty remarks about her voluptuous figure and sensuality, but she's been a huge hit. I'm surprised you didn't know about her before."

"I haven't been going to a lot of movies lately. I've been studying!"

"Berkeley is important to you, isn't it?"

"I want to stay here forever. I love Berkeley!"

Albert broke out laughing. "You're an original!"

"What do you mean?"

"You're so passionate; it's not that common here."

"What about elsewhere?" I wondered if I would fit in better somewhere else.

"All cultures are different."

"Do you mean I'm not a typical American?" I did want to fit in. My mother had always impressed on me the importance of fitting in, yet some people said I was too noisy, too talkative… even too happy.

Albert giggled and reached towards me. A glimpse of his handsome profile and I was in his arms again, snuggling like a frisky kitten. I slid my hand under his shirt. He slid his under my blouse. We were a tangle of arms, legs, and clothes thrown on the floor within minutes.

When I came up for air, I said, "Albert, I'm dying to meet Alexia!"

He laughed. "She'll love you. You're two of a kind. You're hot, too, kiddo! Wait till we get to Cannes."

"Me? Come on. I just want to graduate from Berkeley… and party forever."

We laughed at the absurdity of partying forever and took another dive under his bed covers. The next morning, I snuck out early and dressed for class, not without Maria Dolores spotting me and giving me a dirty look. I also checked my calendar and exam schedule. No exams the week of Thanksgiving. Lady Luck hadn't failed me yet.

I was in Adrianne Koch's office with Albert the day luck failed John Fitzgerald Kennedy Jr., our valiant president, who'd faced off the Russians when they had tried to plant nuclear missiles on Cuba and fought to create the controversial Civil Rights Act law.

I looked at the photograph of the Founding Fathers framed on her wall. Her office was filled with historic pictures, depicting great moments that had changed the world.

"I love your class more than any I've ever taken," I said with a hopeful smile. "I'd like to stay at Berkeley another year and change my major to history." I'd had enough of rat psychology. I knew I wasn't cut out to be a psychologist.

She looked at me in surprise. "History is fascinating," she said. Her phone rang. She picked it up almost midsentence.

I'll never forget her grand dame presence, with her flowing magenta coat and ringed fingers when she heard the news. "The President's been shot," she said. Another student and I exchanged shocked looks. I thought she must be talking about Clark Kerr, the president of Berkeley. When she told us it was President Kennedy, I felt like she'd announced my own father had been shot.

Her phone continued to ring off the hook; the news of the tragedy spread like wildfire. I stood up. Adrianne Koch motioned us away. We nodded, our eyes misting over. I quietly left her office. I remembered my luncheon date at the UCEN as she shooed us out of her office, tears coming from her deep-set, penetrating eyes.

"This... this isn't possible!" I said.

Someone took me by the arm and steered me out of Adrianne's office, past Sproul Hall, and into the student union, the UCEN. By that time we'd learned that Kennedy had died of gunshot wounds to his head, the entire campus was silent. No one could speak. It was incomprehensible, as if Satan had appeared on Earth. In the UCEN, Albert waited for me. He ordered two sandwiches, which we ate in silence. No one said a word. Our world had ended as we knew it.

Soon, there were pictures of Lyndon Johnson being sworn in with a stunned Jackie Kennedy standing behind him, her husband's blood still smeared on her elegant pink suit. The whole nation came to a standstill.

It was a horrible day in the history of the world. Democracy had taken a step backwards.

We separated in the small hallway that separated our studio apartments. Albert kissed me on the cheek and said he'd like to get an early start the nest day.

I went into my studio, where I packed quietly, trying to think of everything both Albert and I might need. I was taking the pill, so there was no need for condoms. Just my nicest skirts and Capri pants, the latest fad for women. We were starting to wear pants in public. I looked out the slatted wooden blinds of my studio and saw Maria Dolores head for Albert's studio. My heart sank, because she was so talkative. I clicked my suitcase shut and headed up the stairs to Albert's. I opened the door to find him and Maria having an animated conversation about Kennedy.

"He was just an ordinary man," she said.

Albert stood up and started to fume. "How can you say that?"

I smiled at Albert and said hello. I also mentioned we were leaving for Hollywood in the morning.

"Albert's studio needs to be cleaned."

"Not tonight," I said.

"What do you know, stupid American girl?" She almost snarled at me. I knew she adored Albert and talked obsessively about orgasms. I'd heard her ranting and raving before.

"I'm not stupid, and I'd like you to leave, right this minute." I put my suitcase down and shoved it to the side. "Why are you so insulting?" I walked past her and put my arms around Albert.

"You little… Ah, the *Americanas* know nothing about love!" she wailed. Then she left.

Albert looked at me for a long time. "I'm… I'm so sorry. She has no right…"

"She's a pathetic woman; she needs to see a shrink or something; ignore her." I squeezed him tighter, held him closer. "She has a lot of nerve saying what she did. Kennedy was noble, brilliant, more than a president…"

"He was my hero," said Albert with a sniff. I realized that he was crying. I kept holding him. He was so idealistic, above the ordinary fray. "I can't imagine the world without him."

We sat down on his sofa and held each other for a long time. Albert barely moved. "He was the first president to invite a black man to the White House," he said simply.

"Yes, he was. He was brave and perhaps too good for the dirty game of politics."

"Too good…" Albert began to cry again. "To die like that."

"Oh, God," I started to cry with him. "I loved him like a father. It doesn't seem real."

We lit candles and turned out the lights to honor Kennedy. Little was said after that, and we went to sleep, side by side, without the bubbly – a goodnight kiss sufficed.

Albert and I still left for Los Angeles the next day, but without the fanfare and high expectations we'd had the day before.

Everything had changed. Alexia still wanted to meet us. She was Italian; the death of our President hadn't affected her as much as if she were an American. I wore dark clothes. So did Albert. We were in mourning.

We decided to cancel the tour along Pebble Beach Golf Course and the spectacular seventeen-mile drive. We had a solemn late breakfast in Santa Cruz, a small town south of San Francisco, and headed for my parents' house. The fact that they were staunch Republicans hadn't entered my mind; I was too tired to think much of anything. Who killed Kennedy kept going through my mind like a flickering neon light. Was it really John Oswald, like they said on the news?

"Albert, how could one man kill Kennedy? He was surrounded by bodyguards, wasn't he?" I gave him a bewildered look. I couldn't believe that some nobody from nowhere had killed the President of the United States.

"That's what they say," murmured Albert in a subdued tone. We exchanged glances as he drove through the lush Santa Cruz country, redolent in pines that gave off the scent of Christmas. Only this was Thanksgiving and there was nothing to be thankful for.

He clicked on the radio. We keened our ears to pick up every word as they described the death of President Kennedy and its implications. Suddenly, there was a break in the news. "Ladies and gentleman," said the newscaster, "Lee Harvey Oswald, the assailant of President John F. Kennedy, has been shot by Jack Ruby, a man with an unsavory reputation, known to have mafia connections."

"No!" I said.

"There goes the testimony," said Albert, quietly.

"This is too convenient! They're up to something." I frowned and tried to make sense of what I'd just heard.

"Never trust a white man," said Albert.

"Never trust…" I looked at him and burst out laughing. Then, I shut up and regretted my irreverence.

But something was wrong, very wrong in Dallas, Texas, and it might be spreading. I wondered if Lyndon Johnson, who had just been sworn in as president, could have had anything to do with it. He had been the governor of Texas before he ran for president and ended up being Kennedy's Vice-President. Little did I know how much the C.I.A. hated John Kennedy for the botched Bay of Pigs and not-so-secret plans to downsize them. He'd even fired John Foster Dulles, the head of the C.I.A.

"Adrianne must know something about this, or at least suspect something," I said. "Can't we call her?"

"Yes, we can," said Albert. "But first, we must meet your parents."

I could tell by the look of grim determination on his normally animated face that Albert wouldn't turn the car around to talk to Adrianne. Not today.

The thought of introducing him to my arch-conservative parents today made me more than apprehensive. I couldn't do it. Not today.

"Albert, my parents are Republicans. They're members of the John Birch Society. Let's drive straight to Los Angeles and postpone meeting them until we return."

"What did they think of Kennedy?"

"They're down on almost everybody," I said, burying my face in a map I took out of the glove compartment. "Besides, we could stop in Malibu for seafood." I did my best to smile, but I think I must have looked a bit grotesque, somewhere between misery and sheer hell.

"We've got to give our full attention to *Venus's Delight,* whether we like it or not. Did you know that Alexia and Alessandro recently married in Mexico, last year?"

"I heard they had problems because he was already married."

"They have to have their marriage annulled because of the Catholic Church. They won't allow divorce in Italy."

"*Mama mia!*"

Albert laughed for the first time in two days. He let out a roar, and I joined in. After that, the world looked more palatable, but I knew the world was no longer in trustworthy hands.

As we drove through Montecito, towards my parents' house, Albert murmured, "It's very beautiful here. I've heard about Montecito. Are your parents wealthy?"

"No, but they like to live in wealthy neighborhoods. Their house didn't cost that much; Santa Barbara is cheaper than Los Angeles and San Francisco; Montecito is even cheaper." Albert swung his fairly new Chevy sedan into the ample roundabout in front of the front door. Luscious azaleas flanked the driveway, and a lovely eucalyptus tree arched over the right side of the house where the bedrooms were. It was a pretty house, but not one of the expensive manors, such as those built at the end of Cima Linda Lane, which was a horseshoe-shaped street with the curving part overlooking some of the hilly part of Montecito and the Pacific Ocean. Our house was modest in comparison.

"Sure doesn't look like where I come from," laughed Albert, coming out of his torpor. "But then, we had…"

"Yes?" I encouraged him.

"Oh, Billy Holiday, people jiving, and a sense of community, black community, it's different, but it's like someone always is looking out for you. Plus, my father was a doctor, so we had more than enough."

I kissed him. "Don't worry. It's deadly dull here. The only good music is down on Haley Street, at the King's Supper Club."

"Are the musicians black, by any chance?" Albert grew more and more animated at the thought of black musicians.

"What makes you think that?" I giggled. "Of course, they are! I've been to some pretty good parties there. It's the liveliest spot in town."

He parked and walked around to my door to let me out. We walked towards the front door, Albert still wearing Navy blue slacks and a tan jacket; I wore a dark skirt and a button-down blouse. We rang the doorbell. My mother answered it. She stared at Albert in shock. "You can't..." she looked at me. "Oh, Inny, how could you!"

My father appeared in the distance, holding a *Scientific American* magazine in his hand. My mother ran past him to draw the kitchen window's blinds shut. She rushed us past the kitchen, into the living room, without offering us a seat. Her face contorted in rage. My father dropped his magazine.

My mother quickly closed the blinds, even though we were nowhere near our neighbors.

"Don't you have any self-respect? You know we don't allow black people in Montecito!"

"This is my good friend and English professor from Berkeley, Albert Curtis, Mother."

My mother walked up to me, raising her hand. Ready for what was to come, I grabbed her hand and turned my face away. Tears welled up in my eyes. We grappled for a moment before she came to her senses.

"Don't talk back to me, Inny. Don't you ever dare do that! As for your English professor from Harlem – he can go back there for Thanksgiving."

"How did you know I was from Harlem?" Albert smiled a contrite smile. "Inny and I are writing a screenplay for Alexia Roma.

She's going to be a screenwriter. You should never be angry at your daughter for succeeding, even if you're jealous."

"Jealous? Of Inny? Writing for that Italian harlot? Hardly," said my mother, sitting down with her arms folded over her crisp, dark blue shirt-maker dress. "Now, tell us what this man really does for a living, Inny." My mother uncrossed her arms and started drumming her fingers on the arm of the chair.

My father sat down on the sofa as inconspicuously as possible. He was unable to cope with the situation. He disappeared into his *Scientific American* magazine, his usual hiding place.

"Are you a pimp? Don't tell me you've gotten involved in something horrible, Inny."

"I teach English literature at Berkeley. I'm also planning to start a film festival in San Francisco."

My mother took a deep breath, stood up, and walked over to Albert. "I don't care if you're the king of Siam. Get out of my house! She stepped towards him as if she were a bull about to charge a bullfighter.

I got up and stood between them.

"Albert is twice as well-educated as we are."

"He's a nigger!"

"And you're Lady Macbeth! You've criticized me, hit me, never a kind word…"

My mother's face turned dark red. "You ungrateful child!" She pushed me. I stood my ground.

"Ladies! Stop it!" Albert tried to separate us, but not before my mother grabbed his Brooks Brothers Ivy League shirt. Albert tried to pull away. The sound of cloth tearing seared my brain. She'd torn the sleeve. I screamed as Albert pulled his shirtsleeve from her grip.

She turned to face me. Her normally smooth, agreeable countenance was contorted with anger. "Inny… I'm going to kill you!"

"You won't have the chance. I'm never coming back here!"

My father stood in the background with his jaw agape. His magazine slid to the floor. He didn't budge. He gasped. "Iris!"

"Let's go, Albert!" I took him by the arm and we ran for it.

"Come back here, Inny! You can't go with that man! Get rid of him and come back with someone who looks like us!" My mother tried to block the front door, but we were faster than she was.

"Faster," I breathed, and we beat it out to the car and jammed out of Montecito as if the devil himself were chasing us. Albert slid behind the steering wheel and took off, the tires skidding on my parents' curved driveway.

The beauty of Montecito faded fast as we got on the freeway and headed toward Ventura.

"Now, you've met my parents," I said.

"I've never met anyone quite like them," said Albert. "I've run into all kinds of crazy white people, but none of them ever attacked me." He winked at me. "Maybe a psychiatrist could help your mother."

"I'll say. I think my father needs to see one, too. But I'm a student, not a psychiatrist. They don't believe in psychiatry, anyway, and wouldn't spend a penny on a shrink. They say Freud was a sex fiend. Of course, sex is a taboo subject in our household. I don't think they even…"

"Do it?" Albert chortled. "Look, at least you got out." He gave me a sympathetic look. Blood trickled down his forearm where my mother had ripped his shirt; her nail had nicked his arm. I found a Kleenex and tried to wipe it off.

"Some things can't be wiped off," said Albert. He sighed. "But we still must forgive."

"I'm sorry I took you there," I said, aghast at what had transpired. They were far worse than I'd imagined, and Albert was right: they needed professional help. I thought of all the secrets behind closed doors in Montecito, with its beautiful façade. *Perhaps the more beautiful the façade, the darker the secrets*, I thought. "We need to be around creative people, joyous people," I said.

"Wait till you meet Alexia." Albert grinned, in spite of himself.

"She sounds so happy, so playful," I said.

"And more!"

"*Amore!*"

"Yes! Alexia Roma is all about love. You'll learn from her. But you must forgive your mother." He turned and gave me a serious look.

"I hate my mother!" I frowned, miserable.

"Unless you forgive her, you'll carry all that anger in your heart and it'll eat you up."

I turned to him with wide-open eyes. The beauty of the Pacific Ocean dazzled me as we drove on, but I couldn't forget what Albert had just said. It turned round and round in my numbed mind.

Chapter 9

Mrs. Johnson walked into the master bedroom, went to the dresser drawers, searched through various articles of clothing, and pulled out a revolver. She looked at it with an uncharacteristic smile widening on her face. She put it back in the drawer and walked into the living room, where her husband sat reading his *Scientific American*.

She strode over to where he sat, immobile, and stood over him. "Craig, we have to go to Berkeley." She crossed her arms over her chest resolutely. She brooked no quarter, and he knew it.

"Now, Iris," he said, trying to calm her. "Inny's always been a bit wild. This will pass, like her other…"

"Other what?" demanded Mrs. Johnson. "She's never been in trouble with the police before; she's always been a good student. The boys have run after her, but she's held her own. This time, she may need some professional assistance."

Mr. Johnson's eyes widened. "What do you mean, Iris?" He was scared stiff of his wife.

"There are ways of dealing with black men who take up with your daughter." She paced back and forth. "I need to contact…"

"Not our relatives!" Mr. Johnson put his hand to his mouth, aghast.

"No, no one we know. A stranger." She paced faster.

"I don't like the sounds of this, Iris." He couldn't believe his ears.

"I'm going to put an end to this! No one must know!" She gave him a look that would have intimidated the Iron Maiden.

Mr. Johnson shrank back. "I don't think he's a Communist," he said, weakly.

"He's black, Craig, black as the ace of spades! I'll not have her seen with him!"

Mr. Johnson turned his back and wandered out onto the patio and into the garden. He picked a flower absent-mindedly. He understood science, not people. His mind wandered.

Mrs. Johnson looked at her husband in the garden, stalked around their spacious house, and sat down to leaf through a book, a detective novel she'd been reading. Then, she sat bolt upright. A look of profound determination came over her face. She stood up, smoothed her elegant dress, straightened the fake pearl necklace around her neck, and picked up the phone. She called the San Ysidro Ranch.

"Hello, could you let me speak to Andronicus, please?" she purred in her most seductive Southern accent. "He isn't? Could you tell me how to get in touch with him? At his father's house? Senator Michael Dorland? Thank you so very much."

She put the receiver down and called information. She got Senator Dorland's number and dialed it.

"Hello, could I speak to Andronicus, please? This is an acquaintance of his." She tapped her high-heeled shoe impatiently while she waited. Then, Andronicus answered. "Hello, Andronicus. You may not remember me, but I'm the mother of a girl whom you'd probably like to forget. No, no, don't hang up! This has nothing to do with the police! I'd like your help!"

Andronicus, stupefied, listened to what the woman had to say, in mild shock. "She's dating a black man? What does that have to do with me? I'm white." He shifted his weight uneasily.

"You'd like to meet with me? You need my help? Mrs. Johnson, I never touched your daughter… You need my help to get rid of the black man? How?"

Mrs. Johnson gritted her teeth. "I don't care how you get rid of him. I'll be willing to…"

"Lady, my father is a state senator. Oh, you know that. Look, I've got some friends over; can I call you back?"

Andronicus hung up the phone and sat down heavily in a large, overstuffed chair in his father's vault room, where the family kept their valuables. He glanced at the vault and fell deep into thought. A smile crossed his face from time to time. *Get rid of a black guy who's fucking Inny*, ran through his mind. His smile broadened.

He picked up the phone and called Mrs. Johnson.

"Would you care to meet me for lunch?" he said as Mrs. Johnson fluffed her well-coiffed brunette hair, batting her lovely long eyelashes ever so slightly. She had lovely porcelain skin that refused to age. Instead, it had a creamy glow to it.

She glanced at her husband, who was sitting on the chintz-covered sofa, the expensive chintz Inny had liked, instead of the usual rug-like material they preferred. Ensconced in the *Santa Barbara News-Press*, he giggled a bit at the funnies. His mild Walter Mitty look emanated from the pages.

"Where would you like to meet?"

"At the Biltmore Hotel's restaurant."

Mrs. Johnson's face flushed in excitement. She hadn't been to a nice restaurant in years. Ever since she'd married, they'd scrimped on luxuries. After all, her husband was only an engineer, not the president of the Washington, D.C., post office. Which was the position her father had held until he was fifty, at which time he quit. He spent the rest of his years commuting between a dairy farm that would later become Dulles Airport and Grandma's house. Grandma knew he met a young women there, but she ignored the situation and sang louder than ever in church. Indeed, they asked her to leave, as no one could hear the other voices. Her daughters knew, too, but said nothing, thinking their mother had gotten fat and it was her fault.

"It would have to be for lunch. I have to fix dinner for my husband." She spoke with a nervous thrill.

All her life she'd been a good girl, maintaining her virginity until she married. Mr. Johnson trusted her implicitly; he adored her.

She dressed carefully for the luncheon date with Andronicus Wyland, adding touches to a fine linen frock, a silver pin her mother had given her, with matching earrings. She no longer had the downiness of youth. Her brown eyes shone in anticipation, and her hair was permed to perfection. She'd put on a bit of weight after bearing two children, but it only made her more voluptuous.

She got in the car and drove to the sparkling Pacific, on which the Biltmore was a crown jewel of architecture and luxury. She parked her car nervously, bumping another's bumper as she did so. She got out quickly, so no one would notice. She ran to meet Andronicus like a schoolgirl.

Andronicus wore a sports jacket that covered some of his heavy build and already-bulging stomach. His reddish hair was slicked back, though an unruly curl or two, along with his thick features, gave him a raffish look. When Mrs. Johnson walked up to him, a dainty clutch purse in hand, he appraised her admiringly. Now he knew where Inny got her looks from. He appraised her with expertise. This woman was truly beautiful, even better-looking than her daughter. He grinned his fleshiest grin.

"Hello, Mrs. Johnson," he said. They hadn't seen each other since he'd picked Inny up the night he'd attempted to rape her, but he remembered her mother as a nice-looking woman. Today, she was so ravishing that he had to catch his breath.

"Oh, hello, Andronicus," she said. "It was so nice of you to invite me here."

"Think nothing of it. Let's sit down, shall we?"

He nodded to the maître d', who seated them near the bay window that had a dazzling view of the ocean, across a large expanse of perfectly kept green lawn with two beautiful eucalyptus trees.

The waiter came and took their order. Mrs. Johnson had scanned the menu, at a loss, but finally decided on clam chowder soup and a sandwich. Andronicus ordered steak and hors d'oeuvres.

Mrs. Johnson blushed at his audacity and her own, sitting in the finest restaurant in Montecito with… with an audacious plan.

They exchanged pleasantries until Andronicus asked, "Did you say Inny was dating a black man?"

Mrs. Johnson turned a deep crimson. "Yes. She says she loves him. I'm afraid they might even…"

"How distasteful," said Andronicus.

"I'm glad you understand. Miscegenation is a crime in Virginia, where we come from."

"What did you say? Mis…?"

"When you marry someone of a different race… It's illegal in Virginia."

"Now I get you," said Andronicus, thinking of his Jewish roots with annoyance.

"It must be stopped."

"Who is the man involved?"

"His name is Albert Curtis. He works at Berkeley, where Inny goes to college." Mrs. Johnson choked a bit on her sandwich and took a hasty drink of water. "She says he teaches English, but I'm sure he's a janitor."

"I'll see what I can do," said Andronicus, wondering why she'd asked him, of all people, to do such a thing.

He smiled at her and put his hand in the air. The waiter appeared instantly. "Wine, please."

"Yes, sir," said the waiter, a distinguished older man. He gave Mrs. Johnson a quick look and smiled.

Andronicus and Inny's mother discussed the finesse of what she had in mind. He sympathized with her predicament and wondered if… After all, her daughter had scratched his bare back till it bled on that horrible evening. Not to mention that she ran away into the arms of another man after denying his advances. Not to mention that he still wanted to fuck her and had been stalking her the rest of the summer.

Mrs. Johnson drank some more wine, and began to get tipsy. She smiled at Andronicus and dropped her linen napkin. A waiter rushed to pick it up. She had already bent down to retrieve it; her dress had a loose cowl; it revealed a generous bosom.

Andronicus smiled, "You're a very attractive woman, Mrs. Johnson. Could I call you by your first name? Iris? You must have been a raving beauty when you were Inny's age. I'm sure you were much prettier than she is."

"You may call me Iris."

Mrs. Johnson tittered at the compliment. She was thrilled to be recognized for her beauty and to hear that she might have been prettier than her daughter. Andronicus grew tired of just eating. He called for the check. When it came, he looked at Mrs. Johnson. She looked at him in surprise. Then, she fished through her purse for what little cash she had. He took her hand. "Don't worry about it.

My father has an account here."

Mrs. Johnson smiled and arched an imperceptible eyebrow. This was more like it.

"Would you like to walk on the beach?"

"Oh, I never walk on the beach." She had turned a bright red from the wine. "But, today I'll make an exception." She smiled like the cat who'd swallowed the canary. "But I don't want to get sand in my shoes."

"You can take them off," Andronicus assured her.

"Oh, no. I couldn't do that," she laughed, a bit tipsy from the wine. Like her daughter, alcohol affected her almost immediately.

The sand was soft and Mrs. Johnson wasn't used to walking in it, so she tottered a bit and almost fell; Andronicus caught her. As he straightened her up, his lips brushed her cheek.

They would talk later.

That evening, Mrs. Johnson hummed a little song as she prepared dinner for her husband and younger daughter, who had just turned fifteen. Her cheeks were still a bit flushed from the excitement of the afternoon. Mr. Johnson complimented her on her unusually high spirits at dinner, although he pushed the hamburger patty and baked potato around his plate, sick of the same dinner, night after night.

"Craig, why aren't you eating?"

"Oh, I was thinking of something else," he said, eyes lowered.

Kendra, their younger daughter, smiled at her father. She was his favorite and basked in his admiration. "I got straight As again, Daddy."

"You're the smart one in the family," he remarked, his eyes resting for a moment on his daughter's shapely breasts, whose outline showed through her sweater set.

Mrs. Johnson cleared her throat. "If only Inny could be so well-behaved," she rued.

Kendra gloated over her mother's remark in silence as she poured more ketchup on her hamburger patty. She raised her head and threw her shoulders back, making her breasts more noticeable than ever. Mr. Johnson looked at them and then choked down a forkful of hamburger patty.

They continued to eat the humble fare, relatively content in the knowledge that they lived in the best neighborhood in Santa Barbara.

"He's the best I could do," she'd often said to Inny. "I should've married Pat Buchler. He made a fortune in real estate."

Chapter 10

As we approached the outskirts of Los Angles, I prepared to observe the women I would meet closely, in hopes of learning from them. I had never learned about love except from my grandmother. Everyone took advantage of her generosity and made fun of her high spirits, not to mention her lack of inhibitions. She sang on the bus and sang and played the old piano in her living room whenever she had a spare moment. I loved her and considered her my soul mother. I'd spent the first three years of my life in her home, while my father was on a destroyer fighting on the Pacific Front during World War II. He returned at the end of the war, in 1945, when I was three years old. In the meantime, my grandmother, who adored her first grandchild and all children, for that matter, had helped my mother raise me. I continually thanked the good Lord for her presence in my young life.

We approached the city limits of Los Angeles. The bitter taste of the encounter with my parents still palpably disgusted us, me more than Albert, perhaps. He could write them off as bitter white people, whereas they had openly rejected me, their daughter. I couldn't change that. Yet they were my parents. I knew I was supposed to love them.

Palm trees lined a beautiful street full of elegant mansions like beacons to paradise. I sat up and stared at the beauty of Beverly Hills, a suburb of Hollywood, in silent admiration. I'd never seen it before and was astonished by the lavish beauty of the rolling grounds that led to each separate mansion. Then, Albert stopped the car in front of one of them. He got out a map, checked an address, and with a sweep of his hand announced, "Voila, the home of Alexia Roma and Alessandro Rossi."

I took a deep breath. "It's so beautiful. I've never seen such a lovely home, even in Montecito."

"Actually, they're just renting while Alessandro prepares to shoot *Venus's Delight.*" Albert opened the car door and walked around to let me out with a proud little strut. He was having fun.

"Are they waiting for us?" I couldn't believe this was real.

"Of course. They need the script; Alexia is dying to read it." Albert cocked his head and preened a bit like a peacock. I had to laugh.

"So let's go!" I jumped out and ran to the front door with Albert right behind me, carrying the script. I rang the doorbell, expecting a maid to answer, or a butler. Instead, Alexia Roma appeared, wearing a dress that could only be described as molded to her voluptuous figure.

"Alberto," she squealed, and hugged him in delight. "You've brought my script and... a friend!"

"Don't you remember my mentioning that I had engaged another writer to help me with the more... shall we say, delicate female parts?"

"*Ciao*, yes I remember!" She hugged me and bussed me on the cheek, French style, or maybe it was Italian style.

I grinned a huge smile at her and put my hand out. "I'm Inny Johnson," I said. "I'm so excited about working with you!"

"Have you seen my movies?" Alexia motioned for us to come in and showed us to the living room with a grandiose sweep of her hand. She was taller than me by a couple of inches, and she was so beautiful I couldn't take my eyes off of her. I had only seen her in her Oscar-winning performance. I looked at Albert for a hint, but he was already busy shaking hands with Alessandro, her producer and husband-to-be.

"You were magnificent! I've never seen such acting. The Americans just don't have that feel for..." I groped for the right words.

"Passion? Earthiness?" said Alexia, helpfully.

"Yes, we're too controlled and... we lack the vitality that comes so naturally to Italians!"

Alexia beamed. I'd said the right thing. She took me by the hand and guided me to the living room. Alexia sat down on a velvet, Empire-style French sofa. I followed suit.

"Of course," she crossed one of her shapely legs over the other, adjusting her skirt, "we plan to go to Mexico to look for locations for the shoot. We hope you can come!"

"I'd love to, but I have to take exams at Berkeley at the end of the Thanksgiving vacation..." I hoped I hadn't said the wrong thing. I'd never talked to a movie star before.

"It won't take but a few days. I'm sure you'll love Mexico."

"I've been to Tijuana, but I'd love to see the rest of Mexico," I enthused. "Where were you thinking of going?"

"Alessandro and I would like to visit Acapulco. I've always wanted to see those cliff divers. I admire their daring."

"They're so famous. I'd love to watch them, too."

"I know we're discussing Albert's screenplay, but maybe you could both come. We could combine business with pleasure." Alexia smiled her dazzling smile and her eyes sparkled with irresistible charm. I'd never seen anyone with such impish, lovely eyes. Plus, they were green.

"I'm helping Albert with some of it." I lowered my voice. "I don't know if he's mentioned it to you yet..."

"Yes, I'm very happy to have a woman give her viewpoint." She winked at me. "After all, we do think differently than men, don't we?"

"I haven't thought about it very much, but I think I could make your lines more feminine and... I'd like Albert to change the love interest in the script... with your permission."

She looked at me with frank admiration. "How would you change it?"

"I think you should have two men adoring you, not a man and a woman. It seems more..."

"Natural?" said Alexia. She winked at me again. Everything seemed to amuse her; she was so easy to please. I'd had no idea she'd be so engaging.

"Yes! Especially for today's audience. We have to consider them, since they buy the tickets."

"Don't worry. Alessandro always thinks of everything. He's a genius. Your script is in good hands."

"The best," I agreed.

Albert and Alessandro entered the room, talking and making gestures. They'd been having an in-depth discussion about the film.

"Let's go out on the town! Let's go to Hollywood Boulevard!" I entreated. I jumped up, smoothed my skirt and walked over to Albert. He kissed me on the cheek.

Alexia and Alessandro exchanged looks tinged with a bit of remorse.

"Not tonight," Albert said.

"We're keeping a low profile, because of... his wife, not that she objects. It's the Church," whispered Alexia.

"Oh! I didn't know."

"We had to have their marriage annulled in Mexico, last year, because the Church wouldn't grant Alessandro a divorce. It's unacceptable in Italy. They won't accept the annulment." Alexia lowered her beautiful almond-shaped eyes in chagrin.

"I'm so sorry. You don't have to talk about it." I was out of my league talking about annulments and marriages.

I must have turned a bit red, because Alexia said, "It's so embarrassing. We have to be careful not to have our picture taken together; we're still trying to obtain an Italian divorce for him, so we can marry, and of course…" Now it was Alexia's turn to blush.

"Of course, I want to have children."

"I'm sure you will, someday. Just relax, and it will happen like magic. That's what I've heard anyway." I tried to look encouraging. Here, my friends at Berkeley were having abortions and this magnificent woman was dying to get pregnant. It was too ironic.

"Don't tell anyone, but I'm hoping… it will happen soon," she said.

"Don't worry. I don't know anyone to tell! My friends are just students." We laughed at my lack of worldliness.

"I'm hungry. Can we have din dins?" I asked.

"By all means," said Albert with a cavalier sweep of his arm, gesturing toward the door to the dining room.

We walked into a magnificent Italian Renaissance dining room with Alexia and Alessandro, both of whom looked relaxed yet so elegant. Alessandro wore evening clothes, and Alexia… Alexia looked like God had made a dress especially for her. Its light golden color enhanced the color of her hair, and her figure was always a source of amazement. Shall we say she was God's gift to men? And always full of energy and thrilled with her life. Her only sore point was that she wanted to have a child with Alessandro, legally.

That the Church wouldn't grant him a divorce was the biggest sticking point. Alexia remained optimistic in the face of everything. After all, she had eaten bread and beans for dinner most of her childhood, and now she was a movie star.

"I hope you like spaghetti," said Alexia.

I had to laugh. It was the last thing I thought we'd eat in such an elegant setting. But I loved spaghetti and said so.

"We love spaghetti… and champagne. Do you have Korbel?" Albert smiled broadly, knowing that they must have champagne.

Alexia nodded her head with a big smile. We sat back in our chairs and prepared for an enjoyable evening. We ate spaghetti the traditional Italian way, with spoons to twirl it around in, although mine fell all over my plate. Alessandro laughed at my ineptitude.

"Don't worry," he said. "Only Italians eat it this way. Eat like an American."

I had just managed to plunge a huge forkful into my mouth.

"I…" I couldn't talk.

Everyone found my awkward attempts at eating spaghetti charming; they loved me; I was in heaven, and Albert looked like he was having the time of his life.

"Do you mean you're the first black English professor at Berkeley?" Alessandro asked.

"And I'll soon be one of the first black screenwriters in Hollywood," responded Albert, tilting his head and then raising it slightly higher than before. "There have been others, but they haven't written for mainstream films."

"You have a right to be proud!" said Alessandro. "America needs more people of color in film."

"The whole world needs them," said Alexia, a bit slyly, as her skin color had been a source of talk in Hollywood. "They thought I should be darker," she laughed. "They'd never seen an Italian like me before. I am not what they call lily white…"

"You don't have to explain," I said. "My parents have drummed the color code into me all my life."

"Which is why you're with Albert?"

I paused to reflect. "Yes!" I said with enthusiasm. Albert smiled wryly.

* * * *

Alexia didn't appear for breakfast the next morning.

"She's not… not feeling so well," said Alessandro. He looked upset.

"What could be the matter?" I turned a concerned face to his.

"You know how much she wants to have a baby…"

"Oh!" said Albert. "Do you mean she has morning sickness?"

"It's possible. She had a very unfortunate miscarriage a couple of years ago. This is so important to us. I'm afraid we must fly back to Italy to see her gynecologist. He thinks she needs more rest." Alessandro looked down. Then, he smiled at us, beseeching us to understand.

"I'd hate for her to have another miscarriage," I said.

Albert kicked me under the table. "What if she is just under the weather?"

"No, she says she recognizes the signs. I've already booked a flight. We'll leave this afternoon. I'm so sorry we can't discuss your script, Albert, but she can read it after she recovers."

Flustered as all got out, and disappointed, Albert said, "Whatever is best for Alexia. I hope she's right and conceives this time. An Italian woman needs a child… to feel fulfilled."

"I knew you'd understand, dear Albert," said Alessandro. "I've felt such a strong bond between us ever since we met in Cannes. Send the script to our room and we'll read it more thoroughly. It has promise. We were also looking forward to collaborating with you and Inny." He smiled warmly at me. I smiled back, delighted that he'd mentioned my name. He was a darling man, half

Alexia's size and almost twice her age, but it didn't matter. They were truly in love.

"I'll bring it myself," said Albert.

"You're so kind. Now I must go; Alexia needs me." Alessandro left in a rush; it was almost as if he'd never been there. Albert was crestfallen.

"Why did she have to get pregnant NOW?"

"If she is pregnant and has the baby, they can make the movie afterwards," I said, trying to console him.

"Inny, you're so naïve." Albert's normally composed face became downcast.

"What do you mean?"

"Things change so fast in Hollywood, and Alexia is going to fly back to Europe. I don't know how long she'll stay interested."

"If it's a good script, she'll want to make the movie," I asserted.

Albert smiled and reached for my hand. I kissed him gently on the forehead. He reached for the bubbly.

We drove back to Berkeley in relative silence, each immersed in our own thoughts. I had another midterm coming up and then finals after Christmas vacation. I wondered how I could possibly spend it with my parents after our horrible falling out. They'd put me through the third degree, and I wasn't in the mood to be yelled at. I decided to stay in Berkeley and lay low. I'd send them presents and a card. Maybe I'd just go home and let bygones be bygones.

When we arrived, we saw Jerry's car parked outside.

"Sally and Jerry must be back from India."

"Delightful young couple," rued Albert with a smirk.

"She can stay with me."

"And you can stay with me." Albert grinned and kissed me. I kissed him back, giggling. We'd have fun.

Sure enough, as I unpacked my suitcase in our studio apartment, I heard a timid, Sally-like knock on the door. She came in, head down, her long bangs hanging lank and uncombed, obscuring most of her low brow and largish nose. She'd lost another round, I figured.

"Tell me about your trip," I said, plopping on the double bed and motioning for her to join me.

"We had servants," said Sally.

"And…?" I smiled to encourage her.

"Jerry made me fly in small planes with him. He knows they scare me to death."

"Do you love him, Sally?"

"I'm afraid of him."

"Why don't you leave him?"

"I don't know what to do."

"You can stay here with me until you find a job and move away from here," I suggested. "You could go back home."

"I've told my parents I'm still going to school at Berkeley.

They'd find out I was lying. They'd find out I flunked out." I put my arm on hers and turned her to look me squarely in the face. Hers was hangdog, with her usually uncombed bangs hiding most of her features. She sniffled. I put my arm around her shoulders.

"Crying won't help, but sometimes it makes you feel better."

"I'm a washout; a failure. You've made your grades and stayed in Berkeley; you'll graduate this spring. You have a future."

Her tears fell on her plain shirt dress, spotting it in places.

"Does he hit you?"

"Sometimes."

That did it. I shook her into a straight sitting position. "Sally, where is your self-respect? You made it through two years at Berkeley; you can go to a state college and finish your degree there. Your parents will give you the money; you know they will. You need to come clean with them."

Sally stared at me and heaved a huge gasp, gulping for air. Then, she started to sob. I let her cry. I had to fix dinner.

"I've got some trout. Have you ever eaten trout?"

"No."

"Me neither. So this will be a first for both of us. Stop crying! Let's have some fun. Come and help me."

Sally staggered into our small kitchen. I unwrapped the trout from the butcher paper. Much to my surprise, I discovered they were whole fish with their heads attached. I didn't realize you could cook a whole fish, so I started trying to cut their heads off with a kitchen knife. They slid all over the sink. Sally started to laugh.

"Now you laugh! This is the worst thing I've ever had to do!" I hacked away, making a hideous mess of one of the trout. I decided to put them in a bowl full of water, where they took on the semblance of live fish. It frightened me, for I had not yet related to anything other than the saran-wrapped meat in grocery stores. I loved the natural world. I didn't want to participate in mangling it.

"Boil them!" yelled Sally, recovering her voice.

"You boil them!" I laughed at the grotesque mass of fish guts I'd created.

I brushed aside my long hair that had fallen over my eyes and turned the burner on high. The water heated up and the fish, instead of swimming, turned white and accusatory. Their blue eyes turned white and popped out. Sally sniffled a bit, sitting on a kitchen chair. In the back of my mind I kept thinking about my exams I had to study for. Lovers, movie celebrities, and battered friends were secondary to my exams in real life. I wanted to do as well as possible at Berkeley and graduate. I always finished what I started, which included graduating from U.C. Berkeley, in 1964.

Kathy began to practice her violin upstairs. Albert played Barbara Streisand's 'People Who Need People' at full blast. His taste in music was impeccable. *Perhaps because he's black*, I mused. Then, I realized that was a stupid thought and brushed it aside.

"I need your help, Inny," wafted through Sally's sniffling.

"Uh-huh."

"I need to have an abortion."

"What?"

Disconnected thoughts reeled through my already fatigued mind. Janey's abortion in my double bed at my former apartment; Alexia Roma so radiantly pregnant that she turned down the role in Albert's screenplay. Kennedy slumping backward, then forward, in the limousine with Jackie lurching to cover him from further gunfire. My mother calling Albert a nigger, tearing his beautiful Brooks Brothers shirt and chasing us out of my own home, which I realized wasn't really mine but my parents', because they were going to disinherit me. An orphan with parents. I laughed at the ludicrous thought of being raised by parents as inhumane as mine.

"Please help me, Inny."

I looked from the fish, whose eyes had turned white and had popped out of their sockets in the boiling water, to Sally, slumped in misery, limp as my wet dishrag.

"I'm trying to help you get away from Jerry! So now you tell me you need an abortion. Couldn't you have gotten a birth control pill prescription? I... I... I have exams to take!"

The door slammed open. Jerry barged in, a wild look in his eyes, blood-streaked from drinking. His largish, ungainly form headed towards Sally. "Come back to our apartment!" he yelled.

"Don't touch her!"

"Wanna stop me?" He staggered towards me, taking a Swiss Army knife out of his pocket. His eyes bulged. I could feel his breath on my face. It smelled of alcohol.

"I know you hit Sally. I know all about your... your psycho, sick ways, and I won't stand for it!"

Jerry's reddened, veiny eyes stared at me. "And you sleep with niggers!"

"I make love with Albert Curtis!"

Sally turned and started to slink towards the bathroom, placed conveniently next to the kitchen in our small studio.

"Come back here, you silly… bitch!" growled Jerry.

"Get out of here or I'll call the police!" I yelled. Jerry opened his Swiss knife and lunged at me.

Dodging him as best I could, I grabbed the nearest weapon, the pan full of boiling fish, and threw it at him. He howled as the hot water hit his chest, sending trout slithering all over the kitchen floor. He kept coming towards me with the knife. I grabbed a kitchen knife and raised it in the air, screaming, hitting a high C.

Jerry lunged at me, grabbing the knife from my hand. I screamed again. He slashed at me but missed in his drunken stupor. I dodged, faster than him. He turned and walked like Frankenstein towards Sally, who shook like a leaf in a storm.

"No, Jerry, no! I'm sorry! I'll never do it again!" screamed Sally, her face white as the belly of a dead fish.

A gunshot rang out of nowhere. I felt the bullet whiz under my arm; Jerry clutched his chest and went down, spurting blood, which mixed with the boiled trout on the floor, creating a bloody mess.

"Call the police!" I said.

Albert ran down the stairs in time to catch the glimpse of a man with a gun in his hand, running down the brick pathway. When he burst in and saw Jerry bleeding on the floor of my studio, he ripped off his shirt and shredded it, staunching Jerry's gushing wound with it. His father was a doctor; Albert knew how to do these things.

I called the police and an ambulance, which arrived in short order along with most of the neighborhood.

"Can we take him in your car?" I asked Albert.

"He's too far gone!" he said.

Albert kneeled next to Jerry to administer mouth-to-mouth resuscitation. I ripped up a towel to replace Albert's blood-soaked shirt. Jerry's eyes rolled towards the back of his head.

Sally howled and sobbed on my bed. Maria Delores ran down the brick path, yelling, "I told you she was a stupid Americana!" When she saw Jerry, she shut up, her face a mass of wrinkles and anger. Kathy stared from the doorway with other neighbors, aghast, her violin still in her hand.

The ambulance team arrived and went to work.

"What happened?" asked a paramedic.

"Gunshot wound to the chest," I said.

Albert stood up as the ambulance crew put more gauze and bandages on Jerry's wound while taking his pulse. They started an intravenous transfusion.

"Fifty-fifty," mumbled one of the ambulance crew. They placed Jerry on a stretcher, careful not to displace the intravenous or any of the other life-saving devices attached to his body just as two stocky Berkeley policemen arrived.

"Don't move!"

"Life or death matter. Let's go!" yelled one of the ambulance assistants. They hefted Jerry's body on the stretcher out of my studio, down the brick pathway and into the ambulance, which sped away, sirens screaming into the freakish night.

We stared at the police, who said, "Don't move! We have to mark the spot where he fell." We cleared a space for them. I watched with irritation as one of them made a chalk outline on the floor of the living room/bedroom section of my studio. The other called for backup over a walkie-talkie, a new device.

"Do you have IDs?" asked the other.

My mind flashed to my wallet, where I had my driver's license. I felt relieved that I'd just renewed it when I turned twenty-one. I showed it to them. Sally had no I.D.

"I lost it in India," she blubbered. Her tear-streaked face turned bright red.

"Yeah. Look, little lady, ya' gotta show an I.D." She cried harder. The officers exchanged looks and starting checking everyone else's identification. When they got to Albert, they hesitated. "Haven't we seen you someplace before, buddy?"

"Please, call me Professor," said Albert. "It is possible that we have met before. I teach large classes of students at Berkeley."

The police exchanged looks. "India and Africa. What next?" Spain was next, because Maria Delores had a passport in the main house, in front of our studios. One of the police officers escorted her to the house. "It's the Americana's fault!" she yelled. I wondered if she might be vaguely connected to this horror show. I'm sure the police did, too, as she rummaged around her disorganized purse, trying to find her passport.

I decided it might not be a propitious moment to call Adrianne Koch, since she was overwhelmed by President Kennedys' recent assassination, which she knew would change the course of history. So much had occurred since then. I began to feel faint.

"I have to take a test tomorrow," I protested.

"I have to teach," said Albert.

"I have to play in the Berkeley Symphony," said Kathy, her violin hanging limply by her side.

My kitchen knife lay on the floor, near Jerry's smaller Swiss Army knife. One of the officers picked them up with a cloth, so that they could take fingerprints.

"Jerry was shot." I said.

"What're those knives doing on the floor?"

"We, um, Sally, um, he threatened me… for accusing him of mistreating my friend." I motioned towards Sally, who cowered in the corner, on my bed, in a near-fetal position.

"So you went after him with a knife?"

"I tried to protect myself with a knife!"

"Why are there TWO knives on the floor, young lady?"

My mind turned to mush. I mumbled something about gutting trout, and yes, trying to protect my friend. The trout, still, were on the floor in spilled water.

"And this guy shot him." They turned to Albert.

"I don't own a gun, much less know how to shoot one! I'm an English professor!" He hesitated. "And that guy was an abuser!"

I looked at Albert in surprise. He'd never called Jerry an abuser, although he hit and tormented Sally constantly. Albert heard it all, because he lived directly above them and noise came through the floorboards. But he'd never said anything before.

"Yeah, sure. Okay, Buddy. We're going to get a search warrant to look for the gun. All these studios, or whatever they are, will be thoroughly searched."

"Now if you'll all kindly come to the police station for fingerprinting."

Albert, Kathy, Sally, Maria Dolores, and I stared at them as if they'd asked us to fly to Mars. Then, we followed them to the police car. We had very few options at this point. Sally blubbered about her parents finding out about her and Jerry; we hushed her.

By midnight, the police were interrogating us at the station. It was a stuffy room with a sturdy wooden desk for the sergeant and less-sturdy chairs for potential inmates. Once again, Clark Kerr had to identify Albert as a member of the Berkeley faculty. Albert kept checking his watch. "I've got to teach two large English classes tomorrow…"

The sergeant gave Albert a baleful stare and put an ink pad in front of him. "Your fingerprints, please."

Albert pressed his thumb into the pad. The sergeant removed it.

"What about the rest?" he asked.

"They're not suspects," drawled the sergeant. A couple of police officers smiled.

"Why is Albert a suspect?" I asked.

"He was at the scene of the crime," said one of the police officers.

"We were at the scene of the crime. Albert heard the gunshot and rushed downstairs to see what had happened."

The atmosphere grew thicker, the lights seemed brighter, and the glare made me feel faint. The officers jostled one another. Albert gave me a look of admiration.

"Okay. Book her."

They took my fingerprints and eventually Sally's and Maria Dolores', over her shrill protests about being Spanish and exempt. Nothing made much sense.

Sally bawled her head off and kept asking about Jerry, who was at Crowell Hospital in the Intensive Care Unit. Hell descended on us, but there was no gun; nothing except for a kitchen knife and a Swiss Army knife. We'd all heard a single gunshot. Albert had seen a stocky man of average height run down the brick alleyway.

"He was white," he'd added. The police gave him a suspicious look. Albert asked if he could use a phone.

"That won't be necessary. We have all the evidence necessary for the moment. One of your neighbors did say they saw a stocky white man get into a sports car and pull away at about the time of the shooting."

"Please, Officer, I have a test tomorrow," I said.

The police let us go home. No conga line. No bubbly. Just home, to a warm bed, and we were grateful for it; at least I was.

"I have to keep a clear head for my exams," I said to Albert.

"Alessandro phoned. Alexia had another miscarriage. The deal's off."

"Oh, God. I'm so sorry." We held hands in the backseat of the patrol car, next to Sally. Kathy rode in the front seat.

"Who would shoot Jerry?" I mumbled, numbed to the core of my being.

"Who would shoot John Kennedy?" responded Albert.

We exchanged looks of commiseration. "I have something to tell you," whispered Albert. "After your test is over." He kissed me on the cheek. I kissed him back.

We got out of the patrol car. I walked hand-in-hand with Albert. Sally walked with Maria Dolores.

"I have to see Jerry," she said.

My life had changed, and so had hers, I suspected.

"Why don't you call the hospital? We all need to go to bed so we can function tomorrow," I said.

Sally hung her head, her bangs in her eyes. "Okay."

She walked into Jerry's apartment. Maria Dolores went into the front house. Albert and I stayed in the hallway, stunned by the turn of events. Slowly, we climbed the steps to his studio and breathed a bit more freely.

"You stood up for me," he said.

I kissed him. We embraced for a long time. I felt the tension flow out of my body.

"You'd do the same for me."

"Do you want to spend the night in my little den of inequity?" His voice took on a lighter, more Albert-like tone.

"Tomorrow night. I've got an exam tomorrow. You know how important exams are." I smiled into his warm face.

"Until tomorrow night."

We kissed.

"I've got something to ask you."

"Do I prefer Barbara Streisand to Billy Holiday?" I quipped.

He laughed and kissed me again. "Will you marry me?" He got down on his knee and looked at me like he would die if I said no. Marriage was the furthest thing from my mind, but I was moved. I kissed him and smiled.

"Albert!" I giggled. "You're so impulsive! I hadn't thought about such a thing as marriage. But, anything can happen when people love each other." I stared at his earnest face, his eyes penetrating mine. I couldn't help but think of my mother's words... '*No one will love you.*'

"What about my...?" I faltered, hesitated. I couldn't say 'my mother.' She'd been so horrid to him.

"Do you think your parents might object?" Albert's tone changed to one of sarcasm.

"They object to everything. They're... They don't love me." I looked at him with pleading eyes. "I don't know what love is, but I want to be loved more than anything."

Albert laughed softly. "What do you think we've been doing?"

"We've been making love, and it feels so good; I know I ought to love you, but I'm not sure... I keep thinking of my parents, even though they've been awful."

Albert looked away. "One has to be sure about such things."

I could hear my mother's voice saying, 'No one will ever love you...'

I didn't know how to respond. My head reeled, for perhaps the tenth time that evening. I turned and ran down his staircase to my studio, leaving Albert speechless.

Albert stared after me. I didn't know what he thought. I was scared to death... of love... and of marriage.

The world turned on its axis. Soon, the morning sun lit up the garden, which had been trampled by the police searching for the gun that came out of nowhere to shoot Jerry.

I jumped out of bed and ran to take my test.

I heard Billy Holiday's peerless voice singing from Albert's apartment. No one could sing like her. Incongruent thoughts ran through my head as I ran toward the Psychology Building to take my mid-term examination.

As I walked out of the Psychology Building with my head still spinning from questions about the results of experiments performed on rats, I thought of Jerry in the hospital. I looked up at the leafy foliage surrounding the path to the commons from Sproul Hall, the building that housed Berkeley's administration, including Dean MacGruder, who had threatened me with perjury not long ago. A large, lovely space with a beautiful fountain off to one side faced the two-story building with marble stairs leading to it. A sense of serenity usually flowed through me when I walked through the commons, but today was different.

Someone had shot Jerry last night and narrowly missed me.

I turned towards Crowell Hospital, Berkeley's student hospital. I walked past the Campanile, Cal's famous bell tower, which had been imitated on its other campuses. It stood sixty feet tall, a noble symbol of academic endeavors. Walking down the tree-lined path that led to Crowell, which loomed large and imposing in the distance, I felt a bit queasy. Jerry shot. Sally distraught. Me? The one to help Sally, if that was possible.

A nurse in a crisp white uniform sat at the registration desk. I approached her and asked if I could see Jerry White.

"Are you a member of the family?" she asked.

"No. I'm just a friend."

"He's in the Intensive Care Unit. No one is allowed in."

I took a deep breath. "I was with him when he was shot."

She looked me over. I stood erect, waiting for her decision.

"You may wait in the waiting room." She returned filling out a form, without lifting an eyebrow.

"Thank you."

I walked down the narrow corridors of the clean, but windowless, hospital. A doctor walked by and I smiled at him. He nodded and went on his way.

At last, I found the waiting room, where Sally sat, twisting a handkerchief in her hands. When she saw me, she started to cry.

"How is he?" I asked.

"They operated on him last night. He's still in a serious condition. The bullet almost hit his heart." Sally sniffled. "It's so awful!"

I looked at her bedraggled hair, which half hid her reddened face. I could tell she'd been through a lot. I put my arm around her shoulders. "It's going to be all right. They have excellent doctors at Crowell Hospital." Sally cried a bit more. Then, she hit me with the zinger.

"My period's late." She looked at me with a tear-streaked face.

I turned and took my arm off her shoulders. "I know."

"Two months."

"Jesus, Sally! Aren't you taking the pill?"

"I ran out."

I put my head in my hands, wondering if there was ever going to be an end to her litany of bad luck or carelessness.

"One thing at a time. Right now, Jerry's hovering between life and death." I looked into her woebegone face with commiseration. She wasn't the first of my friends to have missed a period.

"If he dies, who will pay for the abortion?" Sally asked.

I pushed myself to my feet. My head reeled.

"Come on, Sally! He's in good hands! He'll recover, and you'll get your period. Are you sure it's been two whole months?" I started to pace back and forth like an expectant father. I couldn't believe she could be thinking such thoughts when he was so near death. I didn't like him, but I thought she loved him. Apparently, I was wrong. She was hopelessly insecure and seemed to be incapable of taking care of herself.

A young doctor walked up to us, impeccably dressed in his white doctor's uniform. We looked up at him expectantly.

"Are you friends of Jerry White's?"

"Yes," we said at the same time.

"He's doing better. We'll be moving him out of the ICU into a regular room if his vital signs continue to hold."

Sally stared at the doctor, looking a bit hopeful. "Does that mean he's going to live?"

"We've removed the bullet from his chest. It was close call, but he should pull through."

I breathed a deep sigh of relief. Sally started crying again, releasing her pent-up emotions.

I smiled at the doctor and told him she'd be all right. I'd take care of her. I was beginning to feel like her big sister. I thought of my own younger sister, seven years younger, so bright, so alert, and always a straight-A student. I loved her dearly.

Chapter 11

In Montecito, my mother sat waiting for Andronicus Wyland at the Biltmore Hotel. She sat with perfect posture, hoping she looked younger than her forty-five years. She wore a conservative but elegant dress. She drummed her fingers nervously on the table, looking at the lovely eucalyptus tree in the immaculate lawn in front of the window-vaulted dining room. A waiter had brought her some water in a crystal glass. She took a sip and fingered the white linen napkin at her place setting. She began to smile.

Andronicus pulled into the driveway of the Biltmore in a sports car and snapped his fingers in the air. A valet ran to park his vehicle. He frowned at him for no reason other than he was angry at the headlines of the *Los Angeles Times*. The stock market was down. His father was losing money. His stepfather. He jumped out of the car and ran into the Biltmore.

Mrs. Johnson spotted him at the arched entranceway to the dining room and waved discreetly. Andronicus saw her and nodded as he made his way to her table, brushing a waiter aside in the process.

"Excuse me," said the waiter.

"Watch where you're going," snarled Andronicus.

He sat down opposite of my mother and frowned. He'd shot a man, perhaps killed him, for this woman, and he was beginning to think she wasn't worth it.

My mother smiled and asked him if he was all right.

"We'll talk about that later," he hissed.

"Oh!"

"Just order lunch and act like everything is fine."

"What happened, Andronicus?"

He kicked her under the table.

She kicked him back. Then, she smiled and said, "Sorry."

She's just like her daughter, thought Andronicus. *These bitches are all alike*. He smiled a gratuitous smile, one that emphasized his double chin. Mrs. Johnson looked over her shoulder to make sure no one she knew was there, which was unlikely, because she hadn't made many friends in Montecito yet. Still, she had to keep a sharp eye out, just in case.

"How was your trip to San Francisco?" she asked.

Andronicus flinched. He pursed his fleshy lips and said, "I enjoy the Bay Area."

Mrs. Johnson batted her long eyelashes at him. "Did you see anyone we know?" She hoped he'd finished off his relationship with her daughter. She'd already proven to be too much competition in so many domains that Mrs. Johnson hadn't entered academically and socially. What was worse, she often disobeyed her. Going around with a black man was the penultimate slap in the face. She deserved to be punished. After all, they were from Virginia, and miscegenation was a sin there, not that Inny would ever marry a black man...

"I saw Inny. And some of her friends." Andronicus smiled his ungracious, fleshy-lipped smile.

"Who was she with?" Mrs. Johnson leaned forward, waiting to hear the worst.

"I couldn't get a clear look at them. I only saw them from a distance." He decided to torment Inny's mother, who sat and listened to him with attention that bordered on devotion. She was smitten by his youth and social status. *If I can't get my revenge on Inny, I'll settle for her family*, he thought, a sly look crossing his face.

"She lives in a dumpy little studio apartment near Berkeley. I'd be ashamed to associate with her."

Mrs. Johnson nodded in agreement. Inny should be disapproved of. She should be shot. Well, no... but she must be punished. Afterwards, they could bring her back into the fold. Of course, now that Andronicus was secretly part of the fold, this would be risky. *Oh, she's too much trouble*, thought Mrs. Johnson as the waiter approached to take their orders. Deep down, she still wanted Inny dead. Her own flesh and blood. *If she marries that black man, I'll shoot her myself. No, I want the nigger dead.*

She skimmed the heavy leather-bound menu quickly and ordered a sandwich. Andronicus grinned and ordered a leg of lamb with potatoes. *A sandwich?* He laughed at her under his breath.

"Wouldn't you like something more," he asked, amused that Mrs. Johnson had no idea of what had transpired last night in Berkeley, even though she'd asked him to kill Inny's black boyfriend. She was acting different today.

Women!

"Oh, no thank you. I always have a sandwich for lunch."

Andronicus pushed the heavy chair away from the table full of lovely silverware and porcelain plates. *What a peasant. I want Inny, not this old frau... Although, she still has a nice shape.* He looked at the curve of her breasts under her crisp linen dress with approval. Mrs. Johnson took a deep breath, unused to having a man look at her so intimately. Her husband never did, or perhaps never dared, after… after she became frigid and insisted on twin beds.

"Well, I hope she can find a good job after she graduates from Berkeley," she huffed. "She's costing us a fortune."

Andronicus arched an inquisitive eyebrow. "Are you having financial difficulties?" He hadn't thought of this aspect of their relationship.

Mrs. Johnson cleared her throat. She looked him squarely in the eye. "Mr. Johnson has had, um, some career upsets. That's why we came to Santa Barbara. Things didn't work out for him at Douglas Aircraft, so he had to take another job here. And we have our second daughter to think about."

"Second daughter?" Andronicus's eyes lit up. *Another Inny?*

"Yes, our younger daughter is only fifteen, but we have to plan for her college years as well." She picked up her napkin and twisted it a bit absently. "I don't know what will happen if this job at AFM doesn't work out."

"Perhaps you'd like some financial aid?" Andronicus almost snarled. *So this is what the old whore is after. Fifteen is a bit young though.* Then, his eyes lit up at the thought of a virgin fuck. I can get to her through her mother. "Would you like to walk on the sand like we did last time?"

"Oh, I'm wearing heels." Mrs. Johnson blushed.

"You could take them off." He grinned his fatuous grin at her.

"Well, let me think about that."

The waiter arrived with their lunch. Andronicus snapped his fingers and said, "Two Bloody Marys, please, on the double."

The waiter lowered his well-coiffed head. "Yes, sir." He was used to rude people in this setting.

"Oh, I couldn't possibly…" Mrs. Johnson offered Andronicus her best finishing-school look of indignation. Then, she lowered her head and smiled a mysterious smile, wondering if he could lend them money. They certainly could use it. Such was the birth of prostitution. She fed Andronicus the information he wanted about her oldest and youngest daughters. Andronicus would not let that slippery bitch get by with cheating him out of a good fuck. He eyed Mrs. Johnson and gave her a crude grin, thinking he might continue his revenge today by bedding her in a Biltmore bungalow.

After making torrid love with Andronicus, Mrs. Johnson retreated to the bathroom of the bungalow to comb her hair and make herself look presentable for her husband that night. She put on some bright red lipstick that accentuated her brunette beauty.

She came out of the bathroom, stared at him and said in a steely voice, "Next time, make sure you don't miss." Andronicus let go of her and stared in disbelief. Even he was shocked.

"Sure, Iris, whatever you say," he heard himself say. His thoughts were jammed together. Later in the afternoon, he called to tell her he was going to Berkeley to carry out her wishes. He didn't want her to know he usually botched his attempts.

A few days later, Mrs. Johnson watched her husband eat his breakfast methodically, one forkful of overcooked scrambled eggs at a time, before he left for work. Her mind was five hundred miles away, in Berkeley. Had she really sent a boy, a boy who'd tried to rape her daughter, who was now sleeping with her at will, to Berkeley to kill her daughter's black lover? She looked absently at the hydrangeas that bloomed by the kitchenette windows. "I had to do it," she mumbled. "To protect Inny."

"We have to protect Inny." Mrs. Johnson got up and started pacing around the kitchen.

"What, Iris?" asked Mr. Johnson, hastening to finish his breakfast so he wouldn't be late for his job at AFM, an engineering firm where he had no idea what he was doing, other than trying to make a living. Supposedly, he was helping design machines that scraped away the remaining bowling pins if someone didn't make a strike, which was most of the time. Craig Johnson thought of the days when he was captain of the USS Forrestal, a naval destroyer, when he blissfully rolled with the waves, lobbed an occasional cannonball at the islands near Japan and loved showing off his officer's uniform, loved saluting and being saluted at. That's all he had wanted, plus a nice family to come home to, which he believed he had.

After he was summarily passed over for the rank of captain, something that had been guaranteed to all Annapolis graduates until he came up for promotion, his life changed. The treasury, or someone, had decided to economize by passing over twenty percent of the naval graduates that year; he'd been one of them, due to his miserable grades in Spanish. Mr. Johnson couldn't fathom foreign languages. He'd been at the bottom of his class due to his Ds in Spanish. He couldn't fathom a table being anything other than a table. What the heck was a *mesa?*

He pulled into his parking space outside of AMF, looking dully ahead and nearly running into the car next to him. He'd been in a serious depression ever since he'd been passed over, five years ago. Now, Inny was about to graduate from college and his youngest daughter would be applying for colleges soon. He winced, wiped his nose with its perpetual postnasal drip, opened the car door, got out, and walked stolidly toward his office.

Mrs. Johnson was already on the phone with Andronicus, dressed in one of her prettiest mid-calf house dresses. She thrilled at the sound of his deep, masculine voice and the daring act she'd put him up to. "How… how did things go in Berkeley?" she asked with a girlish trill coming into her voice. She'd never slept with anyone before other than her husband; her sole aim in life was to play bridge, have occasional dinner parties, and be socially acceptable by the right people, who were rich and white in her book. When she scratched Albert's arm and drew blood, everything changed.

Inny had always infuriated her with her independent, headstrong, insulting manner; she knew she'd always do whatever she wanted, but she admired her for passing tests and getting accepted into good schools, which was something Mrs. Johnson hadn't done. Not that she couldn't have, what with her father's wealth and high position as president of the post office in Washington, D.C. but she'd gotten a D in algebra, which convinced her she wasn't smart like her younger sister, who got straight As. Beautiful and sharp-witted, Mrs. Johnson undermined herself and others every time she got the chance. Criticism was her forte.

She was more direct with Andronicus today.

"He and Inny were struggling with a knife! I shot him just in time! I think he's dead!" Andronicus smiled at his skill at lying. He wasn't aware that he'd shot Jerry by mistake.

Mrs. Johnson caught her breath. "You mean that nigger was trying to kill Inny? Oh, what a horrid man!" She imagined a dark man of monstrous proportions trying to drive a knife into Inny's heart. Oddly, a smile crept over her face.

"Not anymore." Andronicus smiled into the receiver of the phone as he rubbed his penis inside his pants. "Could I come over so we can talk about it? Or do you want to meet somewhere?"

"My husband's at work, my younger daughter's at school – come on over! I'll fix you some lunch!"

"Do you have any of that gin you had last time?"

"The Tanqueray? Yes, we never drink. It's for company."

Andronicus continued rubbing his penis until it was hard as a rock. "I'll be right over."

"Fine!"

He jumped up, took a furtive look at the family vault, which was ajar. He deftly pried it open and took a few hundred dollars, just in case they wanted to celebrate up the coast. Then, he ran outside into the bright Montecito sunshine and got into his road-hugging red Ferrari sports car. He took off at top speed.

He'd hardly had any sleep, but he felt alive, invigorated by the excitement of the hunt.

Mrs. Johnson was thrilled to the core of her being. She had a rich young lover who'd killed a black man for her, or so she thought. She'd saved the family's reputation. No one would ever know because she'd threaten to stop Inny's monthly checks to pay for her room and board if she protested. The thought of her headstrong, disobedient daughter agitated her, which Andronicus took for ardor, and led to passionate lovemaking in her own bedroom.

Of course, Andronicus had to leave immediately afterwards; she understood what a busy young man he must be with such a wealthy father. "If only Inny could fall for someone like Andronicus," she mused. She knew her daughter was difficult, and she hoped she could make up for the rejection Andronicus must have suffered at her hands.

Meanwhile, at the bowling pin manufacturing company, her husband stared at a blueprint for the machine that would clear the fallen bowling pins and set up ten new ones. It looked like a foreign language to him. His thoughts began to drift back to the destroyer in the Pacific Ocean when he was young and captain of the ship.

'Aft to the main deck!'

He turned his head with a gleeful smile, which met his boss' deep frown.

"Craig, how is your blueprint coming along?" Mr. Johnson shook his head and smiled.

"It's full steam ahead," he said.

"Where is the device that will replace the fallen pins with new ones?"

Mr. Johnson looked into his supervisor's scowling face. He flinched. "I don't know... I'm having a hard time with that one, Mr. Jones." Craig bowed his head, waiting for the inevitable.

"Perhaps it would help if you took a day or two off to think about it," said Mr. Jones, feeling sorry for the lost soul, who so humbly lowered his head for the blow. Mr. Jones was a nice man.

"Perhaps it would," said Mr. Johnson. He gathered his stylus, pencils, and drawing materials and put them in a zipper bag. "I often come up with my best ideas while sitting in the garden."

"I'm sure you do," said the supervisor, rolling his eyes and wondering where he could find another engineer, if necessary.

Mr. Johnson left early, driving home slowly, wondering what he'd say to his wife. To his surprise, there was a red Ferrari parked in their semi-circular driveway.

Mrs. Johnson opened the front door to find her husband staring at her and Andronicus. They had sprung apart from a passionate embrace on the living room sofa.

"Oh! Craig!" she blanched. "You remember Andronicus, don't you? The nice young man who took Inny to the Coral Casino?"

Mr. Johnson never paid much attention to his eldest daughter's beaux; he just wished she'd hurry up and marry. He couldn't afford her last year at Berkeley. He stuck his hand out and shook Andronicus.' "Oh, yes. How nice of you to visit. Inny's at Berkeley until June." He didn't remember Andronicus. The night she'd knocked on their bedroom door to tell them about Andronicus, only Iris had woken up. Mr. Johnson slept through it and his wife didn't mention it.

"Oh, yes, your wife just told me," stammered Andronicus, astonished at Mr. Johnson's ineptitude. *Didn't he know about that night in Montecito?*

"Since she's not here, I'll be going. Nice to see you again, Mr. and Mrs. Johnson." Andronicus smiled his most ingratiating smile. His flabby face puckered like a fat pumpkin.

The Johnsons smiled back. Mrs. Johnson sucked in her breath; this had been a close call. Mr. Johnson was racking his brain for an excuse for coming home early from work.

Andronicus closed the front door behind him fast as the Johnsons went out onto the patio to mull things over. He wasn't going to take chances like that again.

Just then, their younger daughter opened the passenger door of her best friend Joanie's car. She jumped out, waving goodbye to her friend, a fluff of long blonde hair and skinny legs in a sweater set that showed off her young figure. She started to run to the front door, when she saw Andronicus leaving.

"Oh!"

"Hello!" he said, appraising her with approval. "I was just leaving."

"I see. Well, goodbye!" She held her school books to her chest tightly and ran into the house.

I'll fuck her little sister if it's the last thing I do, he thought to himself. *She's not so bad.*

He pulled into his state senator stepfather's semi-circular driveway, in the heart of Montecito, skidding to a halt. He got out of the car and ran into their stately Tudor-style manor just as his mother was leaving.

"Whatever is the matter, Andronicus darling?" she asked as she adjusted her large purse, which was slung over her shoulder.

"Nothing, Mom, nothing." He ran to his bedroom to sulk for a while.

His mother watched him go and shook her head. *After all I've done for him, he all but ignores me.*

The atmosphere in the Johnsons' living room had turned thick with acrimony. Mr. Johnson had come home early from work.

"I… I just don't understand bowling alley mathematics," he had said haltingly to his wife, who looked more beautiful than ever to him, with her dark red lipstick on her perfect bow-ribbon lips and satiny skin. He wanted to die. "They told me to take some time off to think of more creative ideas this afternoon."

"Craig! What are we going to do?" Mrs. Johnson put her hands on her face.

"I'll find another job. You can always count on me, Iris. You know that." His whimsical little-boy face turned away and his lip tightened. He'd do anything for his family.

"If you could have just made Captain!" she lashed out, hitting him with his biggest failure, one he'd never recovered from.

"Iris! It was just the…" He felt tears welling up in his eyes. It was too much for him. And what was she doing with that young man in their living room? It was their house; he'd paid for it. His head began to whirl. Mr. Johnson slumped over his wife in a dead faint.

"Craig! Craig! Wake up!" She shook him as hard as she could. Then, she moved away from him in disgust. *Why didn't I marry someone with real money?* she asked herself. Then, she remembered Pearl Harbor and how World War II had swept them into each other's arm after a prolonged courtship. They'd married, and she'd become pregnant with Inny. *That was the beginning of my woes.* She looked out the door-to-ceiling glass sliding door that led to their patio, surrounded by lush ferns and flowers. Then, she looked down at her husband, who had started to come to. A look of revulsion came over her normally lovely face.

Craig and Iris Johnson slept fitfully that night. He left before she woke up. He had resolved to find a new job.

Mrs. Johnson woke to an empty bedroom. She got up and scrambled some eggs for her younger daughter and herself. Brenda left for school in a hurry with a quick "Bye Mother." Mrs. Johnson stared at the beautiful wisteria outside the kitchen window as she did the breakfast dishes. Her younger daughter had gotten a ride to Santa Barbara High School, and she had no plans for the day other than buying some cheap hamburgers for dinner. She wondered what would happen if they ran out of money. Little did she know that her husband, who had dressed for work, was parked downtown, looking through the want ads. He had been fired from the AFM, the bowling alley manufacturing company, for failing to come up with any new ideas. He was going through one of the darkest periods of his life and was terrified.

The phone rang. Mrs. Johnson picked it up. "Hello?"

"Hi, Iris. This is Andronicus."

"How nice of you to call. I have nothing to do this afternoon."

There was a pause on the other end of the line. Andronicus realized that she hadn't read the news yet.

"Why don't we meet for lunch at the ranch?"

She knew he was referring to his father's San Ysidro Ranch, where John and Jackie Kennedy had spent their honeymoon. Her heart beat faster just thinking of the romance.

"I'd love to have lunch with you there!"

"I'm busy with some of Dad's clients this morning," he lied.

"Yes, of course. 12 noon?"

"It's a date."

She hung up the phone and ran to the bedroom to look in her closet. Once there, she could only find a dress she'd bought several years ago, which was a bit tight on her. She took a deep breath and put it on. "Why didn't I marry someone like Andronicus?" she asked herself aloud. "Someone with real money. Not just an engineer." She remembered how Andronicus had mentioned something about money. *Well, we certainly need it now, if we ever did*, she thought, pinching her cheeks to give her face a more alluring color.

She frowned at herself in the mirror. Then, she smiled, turned around to make sure her slip wasn't showing, and pinched her cheeks again, which were still as firm as a young woman's. "Thank God my looks are holding up." She heaved a sigh and looked at the clock. It was only 11. She decided to look at the morning paper before leaving to meet Andronicus.

Andronicus looked out over the Pacific Ocean from his stepfather's sun deck. They had a vast estate, yet Andronicus hadn't been able to attract a suitable wife. The ones he liked didn't like him. Especially that wretched president of the Theta house, who was taking him to court for rape. *What a nerve she has*, he thought. *If only they were all as easy as Mrs. Johnson. Of course, she's much too old and married...* he mused. *But she's useful, and she doesn't look her age.* He thought of her satiny skin and curvaceous body. He winced with pleasure as his penis hardened.

Andronicus stretched and put a lazy leg onto the wooden deck of his stepfather's magnificent terrace. He got up and walked into the living room, where a picture of his stepfather's biological son caught his eye. Handsome and popular, he had a hard time competing with Jack, especially as he was going to graduate from Princeton, soon, while Andronicus was flunking out of

Amherst. Jack had also just announced his engagement to a stunner, a winsome and brainy beauty from Vassar. An original oil by Vuillard caught his eye as he walked towards the billiard room with a growing sense of purpose. To his relief, no one was in it or even home when he entered the room. He remembered when he'd played strip poker with his buddies and Inny. *The cunt lost,* he thought with mounting irritation. The door to his stepfather's vault was ajar. Andronicus halted in front of it.

I'll fix her if it's the last thing I do. He turned the lock back and forth with the expertise of someone who knew the vault combination well, opened the vault door, quickly unlocked a strong box with precision that came from habit, and took a few hundred dollars out. *They'll never even notice it's gone. They never do.*

Andronicus smirked at a picture of his illustrious stepfather hanging on the opposite wall, next to some golfing trophies. *He's not my real father anyway. The bitch married this one for his money.*

Chapter 12

Sally and I walked slowly back to our studio on Parker Way, four blocks from the U.C. Berkeley's beautiful wrought-iron Sather Gate. It stood out like an icon in the setting sun.

"What a close call," I mumbled to Sally, her bangs covering the hangdog expression on her face. A stray cat jumped out of nowhere and she screamed. Her nerves were shot.

"Why are you so jumpy?" I looked at Sally.

"He's going to pay for the abortion," she said.

"So you'll sleep with him and get pregnant again?"

She hung her head. Then, she slowly raised her eyes to mine. "Inny, will you go with me?"

"What?"

"I'm afraid to fly. Please come with me. Jerry will pay for your fare."

"Jesus, Sally!"

"It's in Tijuana. I'm so scared."

My mind darted back and forth between leaving her to her just deserts and helping her out of her mess. She was a friend, though she'd hid in the bathroom when Crutches and Ira nearly raped and killed me. I was torn.

We reached the brick path to our studio apartment. As I unlocked the door to ours, a voice rang out. "Bubbly time!" Albert's voice wafted down the stairs. I heard a champagne cork pop.

"Korbel?" I replied with my best Johnson lilt.

"Whatever pleases my love," he exuded.

"Please come with me to Tijuana," Sally muttered through her matted hair.

I gave her a look of contrition mixed with contempt. Then, I ran upstairs to the clarion call of 'bubbly.'

I took the steps three at a time and arrived panting, avidly in need of a good time, which I knew Albert would provide.

Albert laughed when he saw me and poured me a glass of champagne. We clicked glasses and laughed. "Where have you been? Last night was terrible."

"Sally and Jerry are at it again; I tried to talk some sense into her, but she's worse off than ever. He's going to make it though. He'll live to hit her again."

Albert looked at me with twinkling eyes. He was dressed in a dapper plaid button-down shirt and tan slacks. I was wearing a shirt dress I'd made from some fabric I bought at a store. It had bright yellow sunflowers and stood out from the basic beige sweater and skirts most of the other girls wore to class.

He drank some bubbly. "Is she pregnant?"

"How did you guess?"

"When young ladies live with inconsiderate men, that's often the result. What's she going to do?" We drank some more bubbly. He refilled my glass. My spirits lifted. Albert would make this all seem like a bad dream.

"She's going to fly to TJ to get an abortion."

"Good."

"And I'm going with her."

Albert's frowned. He stopped drinking the bubbly. "Why you?"

"She asked me to go because she's scared."

"Of getting an abortion?"

"No, of flying."

His eyes widened in surprise. We both started laughing, laughing harder than I can remember laughing. It was beyond absurd.

"Of course, you told her you wouldn't go?" Albert gave me a professorial stare.

"No, I didn't."

"Inny!"

"I'd like to see Mexico."

"This is not a pleasure cruise."

"I know; I know. I'd be crazy to go. She's a total coward and has shown no signs of changing. I'd be crazy to go with her, but I've been trying to help her since our freshman year."

We clicked champagne glasses. Albert kissed me lightly on the lips. I kissed him back. "That's why I'm going." I giggled.

Albert stared at me as if I'd dropped Sather Gate on his foot.

"Mary Jane had to have one there. She said it was easy."

"Things can go wrong. Besides, I don't like the idea of you going to a foreign country alone." Albert turned his aquiline nose towards the window overlooking our fern-rimmed garden. I admired his handsome profile. "I'm coming with you," he said.

"Really?" It was my turn to stare at him. Then I grinned. "This is not a pleasure cruise, you know. No lavender wigs allowed."

We burst out laughing and wrapped our arms around each other. I could think of nothing more romantic than Albert accompanying me and Sally to Tijuana to get an abortion. Everything about Albert spelled romance, delight, and integrity. He was everything I admired. He would always have my back.

We drank bubbly until it all made sense. I put my arms around Albert and felt his hard, smooth chest. Nothing else mattered. Albert and I wandered down the stairs to my studio and he helped me cook some trout with gourmet potatoes au gratin he'd made the night before. After a sumptuous repast, we wandered back to his studio, holding hands. I spent the night in his studio. Having his arms around me made me feel more secure after that bullet passed under my arm and hit Jerry. *It could've been me.*

Chapter 13

I awoke from a sound night's sleep in Albert's ample double bed to hear footsteps on the stairway that led to his studio. There was a knock on the door. We woke and mumbled in our half-sleep as I fumbled for my clothes, an unnecessary effort, as it turned out to be Sally.

"Jerry's given me the money," she announced.

I stared at her.

"Money? Money for what?" asked Albert.

I turned and walked over to the bed where he lay with the covers drawn up to his neck. He looked so comical that I almost laughed.

"For my, um, for my trip to Tijuana," mumbled Sally.

I stared at her, then at him.

"You're asking a lot of Inny, you know."

"She's my friend." Sally looked at us as if she needed someone to throw her a life preserver.

"Lucky for you, it's almost Christmas break." I turned and looked at Albert.

"Lucky for you that you have a friend as kind-hearted as Inny," he said. "How is Jerry?"

"He's going to recover."

A wry look passed over Albert's usually serene face.

She seemed numb, unable to process what she was asking us to do or what she was going to go through.

"Albert says he'd like to accompany us," I said.

"To TJ?"

"No, to Paris." I couldn't help my sarcastic remark. Sally drove me wild sometimes. It was almost like I was her big sister, trying to help her take charge of her life.

Sally looked down at Albert's Moroccan rug with its natural dyes and rich hues of pale orange and yellows. I'd hurt her feelings.

"I'm sorry." I felt a surge of sympathy for her hapless situation. *Who would want to have Jerry's baby? The guy's a psycho.*

"Um, could we wait a week until Christmas break? I have a bunch of exams to take."

"I guess so."

Albert and I exchanged doleful looks. Then, he stood up and, all charm, offered her a cup of coffee. The atmosphere changed palpably. Sally was smiling by the time we sat down to coffee on Albert's lovely antique wooden kitchen table.

Still on the critical list at the hospital, Jerry conversed with us about the additional passenger by phone. We got him to agree by offering to bring back some Tequila. *Just what this man-beast needs,* I thought while looking down into the fern-filled garden in front of our studios. It looked so green, so peaceful. I couldn't help but resent Sally's unwanted pregnancy.

I trundled downstairs, sat in the old wooden chair in front of my Formica kitchen table, and opened my Skinner's rat psychology book. I tried to memorize as I read, taking careful notes in my notebook. "The Skinner jumping stand experiment proved…"

The next week passed with a blur of exams and preparing for the trip to Tijuana. A private plane would take us to the clinic where the abortion was to be performed outside the city. That was all I knew.

Sally and I packed our overnight bags with essentially the same things: toothpaste and a toothbrush, some blue jeans, and a light jacket, in case it got chilly on this winter's night south of the border. The only difference was that Sally packed a lot of Kotex and tampons. We didn't know which would be most effective, so she packed both.

She gave me an apprehensive look through her eternally unkempt, overlong bangs, which covered a bit of her beaked nose. I met her eyes and smiled.

"Don't worry. Mary Jane had her abortion in TJ and said everything went smoothly. She said the doctor was a good one."

"But we have to *fly!*" Sally's eyes widened as if the plane had already crashed.

"Flying is safer than driving," I repeated what I'd heard and knew to be true.

"But a car is on the ground!"

I turned and faced Sally squarely. "When are you going to stop acting like such a baby?"

She averted her face. I had no idea what she was thinking. I kept packing my bag on my double bed, which had seen more than enough action, I thought, thinking of Crutches and Ira.

Albert breezed by singing one of my favorite Fats Domino songs, 'You Were My Thrill on Blueberry Hill.' "…love's sweet melody…"

I chimed in, "So we're apart…"

He poked his head in my doorway. We burst out laughing.

"TJ time," I trilled.

"You broke my heart when you said we'd part…" he spoke directly to me. "Ain't that a shame…"

"Now get ready! The plane leaves in an hour," I said and saw Sally searching her purse for the money Jerry had given her at the hospital. He'd been taken off the critical list by this time and would be home soon. She knew she had to pay cash.

Albert tripped up the stairs, light as Fred Astaire, still singing. *How could I not adore this man?* Maybe I did. Of course I did. But marriage? I was only twenty-one although in the early sixties, girls were still marrying in their teens.

Within ten minutes, Albert swooshed down the stairs from his studio and propelled me and Sally to his waiting car. He drove to the Oakland Airport as if he were catching a plane to the Cannes Film Festival, light-hearted and happy. His mood was infectious. Sally perked up and her TJ trip seemed like a caper we'd watched in the movies.

A small four-seater plane awaited us near the edge of the tarmac. The pilot waved us over and we grabbed our bags and ran, hustling up the removable stairs to get in. Sally sat in front of Albert and me. His hand fumbled for mine. We clasped hands. His strong hand in mine felt warm and reassuring. It felt like it belonged there. Sally turned before takeoff and gave me a terrified look.

"Sally, if the plane crashes, we'll die with you, so cut it out!"

The pilot turned and gave us a brief frown. Then, he taxied the small craft down the runway and made a smooth takeoff. Sally leaned over and put her head in her skirt the whole time.

When we were above the clouds, looking down on the magnificent Bay Area, the Golden Gate Bridge barely visible, I said, "You can come up for air, Miss Sissy Pants."

A hand slid back toward mine. It was Sally's. I took it. Albert looked at me holding the hand and started to laugh. It was beyond comical, except that, of course, this scared friend of mine was about to have her first abortion. With her track record, I had no idea how many more she'd have to have. Back in the sixties, abortions were illegal, and you were thankful if someone would pay to fly you south of the border to have one. They were still illegal in Mexico, too, but the money seemed to matter most, not to mention the need to correct an ill-timed pregnancy, which could have been prevented with contraception.

Albert and I marveled at the beauty of the California coastline as we flew along, just low enough to be able to take in the sights. Sally's head remained in her skirt most of the time. The sun began to set as we neared a small runway outside of Tijuana. The plane landed with a bit of a thump. We had arrived.

Albert jumped out to help us out of the plane. I shook hands with the pilot, who looked to be a Mexican national, and practiced my Spanish on him. "*Muchas gracias, señor.*"

"*No hay de que,*" he replied. "I speak English." I laughed at my faux pas. Sally smiled, grateful to be on solid ground.

A late-model Chevy awaited us. We got in and the driver whisked us over the hills to a ranch-style home, replete with cacti next to the doorstep and chilies hanging on the porch. The driver opened the front door and asked us to be seated on a comfortable sofa in what looked very much like someone's living room. The inlaid tile floor gleamed as if it had just been mopped. I glanced at Sally. She was cool as a cucumber. Some people would be more afraid of going to the dentist.

An amiable-looking middle-aged Mexican woman approached us, all smiles. This hardly seemed like a place that performed abortions, but who was I to judge?

Albert and I exchanged looks. "What about din dins?"

"*Queremos comer una comida,*" I said in my textbook Spanish.

The woman snapped her fingers. "*La cena,*" she said.

"*Si, señora,*" I heard from what must have been the kitchen.

"*Pronto!*" the woman said.

Just as we were about to sit at a lovely wooden dining room table with twisting, hand-carved table legs that turned into lion's feet, the amiable-looking woman came to the doorway and said in pretty good English, "Who is the *señorita*?" Sally walked over to her and stood erect. She reminded me of someone about to face a firing squad.

"I'm the *señorita*," she said with a terrible accent.

The woman led her away.

"*Cuando*, um, when will she be back?" I asked.

"Soon," said our hostess. "Don't worry. The doctor has experience."

Albert and I exchanged worried looks.

"I wish I spoke Spanish," he mumbled under his breath. "I'd like to talk to the doctor."

He hesitated for a moment, looking down at the colorful tiles that covered the floor. "My father is a doctor. I'd like to speak to the doctor."

"He only speaks Spanish, *señor.*" She smiled in an ingratiating manner that didn't inspire confidence.

"I could translate," I offered.

"*El medico* doesn't like to be disturbed. Please." A servant appeared with plates of rice, beans, and something that resembled enchiladas. "Sit down."

Albert and I sat and ate in silence. We had no idea what was going on. A chill began to make its way up my spine. "Albert…"

We stared at each other while eating forkfuls of rice and beans.

"I don't think there's much we can do at this point. We've come this far. Try to eat and then we'll find out how Sally's doing."

The meal turned out to be a substantial one, with *flan* and other Mexican delicacies following the main course. It seemed incongruous with Sally's abortion. We finished and sat in silence, lost in our own thoughts.

The amiable woman came in and cleared the table. "Your friend is fine. She's sleeping now."

"Can't we see her?"

"*Mañana.* Your plane leaves at five o'clock tomorrow morning. Before light."

"Where can we spend the night?"

"On the *terraza.*"

I wiped my mouth on the cloth napkin. "Could we go there now?"

"Yes. Follow me."

Albert stood up, brushing a crumb from his Brooks Brothers slacks. I did the same. The woman led us to an empty tile-covered terrace, which looked like a jewel in the moonlight. She tossed some blankets at us and a couple of pillows. Albert laughed. "Mexican hospitality."

"The best," I said and started making beds for us to lie on.

"Just look at those stars!" Albert enthused. "I can see The Milky Way, Orion, the Big Dipper…"

I looked at the star-studded night sky, clear as day. No city lights to dim the beauty of the night. I put my hand in his. He pulled me towards him. We embraced for a long while. Then, we laid down on our makeshift beds.

"Ouch! These tiles are hard!" I said after a quickie.

"Just look at the sky," Albert said.

I looked up at the sky with Albert. "Orion's Belt points to the Pleiades… and the Little Dipper…" Albert was entranced. We stared at the sky for an hour or so. It felt like we had box seats to the best show on Earth. "The world is so beautiful… endlessly enchanted and magical."

"I've always loved nature. Ever since I grew up crossing streams on fallen logs to walk to school with my girlfriends. We were always joyful, filled with glee. That was in Arlington, Virginia. Then, my father got ordered to

Coronado, California by the Navy. Why do we need a military? Why do people kill each other? Animals don't."

"William Blake had a lot to say on the subject. It's all in the human brain," remarked Albert.

We marveled at the gorgeous stars a bit longer, wishing we could be on one.

"I love nature," I finally mumbled, just as Albert reached over and kissed me.

"I love you," he said.

I returned his kiss. I kissed his lips, the nape of his neck, his shoulder. Our bodies sought each other as if an ancient ache that needed pleasure to heal. We made love until we couldn't bear the pleasure anymore. We fell asleep on the hardest of tiles under the magic of the night. It was dawn before we knew it. Too soon. We scrambled to get into our clothes and see Sally, who smiled with relief.

They hurried us back to the small plane and we were airborne before you could say Jackie Robinson. I held Sally's outstretched hand. She put her face in her skirt.

"Sally! We're in the air. We're fine! Are you okay? What happened?"

She took her face, half covered with her too-long bangs, out of her lap. She smiled. "It was over in a minute. And it didn't even hurt. I didn't feel a thing… Well, maybe a twinge."

I detected a trace of pride in her face. Perhaps even the beginnings of courage.

"Congratulations! You've survived your ordeal! Are you sure you are all right?"

"A bit woozy, but that's all."

Albert and I exchanged looks. Woozy didn't sound good. I hoped that we'd be back in Berkeley within an hour. I looked down at the ocean beneath us. It looked so deep and blue. A few white caps, but very serene. It calmed me. Albert took my hand and squeezed it. I kissed him. *Marry Albert Curtis* ran through my mind. I pictured my mother's face. Then I laughed.

"What you laughing at?" he asked gruffly. He frowned at me, a furrow creasing his normally smooth brow.

"Oh, nothing. I just have a funny sense of humor."

He nodded in bemusement. "I'll say." He hesitated. He cleared his throat. I looked into his dark brown eyes, which were somber and brooding today. "You don't really know me," his voice faltered. I realized that I took him at face value. I'd never thought of him as a complicated person. A person with…

"I have a few skeletons in the closet."

"Don't we all?" I answered, encouraging him to continue.

"My past was… I don't want to say I was exploited… Just a lonely black kid studying English in a nearly all-white university."

Sally had already fallen asleep in the seat in front of us. She had lost her fear of flying.

"It must have been awfully hard, but you graduated with a doctorate." I tried to sound upbeat.

"Jerry has lived downstairs from me for many years. He… he…"

I turned my head and stared at his chiseled profile. I prepared for the worst.

"He seduced me when I was a junior. I was still a virgin…" The plane lurched and so did my heart.

"Jerry? That… that abusive, sadistic, disgusting excuse for a man?"

"I was grateful for his friendship. I didn't ask questions. I submitted to him… like a slave, a sex slave." Albert lowered his eyes. I grabbed for his hand and squeezed it.

Tears filled my eyes. I turned to him and saw that he was crying, too. I leaned in and kissed him. We embraced for a long time. The thought of Jerry taking advantage of Albert sickened me. I felt as if we were on a par, the same. We'd both suffered at the hands of others, yet in different ways. A warm feeling of compassion and love suffused me and I held him tightly. "I love you, Albert. I'll never hurt you."

"I hope not," he whispered in my ear. It tickled and made me laugh. We both started laughing involuntarily, wildly. We held each other and kissed, sliding our hands over each other's bodies. I'd never felt closer to another human being. Maybe I should marry him.

Albert held my hand as we landed in the Oakland Airport. One big bump and our small aircraft came to a halt. I had a paper to write. Albert had to teach a class. I looked at Sally. Her face was a bit ashen.

"Are you okay?"

"Yes. The doctor was so nice. I'm just tired and a bit woozy."

Albert frowned. "What do you mean by woozy?"

Sally smiled through her bangs. "Just a little bit dizzy and…"

She fainted. Albert grabbed her, hoisting her into his strong brown arms as we ran down the tarmac.

"Call an ambulance!" I yelled.

* * * *

Albert and I paced outside of the Intensive Care Unit at the Oakland hospital the ambulance had taken Sally to, the one closest to the Oakland

137

Airport where we'd just landed. The cold, sterile hallway, devoid of lovely paintings of nature that had lined the hallway at Crowell Hospital in Berkeley, hardly reassured us. An older, tall, spare doctor emerged from Sally's room, a worried look on his face. He looked like he'd seen more than his share of emergencies.

We ran towards him, hoping to hear she'd be all right.

"She's lost a lot of blood. We've given her a transfusion. Her condition is still critical."

"How critical is that, Doctor?" I asked.

He looked into my eyes. Then, he stared at Albert, who stuck out his hand and introduced himself as a Professor Curtis. Standing erect, his gaze meeting ours, he explained that she'd hemorrhaged, which meant she'd lost a third of her body's blood supply. It could affect the brain, but he thought she'd pull through and be back to normal in a day or so.

He frowned. "The doctor who performed the procedure cut a vein. This should never happen." Albert and I looked at each other, scared to death for Sally.

"Thank you very much, Doctor. My own father is a doctor and has had to deal with similar procedures that were... ah... poorly preformed."

"No woman should have to go through this," I murmured. "Another friend had this procedure and she was fine. But we're playing Russian roulette with women's lives."

The doctor gave me a knowing look. "We've notified her parents. They should be here shortly."

I pictured Sally's sweet, pudding-faced, middle-class mom who'd let me spend the night with Sally's family after spring break, in our freshman years. She'd remarked that I was the kind of friend she'd hoped Sally would make. She was impressed, because I'd passed all of my classes and done research in the Berkeley library. Sally had gotten a couple of Ds and could flunk out. "I'll wait to talk to them," I said.

Albert had to go to his office to correct papers and get grades ready. His elegant face filled with compassion, he left me, whispering, "That was no doctor who performed the procedure."

The horror of what Sally had gone through hit me. I sat down and nodded.

"Why don't you come with me?" he asked.

"I want to talk to Sally's mother. They can give me a ride later."

"Thank you, Doctor." Albert stuck his hand out and he shook it. I looked on, stupefied by the turn of events. Too much tragedy was entering into my friends' lives.

Hours later, after missing my flight to go home for Christmas, I learned that Sally had hemorrhaged from a coat hanger-style abortion that had not been performed by a doctor, very likely. They thought she'd pull through, but they couldn't assure me of her full recovery. I reeled in shock. I didn't know what I'd say to her parents.

Albert kissed me sweetly as he left the hospital. I felt unmoored.

Jerry had been released from Crowell Hospital, and although he still wore bandages, he was able to come to the hospital to see Sally.

"This is your fault!" he raged.

I began to cry. "I thought everything was going to be all right." I wiped my teary eyes. "She begged me to go with her, so I went as a favor. YOU should have been there! You got her pregnant."

He slugged me. I went down and the nurses ran to intervene.

I came up spluttering as Jerry yelled, "She took her to TJ for the abortion! It's her fault!"

The nurses did their best to restrain him. One phoned the police.

"No, don't call the police!" yelled Jerry.

He gave me a filthy look that was worse than the sock in the jaw. I wanted to help Sally, but I wasn't responsible for her botched abortion. The doctor in TJ was. It turned out it was a midwife/abortionist who'd used a coat hanger.

Jerry almost exploded when he heard the word 'coat hanger.'

"I paid five hundred dollars for a D-and-C-type abortion!"

"If you paid for it, and you and Sally decided to go through with it, it's your fault!"

"Cunt!"

"Stop it! This won't help Sally!"

We exchanged furious looks and then sat down on the vinyl-covered chairs in the lobby, looking morose. *A coat hanger abortion. Why didn't they tell me?*

I was in over my head, but I had to stay, for Sally's sake, or what was left of Sally. I couldn't bear the thought of seeing her mother, whom I had met at their comfortable home, in Walnut Creek when we were freshman. She said I was the kind of friend she'd hoped Sally would make. I even went to the library. I didn't mention that almost everyone at U.C. Berkeley went to the library, at least, to do research, or that her daughter was somewhat of a joke in our sorority for her lack of organizational skills.

She was an awfully sweet girl, and she didn't deserve this, that much I knew for certain.

Chapter 14

Andronicus stretched, yawning after an uncomfortable evening waiting for Inny outside of her studio. He'd waited in his sports car, cramped behind the steering wheel, till two in the morning. Fingering the gun in a holster inside his suede jacket, he heard a scraping noise on the sidewalk. He looked up to see a heavy-set man on iron crutches making his way towards him. He almost drew his gun, because the fellow looked menacing, and so did his companion, slighter and taller in build.

Crutches swaggered toward Andronicus, then turned down the brick pathway to Inny's studio. Andronicus stared after him. He watched him go to her door and knock. When there was no answer, he made his way back, his iron crutches scraping loudly on the bricks. Andronicus blocked his path.

"Hey, whatcha want?" asked Ira.

"What are you doing here at two in the morning?"

"We're here to see Inny," said Crutches, a surly grin on his face. Ira grimaced as he stood next to him. Together, they looked menacing.

"How did you know it was Inny's place?" asked Andronicus. He snarled a bit as he spoke, somewhat like a bulldog growling at the smell of fresh meat.

"I've been here before. She's a friend of mine," laughed Crutches. "We've been in tight places together and we get along just fine."

"Tight places?" Andronicus's blood started to surge. He felt his throat tighten.

"Well, sorta. Anyway, we're friends. Tight friends."

"Why are you waiting out here for her?"

"Hey, that way I'll be sure to catch her."

Andronicus stepped back and studied the two men. The one on crutches had a heavy, thick-browed face, older than his years. The other one looked like a Russian spy he'd seen in a movie, thin and wiry, with a mean look.

"Inny's parents live in Montecito," asserted Andronicus, trying to impress them.

"Yeah, she's one fancy bitch all right."

Andronicus smiled slowly, his upper lip curling over his gums. "Do you want to fuck her?"

Crutches stood his ground. "That's my business."

"Do you need any help?"

"I got all the help I need. I'm capable of fucking women."

Andronicus looked at the iron crutches. "I don't doubt it. I just thought I might help you."

"Yeah? How? She a pretty slippery bitch."

"Watch who you call a bitch!" Andronicus pulled out his gun. Crutches and Ira stared at it.

"Put that rod away," said Crutches. "Who are you trying to impress?" Andronicus put it back in the holster inside his jacket.

"That's more like it," laughed Ira. "So, where the hell is she? This place is dead as a doornail. Nobody home."

Andronicus laughed, "I guess our timing's bad. We could try again next Saturday night." He mopped the perspiration from his brow. These guys made him nervous.

"She's got a black boyfriend, I hear," mumbled Crutches.

"I'll keep that in mind," said Andronicus, suddenly feeling his confidence surge. "Girls who sleep with black guys deserve what they get."

"Yeah. They're all bitches," mumbled Crutches. He turned and started to walk away.

"Why don't we all do her?" Andronicus called after him.

"Nah. That's playing dirty," said Crutches. "Two's enough." Crutches turned and looked at Andronicus' late-model sports car. "Rich kid, eh?"

"Went to Amherst," snarled Andronicus as he put his gun back in its holster.

"Snot-nosed Ivy League brat. I've known guys like you." Crutches leaned forward on his metal crutches so that his muscular shoulders and arms bulged. Andronicus instinctively stepped backwards. That's when Crutches hit him with one of his metallic devices, flat across the face. Andronicus recoiled and turned to run, but he wasn't fast enough. Crutches and Ira jumped him on the sidewalk, Ira pulling him up to punch him in the face, Crutches continuing to slap him with his iron rods. Andronicus started to scream. A young couple coming home from a date spotted them. Crutches and Ira scrambled to make a getaway, Crutches moving fast as lightening on his metallic rods, leaving a scraping noise in his wake.

"Need some help?" asked the young woman. She held out her hand as her date stooped to help Andronicus to his feet.

Andronicus shook his bloodied head and said, "Nah, I'm okay."

"You don't look okay."

Andronicus wiped blood off his face. "Shit like this goes down all the time. It's just a quarrel between guys … over a bitch!"

The couple looked at him, horror written on their innocent young faces, as he walked over to his Ferrari, got into it wiping blood from his brow and swearing under his breath. Crutches and Ira stopped running to laugh as Andronicus started his car and pulled away, wiping blood that flowed freely from his nose. "It's the bitch's fault. Everybody wants to fuck her," Andronicus mumbled. "Even that psycho cripple!"

Maria Dolores stared after him from the front window of the Victorian house that was in front of the studio apartments Inny and Albert lived in.

Andronicus glanced at the house. She closed the curtain and drew down the shade, running to the bathroom to fix her hair a bit before going downstairs to see what had happened.

Andronicus drove resolutely towards Santa Barbara, towards Montecito, where he figured he'd borrow some more money from his stepfather's vault. He thought of Mrs. Johnson, her willing body giving way to his thrust at the Biltmore cottage. That was getting too expensive. He remembered her husband's dumbfounded look when he caught them together. *That guy's unbelievable. How could he not grasp that I was doing his wife?* He had never met anyone as naïve as Mr. Craig Johnson, who believed his wife to be as chaste as a vestal virgin.

The image of their fifteen-year-old daughter flickered through his foggy mind. His lip curled up in a half-smile. *The younger the better, they say.*

Chapter 15

Andronicus pulled into his stepfather's carriage-style driveway and parked the Ferrari in one of the three garage slots. He took out an old shirt and mopped his face with it, trying to look presentable. It was almost seven in the morning, and the family would be getting up. He slid out from behind the steering wheel to encounter his older half-brother, the true heir to Senator Dorland's fortune.

"Hey, Andronicus!" Kevin walked up to him, tall, slim, and clean-cut as a new penny. Andronicus knew only too well that he was his father's favorite. He never could figure out why the senator had adopted him.

Andronicus slid out from behind the steering wheel fast, trying to avoid his half-brother's inquiring look. Too late. Kevin stood in front of him.

"Where were you last night? You had your mother worried sick." Kevin mustered a sympathetic look for the black sheep of the family. Andronicus had been in and out of trouble for years, ever since his dad married his stepmother. Nothing too serious and the judges usually dismissed the charges. Kevin didn't question why.

"Oh, yeah, Kevin!" Andronicus looked up at him and laughed. "Just having a good time. Must've drunk a little too much."

Kevin looked at his watch. He would be late for work if he got into it with Andronicus, and he knew Andronicus wouldn't tell him the truth. "I've got to get to the office," he said as gently as possible. He tried to be gentle with Andronicus, knowing he was troubled and that he could fly off the handle if cornered.

"Yeah, big brother, go to work like a good boy." Andronicus averted his face to try to hide his wounds, which include a gash in his forehead where Crutches had hit him with his iron crutch.

Kevin saw them anyway. "Man, that must've been some party! Why don't you see a doctor?"

"Nah. Just a minor scrape. Nothing to get excited about."

Andronicus turned his back to his brother and headed towards the garage. Kevin stared after him. He shook his head, perplexed. Then he slid in behind

the wheel of his Mercedes Benz. He was the biological son of Senator Dorland. He had a good deal and didn't want to rock the boat.

Andronicus slunk into his spacious bedroom, furnished in the latest French rustic style. His mother always took care of the house furnishings and parties. She knew her role and played it well. He knew she wasn't happy that he'd flunked out of Amherst. And she and the senator expected him to enroll in another school. Instead, Andronicus had learned the family vault keyhole numbers and could open it in seconds. No one ever offered him money, so he took it. *After all, as the adopted son, I'm entitled*, he reasoned.

He took a long shower and put Neosporin on his head gash, plus a large Band-Aid that hid it well enough. As he combed his hair and looked in the bathroom mirror, he figured he could tell anyone who asked that the scrape on his chin came from shaving while under the influence. They knew he drank.

Feeling renewed, he looked out his window at the Santa Barbara Channel Islands, whose contours stood out like sentinels in their stark beauty today. *I'll bet Iris would like to see those.* He smiled as he thought of his married conquest. He turned and walked towards the living room phone to give her a call. As he passed his mother's bedroom, he glanced in and saw her jewelry flung carelessly on her vanity. A smile crossed his face. He listened for sounds of a human presence. Hearing none, he slipped into his mother's room and took what looked to be pearl necklace from her vanity. *She has so much jewelry... She'll never miss this.*

He admired the double-stranded pearl necklace and then fumbled for a box to put it in. Footsteps resounded on the staircase. He slid the necklace into his pants' pocket and walked into the hallway, cool as a cucumber.

Sure enough, it was his mother.

"Were you looking for me, Andy?" she asked. She always called him by her pet name, which annoyed him, but he was used to it by now, having heard it all his life.

"Um, yes, Mom." He grinned his most affable grin at her and she smiled back. "I was thinking about colleges."

"Just what I wanted to hear," she beamed her approval. Then, she saw the Band-Aid on his forehead. "Did you hurt yourself?"

"Nah. I just hit the side of the pool when I was swimming last night."

"Oh. I thought you went out last night. I couldn't find you anywhere." Her high forehead furrowed into a familiar frown. She had been helping Andronicus cover his tracks for years. Now, she began to doubt her results.

She took off her horn-rimmed glasses and scrutinized her son. She knew he was in trouble.

"Oh, Mom, you know how the guys are here. Drink a few beers, go for a swim at someone's house… If you hit your head on the side of the pool it's all in good fun."

She stepped closer to him and adjusted his shirt collar, noting the scrape on his chin. She doubted that he was telling the whole story. "Look, Andronicus, don't you think it's time to enroll in a nice university like USC? It's easy to get into…"

"You mean like Jim did after he flunked out of Berkeley? Pay for your diploma?" He pulled away from her and started to scowl, the precursor to one of his tantrums.

"Now, Andy, it's strictly up to you," she quickly backed down, trying to avoid his notorious bad temper. She wondered what she'd done to deserve such an offspring.

"Okay." Andronicus replied. "Then leave it up to me." He turned heel and left her feeling sad and rejected. She knew she'd have to talk to her husband about it, and she knew he was unhappy with Andronicus as well. Seeking solace, she went into her bedroom and changed clothes, putting on one of her most expensive dresses for effect. She went to her vanity to look for some jewelry to set it off. She saw her pearl earrings, a diamond bracelet worth several thousand dollars like the one Swann had given his mistress in Marcel Proust's *Remembrance of Things Past*. But try as she might, she couldn't find her favorite pearl necklace, the one with double strands. She was sure she'd left it there last night.

Andronicus picked up the phone in his bedroom to call Mrs. Johnson.

"Hello?" she answered.

"Hi, it's me."

"Oh, I'm so glad you called. I was just about to go grocery shopping… but it can wait. I've missed you."

Her younger daughter ran into the kitchen where the phone was, ready for school.

"Oh, I'm going to take Kendra to school now. Can you call back?"

"Just meet me at the Biltmore for lunch." Andronicus felt a sharp pain in his forehead. *That damn shit hit me hard.*

"I've got something special for you."

"I can hardly wait!" She hung up and grabbed the keys to their second, older car to take her youngest to school, thinking that she'd have to change clothes if she were to dine at the Biltmore. *I really need nicer clothes. Maybe Andronicus can…*

Kendra got out of the car, clutching her algebra and history books, her nubile fifteen-year-old body not yet filled out. Inny got her mother's good looks, but Kendra was considered the brainy daughter, the one they'd count on in their old age.

Mrs. Johnson watched her youngest daughter trip up the stairs to Santa Barbara High School. A friend joined her, and they walked into the lovely Spanish-tiled school. The thought that she'd soon be in college, reeled through Mrs. Johnson's head. She knew they couldn't afford it. Their trust fund for Inny's college was almost depleted, and they hadn't felt rich enough to get one when Kendra was born. *Why couldn't they just get married like me and my sister did?*

Mrs. Johnson looked in the rearview mirror, put on some fresh lipstick, and turned toward the Biltmore, only a quarter of a mile from the school. Santa Barbara was small and convenient, especially for those grasping for the rung in the social ladder ahead of them. She felt a bit disgusted with herself for associating with Andronicus, but she did have to punish Inny for consorting with that black man... Not to mention her husband was about to lose his engineering job, a thought that made her shudder.

She marveled at the beauty of Butterfly Beach as she pulled her car into a convenient parking spot near the balustrade which overlooked the beach and a view of the bluffs next to them. Then, she took a pair of high-heeled shoes from underneath the driver's seat and took off her normal-housewife, flat shoes. No sweeping floors for her today.

Mrs. Johnson got out of the car, adjusted her high heels, and walked into the Biltmore Hotel looking as regal as a queen. After all, she was the daughter of Audus T. Davis, the former president of the Washington, D.C., Post Office, a position that had enabled her mother to attend numerous White House dinners. *My mother even talked to President Harding's wife*, she thought, airily. That her mother had to take a streetcar to get to Washington because her husband refused to use his political clout or escort her to such events... That was another story. Mrs. Johnson's biggest chagrin was not having married better, that is to say, richer. Known as a conceited beauty who had a mind of her own, Craig Johnson was the only one smitten enough to marry her.

Andronicus sat with his back to the entrance of the dining room, staring out the window at the huge eucalyptus tree in the green area in front of the hotel. Mrs. Johnson walked up behind him. Feeling girlish, she put her hands over his eyes and said, "Guess who!" When he turned around to face her, she quickly withdrew her hand and surveyed his puffy face and the scrape on his chin.

"What happened, Andronicus?"

He laughed a guttural, manly guffaw. "It's nothing. Just tripped on the landing and landed on my face."

"Is that all?" she commented drily. Mrs. Johnson could see through a lie with laser-like vision.

"Isn't it enough?" he asked.

She turned her head so he could admire her perfect profile. "I don't really know what enough means, Andronicus."

"Well," he stammered a bit, sensing she'd detected his white lie. He took the pearls out of his pocket. "These are for you."

The double-strand pearl necklace gleamed as bright as the silverware on the table. Mrs. Johnson took the necklace and gasped, "Where did you get these?" She knew that necklaces in pockets had often been pocketed.

"At the local jeweler." Andronicus kept a straight face.

Mrs. Johnson put them on, fumbling with the clasp behind her neck. She noticed that people were beginning to stare at her, so she put her hands in her lap. "Andronicus. People are staring."

"Don't let them bother you. You're the most beautiful woman in the room. That's why they're staring."

Mrs. Johnson smiled a cryptic smile. "How did it go this weekend?"

"I stayed home. I didn't call because I knew your husband would be there."

The waiter approached them. "Cocktails?" he asked.

"I'll have a whisky soda," said Andronicus without hesitation.

"I'll have a cup of coffee, please," said Mrs. Johnson, her Southern good manners firmly drilled into her by her own mother. Please and thank you were the first words she'd learned, and she'd taught them to her daughters. To be ungrateful was the worst sin in her book.

"Send the waiter over. We're ready to order," said Andronicus.

Mrs. Johnson scanned the menu looking for something that cost under twenty dollars. She couldn't bring herself to be careless with money. She glanced at the pearl necklace on the table. It looked obvious that he was trying to please her, so she scooped it up and put it in her purse. "I'll put it on when you can help me with the clasp," she murmured to Andronicus, who smiled his approval. Under her breath she said, "I thought you were going to get that nigger Inny's sleeping with."

"All in due time, Iris," said Andronicus, growing a bit apprehensive. He took a swig of whisky soda, making a loud slurping noise, which annoyed Mrs. Johnson.

Mrs. Johnson turned and addressed him in her most imperious tone of voice. "You can't marry a black man where I come from. Nor can you sleep with one. They'll put you in jail."

Andronicus stared at Mrs. Johnson's lovely oval face, her perfect features set in satiny white skin. To hear her speak with such an authoritarian tone

147

shocked, even scared, him. There was a side to her that he hadn't realized existed. *Women are such unpredictable bitches.*

"I thought you'd agreed to take care of this problem over the weekend," she continued, gathering steam in her Southern veins, where many a civil rights issue was being fought at this very moment with Bobby Kennedy at the helm as attorney general.

The woman at the table next to them turned around and gave them a suspicious look. Andronicus didn't know if it was because of their age difference or what Iris had said. *Iris. She was Mrs. Johnson. Enough of this Iris bullshit.*

"I thought *you* didn't want to attract any attention," Andronicus lowered his head and pursed his lips with irritation. He also managed to down about half a glass of his whisky soda.

Mrs. Johnson looked over her shoulder just in time to see the curious woman turn her head away.

"Well, I never. You know how discreet I am." She looked at Andronicus. "Why don't we eat lunch?"

"A capital idea," he sneered.

The waiter arrived, perfectly attired in formal black pants and white jacket, took their order, and vanished, as he'd been taught to do.

They waited for what seemed like an eternity to Andronicus. Suddenly, he couldn't stand Inny or her mother. *What the fuck am I doing getting involved with these people? My dad could buy and sell them.*

"How is your father, um, stepfather?" asked Mrs. Johnson to fill the time.

"He's my father! I'm legally adopted."

Mrs. Johnson recoiled at Andronicus' admonition. She looked at the crystal chandeliers overhead and they seemed to spin. She felt ill. She excused herself and went to the ladies' room to regain her composure. As she sat at the vanity, she wondered what she had gotten herself into. *If only Inny would have married that nice Jim, none of this would have happened.*

She dabbed at her eyes, which had teared up a bit. Then, she straightened herself and marched back to the Biltmore Hotel dining room where Andronicus was sitting. The waiter was already serving lunch, and Andronicus had already started eating. *No manners whatsoever.*

After Andronicus picked up the check, signing his father's name, they made their way towards one of the Biltmore bungalows. Andronicus unlocked the door and made a sweeping gesture with his arm. Mrs. Johnson caught the sarcasm in his gesture but walked in and admired the gilt-framed mirrors, the plush carpeting, and small chandelier hanging over the bed. The bed. She looked at it and then at Andronicus. He no longer seemed like the dashing young scion of a state senator, but a soft-bellied lout with a beat-up face. She wondered what had really happened at Berkeley. Remorse began to tinge her feelings.

Andronicus stripped off his button-down shirt and trousers that had cost nearly a thousand dollars, jumping onto the bed with relish. He looked like a beached whale in his underwear, only whales were beautiful and Andronicus was not.

"Well, Iris?" He looked at Iris Johnson, dressed to the nines in a navy-blue suit with a frilly white blouse underneath.

She looked like she was about to bolt out the door, so he stood up and grabbed her by the waist. "You look lovely, my lovely," he crooned.

Mrs. Johnson was at a crossroads. The night her oldest daughter had come to her bedroom door and said she'd been raped flashed before her eyes. By this time, Andronicus had relieved her of her jacket and was undoing the buttons on her frilly white blouse. She thought of the money they needed to send their younger daughter through college. The daughter that made straight As and was the apple of her father's eyes. He called her 'Daddy's Little Helper.'

"My husband has lost his job," she announced, as if speaking to a firing squad.

"Tsk, tsk," said Andronicus, walking around towards the back of her to unzip her skirt.

"We desperately need financial help. How much can you give us?" She couldn't believe her own words, but she was terrified by her husband's unemployment and saw no way out.

"Let's talk about that next time," whispered Andronicus blowing on her neck as he took her slip off.

Thoughts reeled through her mind like fish in a net. She felt trapped. She turned to face the fat slug and shoved him away.

Andronicus reeled, stepping backwards. Then, he lunged at her. She began to scream.

"Shut up, Bitch!"

He tried to cover her mouth, but she had a good scream and wouldn't stop. That's when he slugged her, squarely in the jaw, cutting her lip. Mrs. Johnson went down, unconscious. Andronicus laughed. He couldn't stop laughing as he mounted her and came, copiously.

"They're all bitches!" he repeated his mantra.

After lying next to her inert body for a few breathless minutes, it occurred to him that he might have killed her. He checked her pulse; she was still breathing and had a pulse. He ran to the ornate bathroom of the Biltmore cottage and got a glass of water, which he threw on her face. Her fingers moved and she began to stir. Andronicus breathed a sigh of relief. He'd make it up to her. He'd give her a thousand dollars, he'd...

Mrs. Johnson lifted her head groggily. "Where am I?"

"Don't worry. I'm here. Here. Have a sip of water. You passed out. It must have been something you ate."

He dressed her as quickly as possible, which was difficult, as she was like a lump of clay. This could mean trouble, and he knew it as he struggled to button the tiny buttons on her frilly blouse.

He drove Mrs. Johnson to her home on Cima Linda Lane in her car. She was conscious, but her jaw and even her teeth hurt from where he'd punched her. She wasn't sure what had happened. "Inny can't have a black boyfriend..." she mumbled as Andronicus took her by the arm and helped her to the front door, hoping her husband wasn't at home. She slumped onto the chintz-covered living room sofa. Andronicus beat a safe retreat, not noticing that the pearl necklace had broken, leaving strands of pearls on the sofa.

Mr. Johnson was applying for another engineering job in Santa Barbara and filling out application forms for almost any job, in case they didn't accept him. He was worried sick. He said a silent prayer as he waited to be called in for the interview, during which he'd stammered and blushed, for he was deeply ashamed of being such a poor provider for his family.

Andronicus ran all the way back to the Biltmore to retrieve his own car and drive home. He was panicked. Guilt was written on his face as he got out and ran into his mother.

"I can't find my pearl necklace!"

"Mom, you have a million pearl necklaces. I don't know how you keep them straight."

"I'm quite well-organized, and it's thanks to me that you've got a rich daddy," she turned on him, coldly. "When are you going to enroll at USC?"

"Right away, Mom! Right away!" Andronicus ran to his bedroom and threw himself on his bed. He'd flunked out of Amherst and couldn't get a girl his age. He was overweight and unattractive, and he knew it. He started to cry in his pillow.

Mr. Johnson pulled into his eucalyptus and fern-lined driveway with a heavy heart. He missed the Navy, captaining a destroyer with sailors saluting him. He loved the roll of the ship on the open ocean. He loved cutting all ties from civilization except for the radio contacts he made with his superiors. To him, the ocean was a constant, always there, a beautiful deep-blue without limits. He had felt free on the ocean. Now, he felt like he was a prisoner of society, unable to do its bidding. He firmed his lower jaw and got out of the car, a slight man of graceful bearing. He looked more like a ballet dancer than a ship's captain. Maybe that's why they'd passed him over for captain. He'd never know and always blamed himself. Now, he had to face his wife with the worst news of all. He was out of work. He scratched his blond head, looking down at the driveway, suddenly finding cracks in it that needed to be paved over. Silent for a few minutes, he took a deep breath and resolved to tell his wife the truth, face-to-face. He knew she suspected it, but he had to say it and hung his head in chagrin.

He unlocked the front door and walked into the vestibule, which had a shelf decorated with seashells on one side. Then, he looked into the living room.

"Hello, Craig," said Mrs. Johnson.

"Hello, Honey," he replied. He pulled on one of his ears, a nervous habit he'd developed of late. "How was your day?"

Mrs. Johnson rubbed her chin where Andronicus had socked her. "Just fine, dear. I left Kendra off at school and did some grocery shopping."

He sat down next to her. They stared at one another for a minute.

Mrs. Johnson was so groggy from the blow to her chin that she couldn't think straight. She felt like she was looking at a stranger, but she knew it was her husband.

"I'm... well... I'm..." Mr. Johnson couldn't find the nerve to tell her he'd lost his job, right off the bat. Instead, he felt around the sofa for his *Scientific American,* which he'd stuffed in it somewhere. Instead, he came up with a pearl, a lovely pearl. He stared at the pearl as if he'd never seen one before. Then, he turned to his beleaguered wife and said, "Iris, you've broken your pearl necklace, the one I got for you while on shore duty in Japan." He couldn't believe someone as careful as his wife had broken her favorite pearl necklace. A look of shock came over his face.

"Oh, yes, how careless of me," said Mrs. Johnson, looking desperately at the sofa to see if the rest of the necklace Andronicus had given her was visible. She found a few other pearls, which she grasped in a tight fist. *I... I can't let Craig find out about... Andronicus.* She gulped down air and breathed very fast, as if someone were about to hurt her.

Mr. Johnson looked at his wife's lovely oval face, her hair mussed and her lipstick smeared. He saw a fairly large bruise starting to form on her jaw. He gasped, "Iris, what's happened to you?"

Mrs. Johnson stood up and smoothed her dress. Mr. Johnson noticed she was wearing heels.

"Why are you wearing high heels in the afternoon?"

"Oh, I had to meet with one of Kendra's teachers..."

"Is there anything wrong?" Mr. Johnson blinked his eyes, partly to hold back tears and partly out of concern for his youngest daughter, his favorite. In all fairness, he'd never really gotten to know Inny, since he was either fighting a war or had sea duty. So he considered Kendra his real daughter. He didn't understand his rather brazen older daughter at all. She rather frightened him with her ready laughter and confidence… and all those wealthy boys running after her. She wasn't at all like his sisters in Salt Lake City, nice girls who married right out of high school or shortly thereafter.

Mrs. Johnson felt her neck to make sure the necklace was completely gone. "No, everything's fine, dear." She smiled with a look of contrition. "Guess I'd better start dinner now."

"But… but it's only three in the afternoon." Mr. Johnson couldn't comprehend why his wife would dress up in the middle of the day. "Did you fall down? Where did you get that bruise on your jaw?" He floundered in a sea of doubt. She always wore a simple house dress and flat shoes during the day. The world was too complicated for him.

"Um. I want to put a roast on to simmer," said Mrs. Johnson, blinking hard, flummoxed. What had happened at the cottage in the Biltmore? She felt a tingling between her legs, so she knew Andronicus had made love to her. But she couldn't remember anything, except… then she fainted.

Mr. Johnson took her in his arms and placed her on the sofa. Then, he ran to get some water. When he came back from the kitchen with a glassful of water, his wife stirred slightly. He breathed a sigh of relief. At least she was alive. What had she done to get so upset? As he doused her forehead with water and then held her head up so she could take a sip, she moaned. *Is she in pain? Should I call a doctor?* Craig Johnson was beside himself. He took her in his arms again and walked slowly back to their bedroom, with its beautiful view over their backyard garden, and lay her down on his twin bed.

The family dog was on her bed, as usual. He couldn't stand the way she spoiled the dog, a Labrador mix… Treated him better than she treated her own husband, who was doing his best to… support the family. Thinking of his rejections at job interviews, Mr. Johnson put his head on his wife's chest and sobbed like a child. The broken pearl necklace, the high heels in the middle of the day, and the bruise on his wife's jaw were too much for a simple engineer from Salt Lake City.

When Kendra came home from school, that's how she found them. "Mother, Daddy! What's wrong!"

Mr. Johnson raised his tear-streaked face and looked at his favorite daughter, dressed in a sweater set and skirt. Her breasts had become shapely as she matured; he couldn't help but stare at them.

"Daddy, why are you staring at me like that?" Kendra felt scared. Her parents had never acted like this before. She'd never seen her father with tears in his eyes or her mother slumped onto her father's bed like this.

Her mother was always bright, alert, and in full command of her senses. Kendra felt a bit dizzy herself.

"Why don't you take Sox for a walk?" Mr. Johnson asked.

"If that's what you want me to do, but what's wrong with Mother?"

"I… I don't know. She fainted in the living room."

"Fainted? Aren't you going to call a doctor?"

Mr. Johnson looked at his daughter with sorrow in his eyes. "We can't afford a doctor."

"What?"

"I just lost my job, Kendra!"

A look of surprise and then sympathy crossed Kendra's naïve fifteen-year-old face. She had platinum-blond hair and a sweet smile, a reassuring smile. Only now she was frowning.

"Can't you get another one? Will we have to move?" She stepped towards him and offered him her hand. He took it and put his face against it.

Kendra felt out of place in her parents' bedroom with her father and mother acting in a way she'd never seen them act before. She withdrew her hand slowly. She could feel her heart pounding in her chest. She knew something was terribly wrong.

"Daddy, I'll take Sox for a walk. Will you be all right?" She looked directly into his gray-blue eyes, which were clouded over, and his tear-streaked face.

"Yes, yes, of course." He continued to stare at her young breasts bulging through her cashmere sweater set, wondering how much it had cost. He was scared to death. He managed to stand up. Taking a deep breath, he said, "You don't have to worry, as long as you have me. I'll do whatever it takes to support my family."

Kendra looked at her mother, who started to cry. Her father sat down next to her on the twin bed and stroked her hair. "Don't cry, Iris. You have me. Don't worry." He took a deep breath to calm his emotions. He'd gone to Annapolis and loved the Navy. He thought he'd be a naval officer his entire life, until he was passed over for captain. That rocked his boat – the family's boat. He had to retire after twenty years of service on a partial pension and seek employment as an engineer or be looked down upon for the rest of his life for not making captain. Rank meant everything to an Annapolis graduate and his colleagues. He didn't even know why he'd been passed over, except that his class standing was in the bottom half due to his bad grades in Spanish. Foreign languages didn't make sense to him. Now his wife was dressed for a fancy party in the middle of the day and had fainted. He knew something unusual had happened – that bruise on her jaw. He shook his head in wonderment. And he'd been turned down for a job. His whole world shattered before his eyes, he could only stare dully at his daughter's breasts. He was in shock.

The dog had wandered over to Kendra and looked up at her. Kendra petted Sox, the pet she'd always loved. She looked at her parents. Confused by the flood of emotions, she turned and ran out of the house with Sox.

They ran to the grassy hillside at the end of Cima Linda Lane that overlooked the ocean. The Channel Islands stood out like sentinels, sharply outlined by the cloudless day. Kendra and Sox sat and stared at the gorgeous view, the ocean so vast and calm which contrasted so sharply with what she had just seen. She took a deep breath and hugged Sox, who put his head in her lap. The serenity of the view of the calm ocean filled her with a sense that all was as it should be.

Chapter 16

I had to go home for Christmas. My mind wandered to my mother telling me I was disinherited. Surely she didn't mean it. Christmas was always spent with family; I had to go home. Yet, here I sat in a hospital, with a friend who might not recover from an illegal abortion, waiting for her mother to arrive. I was scared stiff.

Sally's mother arrived alone; her husband had stayed at work. Besides, the fact that Sally was not his biological daughter ran through my mind. I wondered if he cared for her as one of his own. Her mother resembled Sally somewhat, in that she had a longish face, but she was far heavier than Sally. She looked every bit the comfortable, sweet-faced mother from middle-class America in the early sixties. Except that her eyes were red from crying.

"How could this happen?" she asked. "Sally is a nice girl. Things like this don't happen to nice girls like my daughter." She opened her vinyl purse and took out a Kleenex, which she dabbed at her eyes with.

"It shouldn't have happened," I agreed with her. "But..." I was at a loss for words.

"But what?"

I took a deep breath and said, "Sally was having a relationship with a man."

"What kind of a man? Where is he?" Her mother's voice became shrill and angry.

"He's in the hospital, too." I was in over my head.

The double doors to Sally's Intensive Care Unit opened. Out stepped a doctor. We both stood up and ran to him. "How is she?" I felt my head spin. Sally couldn't die. I'd die if Sally died. It would be partly my fault.

"She's hemorrhaged a lot of blood. We've given her a transfusion and taken tests. It doesn't look like there is any brain damage."

"Brain damage?" Sally's mother looked as if she had been hit by a truck.

"This is Sally's mother, Doctor..."

"Doctor Elder." He smiled a contrite little smile.

"How could this happen to my daughter?" wailed Sally's mother.

"It's the result of... of an illegal procedure with poor equipment..." He didn't want to say a botched coat-hanger abortion.

"Why didn't she tell me?"

Dr. Elder pulled himself upright to his full, trim height. He was tall and spare, with slightly graying hair. "I'm afraid that many children are afraid to tell their parents. Right now, we have to wait for her to regain consciousness." He looked into Sally's mother's teary eyes with a glimmer of compassion. I began to like him much more.

"When will she regain consciousness? Do you know?"

"No one knows exactly. Her body has to recover from the trauma of the hemorrhage. I can't predict anything for certain."

A nurse in traditional white nursing garb walked past us, guiding a gurney with a patient on it. We paused to let them pass. I glanced at the patient. She looked moribund.

I wanted to go home. To Albert, and then to Montecito to celebrate Christmas with my family. I wanted something stable and strong that would see me through all these horrors: Jerry's, Sally's, and my racist family dead-set against my having anything to do with Albert Curtis. Maybe I would marry him. I just needed some time, some perspective to think about it. Marriage was more than I had bargained for, and Albert was twelve years older than me. I wanted to study, to do things, travel, get to know the world, work – spinning thoughts ran through my head. Yet I loved him. I was sure I did.

We heard the doors banging open to the waiting room. Someone was entering in a wheelchair with a bunch of flowers hoisted high above him like a beacon in the night. As the person wheeled himself closer, I recognized Jerry with a bandaged shoulder and a dozen red roses in his other hand, wheeling towards us as if his life depended on it.

I stared at him in disbelief. He wheeled directly in front of Sally's mother, who looked equally surprised.

"Where's Sally?" His face broke into a smile, the first I'd ever seen on him. His hair had been cut and he looked almost presentable, minus the bandaged shoulder. He was in better shape than Sally.

"She's in the ICU," responded her mother. "Who are you?"

Jerry put the roses carefully across his lap, across the nice suit pants he was wearing. I'd never seen him dressed so well. He stuck out his hand and shook hands with Sally's mother, saying, "I'm Sally's fiancé. I want to marry her."

I did a double-take, looked for a chair, and sat down, or nearly fell down.

"Sally's still in the Intensive Care Unit," said her mother, her anxious face trying to make sense of this newcomer brandishing roses and a marriage proposal.

"We've got to get her out!" Jerry spun his wheelchair around to face me.

"That's up to the doctors," I said, averting my eyes to avoid his. "You're the reason she's here."

"What?" exclaimed her mother.

"Sally's here because Jerry got her pregnant and paid for her to have an abortion in Tijuana," I said with as much composure as I could muster. Apparently, it wasn't enough. Her mother started to scream.

"An abortion! In Mexico! And I thought you were such a nice girl, Inny," her mother yelled at me, her face a purplish mass of pudding face wrinkles.

Then, she turned to Jerry in his wheelchair. "You look like a decent fellow. You say you want to marry Sally? Why didn't you marry her before this happened?"

Jerry's face blanched. It was the first time I'd seen him look nonplussed and halfway human. He lowered his head and said, "I wish I'd done that. I didn't know how much I loved her until…"

The nurse came out of the Intensive Care Unit. We walked and wheeled ourselves over to her with looks of hopeful expectation on our faces. She stood tall and imperious with her white nurse's outfit and hat over a well-kept, dark-haired bun.

"How's my little girl?" asked Sally's mother.

The nurse managed to almost smile at her. At least she grimaced in a pleasant way. "She's showing signs of improvement."

Jerry wheeled himself directly in front of her. "I must see her."

"Who are you?"

Jerry pulled himself up as much as he could in his wheelchair and brandished the roses. "I'm her fiancé."

The nurse gave him a knowing look. "No one can see her for the time being. She's still in critical condition." She pushed her nurse's cap back and adjusted her bun at the same time.

Jerry thrust the roses into her hands. "Couldn't you give her these roses? Tell her Jerry sent them and that I love her." He gave her an imploring look. He almost looked sweet. I couldn't believe I was watching the same man who'd locked her out in the hallway in the dead of winter.

The nurse gave a curt little nod. "All right. If you insist," she said. She took them and disappeared back into the Intensive Care Unit.

Jerry put his head in his hands and began to cry. We all began to cry. A doctor in whites with an operating apron walked by and shook his head. I felt like I was going to burst with sorrow. This doctor who had seen so much pain, so much agony and death, had the compassion to let us know he understood our pain.

Our emotions poured out in wet tears. When we finished crying and were merely sobbing, we stared into one another's eyes and saw our common humanity. We all loved Sally. We were all connected and would stick together, even though Jerry had been horrible to her. He'd had a change of heart; there is always hope that love will triumph over hate and restore love. Sally's mother sniffed and I held her close.

A nurse came out of the double doors that led to the Intensive Care Unit.

"She's opened her eyes! We put the roses in her arms and she opened her eyes. She smelled them and tried to smile. We told her they were from Jerry. She stirred and looked at us. She looked happy. It's a breakthrough! She's regaining consciousness!" The nurse looked at us with wide brown eyes. She was black and wore her white nursing outfit with pride. I jumped up and hugged her.

"Thank you! Thank you for all you've done for Sally!"

"Oh, the doctors did it... And the roses!"

"Could we see her now?"

The nurse grinned and nodded her head.

"And you were wonderful!" my smile enveloped the black nurse.

She stepped back in surprise. "Why... why thank you! I don't get compliments like that every day... especially from..." She stopped short, realizing what she was about to say.

"...from white people? Don't judge me by the color of my skin! I may be white, but I love people of color! My fiancé is black!" I said.

"My, my," she grinned. "You are something else. God bless!"

"When can we see her?" asked Jerry, scooting his wheelchair next to her.

"As soon as the doctors stabilize her vital signs." The nurse wiped a tear from her eye. She was moved by our display of love. Love is the answer, I realized.

"I must see her now!" bellowed Jerry. "I'm going to marry her!" He spun his wheelchair around in glee.

"You should've done that before all this happened," admonished the nurse, suddenly somber. "I see too many girls like her. Some of them don't make it." She stared into our startled eyes. "But I'm sure Sally will. The roses brought her around."

Jerry beamed at her. "I used to think black people were useless scum, but I was wrong. You've got the biggest hearts, and you're helping save my lifeline, my fiancée!"

The nurse took his hand. "We're all in this together, little white brother. Ain't nobody different, just some mean, some need to understand each other."

She wiped a tear away and beamed at him. I think he would have given her a dozen red roses if he'd had them.

A doctor in scrubs came out of the double doors, grinning from ear-to-ear. He announced, "Sally's vital signs have stabilized. The worst is over. She'll be all right."

Jerry wheeled his chair in happy circles. Sally's mother and I breathed a huge sigh of relief. "Thank you, doctor. I can't tell you what this means to us."

"All in the line of duty," he replied a bit more gruffly to hide his emotions.

"When can we see her?"

"We're observing her closely. I think you could see her for a minute. The nurse escorted us to Sally's room. We entered quietly, practically on tiptoe. Sally lay in bed holding the roses. She smiled a big, toothy grin that lit up the dim hospital room when she saw us. We crowded around her. Her too-long bangs were pinned back. I stared at her in admiration. "You pulled through. You were courageous! I'm proud of you."

Sally's face lit up. Her best friend had told her what she longed to hear. Jerry held her hand, staring into her eyes with love.

"You helped me. I'm so grateful to be alive."

"Why don't you get something to eat in the cafeteria?" suggested the nurse.

We looked at her and then at each other.

"I could use some food," said Jerry.

We nodded our consent. Jerry started to wheel his chair towards the hospital cafeteria. It squeaked as he turned, making lots of noise, but we didn't care. We followed him. I turned and shook the doctor's hand, thanking him profusely. The tension of all we'd been through got to me. Tears streamed down my cheeks. The doctor smiled and offered me a Kleenex. I blew my nose in it, which alleviated some of the tension, and we laughed in spite of ourselves.

Chapter 17

Returning to my snug little studio behind the large Victorian house on Parker Avenue, I felt joy surge in my heart just at the sight of it. I wondered if Albert was home. First, I had to pack to take the train home for Christmas. Thoughts of my mother attacking Albert, my father always hiding behind his *Scientific American,* streamed through my overtaxed mind. So much had happened. I needed a sanctuary. I needed to get away. I hoped my parents would provide that sanctuary, or at least the lovely trees and walks through meadows with ocean views that surrounded their house would. I'd find my own sanctuary. I also had essays to write for Adrianne Koch's class. I'd chosen Ben Franklin, my favorite American.

I unlocked my studio door to find a note under it. 'We'll be back,' it said. Strange. Who would leave such a note under my door? Who was 'we?'

I ran to the closet where I kept my suitcase, pulled it down from the top shelf, and then ran to my dresser. I opened the top drawer, which contained my panties, slips, and pajamas. I started to stuff them in my suitcase, along with a pair of jeans and some dresses. I didn't have a lot of clothes. I finished packing in ten minutes. That's when the phone rang. It was Albert.

"How's Sally?" There was a note of anxiety in his voice.

I slammed my suitcase shut and told him that she was fine, that her mother had arrived, and so had Jerry, with a dozen red roses and a marriage proposal.

"What?" Albert's voice hit a high C.

I laughed. "She's coming around. She's going to be all right!"

"That was a close call," he said. "Would you like to come up for some bubbly?"

"I'd love to, but I have to catch the train to go home for Christmas. I need some time out. Back at the crazy house… in Montecito… I'll be up in a few minutes!"

We laughed at my staccato sentence. I was talking like I'd been given a shot of vodka. "Here I come!" I announced to myself.

I ran up the stairs to Albert's sweet little studio. He opened the door and we hugged each other for a long time.

"It's been a bit much," I gasped. "Sally and Jerry…"

"Maybe you do need to go home. Will you be okay?" He looked at me to see if I'd wavered.

"Sure. I'll walk in the woods and cleanse myself. I'll be fine. If my parents give me a bad time, I'll ignore them. I'm good at that. Been doing it for years," I giggled.

He kissed me on the neck and down we went. No bubbly. Just loving. Afterwards, he asked me if I needed a ride to the train station.

"I'd love a ride to the train station! I wish I could take you with me!"

Albert stared into my deep blue eyes. "Maybe next year."

"Oh, Albert. My mother is so impossible. I don't want to subject you to her."

"Don't worry about me. I'm pretty tough. Now, go get your suitcase."

As I gave Albert a peck on his cheek before scooting down the wooden staircase to my studio, Andronicus parked his Ferrari outside the large Victorian house in front. He grunted with annoyance as he pulled the handbrake. He'd just driven over three hundred miles from Santa Barbara to even the score with Inny and shoot her black boyfriend. Maybe he'd shoot them both. He chuckled at the thought. His depravity amused him. *That bitch deserves what she gets.*

He felt for his thirty-six caliber gun in the inside pocket of his jacket. He fondled it for a moment. He'd parked his car, one of his father's older sports cars, a few spaces behind the entrance to the four studios behind the imposing house. When he got out, he saw two men in front of it. One of them was thin and wiry. The other looked misshapen. As Andronicus walked towards the brick pathway that led to the studios, he realized that the misshapen one was the man who'd beat him up the last time he was here.

Andronicus stretched and laughed a wicked little laugh, feeling elated that he was about to even the score. The two men turned and watched him approach. They stared at him and he stared back. When he was close enough to assess them carefully, he stopped. "Where the hell did you come from?" growled Crutches.

He moved towards Andronicus with difficulty, placing his metal rods on both sides of his bulky form as he pulled himself up to face him, nose to nose.

"Get outta my way, fucker!" Andronicus said.

"Wanna make me? What are you doing here anyway?" Crutches questioned.

"I'm here to see Inny. Outta my way, Cripple!"

Crutches hit Andronicus' shoulder with one of his metallic rods. Andronicus yelled and jumped back.

"Plus, I'd never see you in a lavender wig again in a conga line."

"You should write a book, Miss Inny. Now, roll that window back up. You're giving me a chill!"

I gave a little snort of laughter. Then, I started going through my purse again. Before I could count my money, we arrived at the train station. I jumped out of the car. Albert grabbed my suitcase and jumped out with agility. He grabbed my hand. He couldn't help but feel his heart strings flutter. I guess the emotion of the moment got the better of him. He grabbed me by the waist and kissed me on the mouth. "I'm going to miss you!"

"I'll be back soon. But I'll miss you more than you can imagine. My love!" I took my suitcase from him and ran towards the train. Albert ran after me, exhilarated by my latest declaration.

Andronicus ran right behind them, a bit off to the left, with a few other passengers in front of him. His face, bloodied and grotesque from his encounter with Crutches and Ira, caught the attention of an occasional passerby, but no one stopped him.

I kissed Albert goodbye, holding a history book Adrianne had given me in one hand and the suitcase in the other. I got on the train and sat down in the first empty row of seats I could find, so I could read without distraction. I was well into the *Battle of Waterloo*, a historical account of Napoleon and Lord Wellington fighting one of history's most famous battles that would change the course of nineteenth century European history. Bloody limbs and disembodied heads flew through the air after cannons roared in this face-to-face, saber-to-saber tale of a battle that still connotes defeat, for Lord Wellington defeated the great Napoleon's army against all odds and by a thread. It all had to do with timing and soldiers who would fight to the death.

Andronicus staggered along the aisles of the train until he spotted me in my seat, engrossed in the *Battle of Waterloo*. He laughed under his breath. Then, he sat in the empty seat next to me, waiting for me to acknowledge his presence. Napoleon's elite cavalry, which included a few women passing for men, charged Lord Wellington's line of battle-hardened soldiers, hidden just behind a rise in the terrain that would give them the upper hand and finally save the day for the British, Germans, and Belgians who fought tenaciously with one goal: to defeat the man who had almost conquered all of Europe and Russia. I caught my breath.

Andronicus' emotions played havoc with his senses. Elated from having shot the miserable Crutches, whom he considered one of his many adversaries, he shifted his considerable weight in an attempt to get my attention. Annoyed that someone was interrupting my concentration, I turned away from him and read in an uncomfortable position, right under the reading light above me.

Andronicus fumbled for a handkerchief to wipe the blood from the facial wound Crutches had given him. He elbowed me hard in the process. I turned even further away from him. Clearing my throat in annoyance, I kept on reading as Napoleon's best cavalry lost its first line of horses and riders, whose fallen bodies created chaos. The second line tripped and fell over the downed horses and riders and were taken down themselves. No amount of heroism could change the course of this part of the battle. I read on, transfixed by mixture of valor and violence.

Meanwhile, Andronicus, the opposite of valor but quite definitely violent, sat within elbow-rubbing distance of another of his adversaries – Mrs. Johnson's uncooperative daughter. He'd never forget, in his tiny mind, the night she'd told him she'd do it with him, then slid out from under his expectant body to… to the arms of Jim. He'd heard they'd dated for the rest of the summer and had even spent a week in Berkeley together. He was infuriated that she was currently ignoring him for a silly book… and had a black lover.

A porter made his way down the aisle, collecting tickets. When he got to me and Andronicus, I searched my purse and handed him my ticket with a polite 'thank you.' Andronicus had none, so he had to buy one.

"A ticket for Santa Barbara, please," he growled. He searched for his wallet. "Could you come back in a minute, please? I can't find my wallet." The porter gave him a knowing look and moved on.

Shock ran through my brain. How could I help but recognize that curt voice? I lowered the *Battle of Waterloo* to look at the back of Andronicus Wyland's head, hair tousled with dirt and blood in it. The incongruence of the valiant soldiers with the man who'd tried to rape me sent a chill down my spine.

The porter passed on to the next set of passengers, seated behind us, punching train tickets.

I swallowed hard as Andronicus leered at me with a slight snarl. He could've been a wild boar as far as I was concerned. I grabbed my book and purse and stood up. Andronicus grabbed me by the hips and pushed me back down.

"You… filthy… pig…" I breathed.

"Shut up!"

"Let me out of here!" I stood up, but he grabbed my book, teasing me with it.

"That's my professor's book!" I tried to grab it back, only to come close to his bloodied face. Disgust coursed through my body.

"Well, aren't we the good little Berkeley student?" said Andronicus in a voice that dripped with sarcasm.

"I'm going to graduate," I asserted, trying to wrest the book out of his hand behind his back.

"If you should live so long."

Ire mounted in me, but I also felt cold, paralyzing fear. For a moment, I hesitated. That's when Andronicus reached for his recently discharged gun, inside his jacket.

"Tickets, please," said the porter, standing over us. He smiled until he saw the bloody gash on Andronicus's forehead. "Do you need a doctor?" He drew back in surprise.

Andronicus fumbled for his gun. I saw it on the inside of his jacket. "He's got a gun!" I screamed.

"Shut up, Bitch!" Andronicus put his hand over my mouth. I bit him. He yelled.

The passengers had already been watching the struggle, wondering if it were a lover's spat. The porter turned and pulled the train's emergency cord. Everyone was thrown forward as it screeched to a halt. Andronicus hit the seat in front of him. He dropped his gun. I scrambled for it. When the porter got there, I was pointing it at Andronicus.

"What... What's this?" The porter turned pale as a ghost.

"He... He's dangerous!"

Some of the passengers got out of their seats. When they saw a gun in my hand, they stopped dead in their tracks.

"Drop that gun!" An off-duty police officer who had been following the altercation pulled his own gun and pointed it at me. I dropped the gun, only to see Andronicus pick it up and fire at the police officer, who clutched his stomach and went down. The passengers screamed in panic.

Andronicus turned and faced the passengers. "Don't move!" He grabbed me by the waist and forced me down the aisle. "This is where we get off, Cinderella!"

I took a deep breath, made a run for the doorway, and hurled myself onto the ground next to the train, praying I wouldn't die. Rolling down the bank of dirt and brambles next to the train tracks, I ended up lying face down in some weeds. I knew I had to keep going, but my right arm hurt. Pain shot through it. I wondered if I'd broken it.

The thought that Andronicus would soon be behind me ran through my brain. I picked myself up and started to run, at a slow, nightmarish pace, panic-stricken.

Andronicus jumped off the train, rolled, and stood up. He looked both ways. He spotted me running through the underbrush and ran after me.

The porter jumped off and ran behind us. The safety of his passengers uppermost in his mind, he charged towards Andronicus.

Andronicus turned and fired his gun at the porter, who clutched his gut and pitched forward. I screamed and ran towards a highway in the distance. I ran as if the devil himself were chasing me, because Andronicus came as close to the Antichrist as anyone I'd ever known. I ran for dear life, invoking God, Jesus, and anyone who cared to save me.

Andronicus charged at full speed behind me, but the head wound sustained from Crutches' metal rod was beginning to take its toll. Dizzy, he faltered, grabbing onto some weeds as he stumbled and fell. I ran on in sheer panic. I managed to reach the highway and started waving my arms at the cars.

Cars whizzed by me, the drivers leery of a woman waving her arms in the middle of the night on a highway. A Chevy sedan swerved off the road and came to a lurching halt. Two people were in it, a man and a woman. The woman opened the passenger door. I could see the outline of her form in the dark. She was wearing a thick woolen coat and a scarf. Her face was dark, but there was a look of concern of it.

"What's wrong with you?" yelled the woman, frightened by the bizarre situation.

"Andronicus Wyland is trying to kill me!" I yelled back. I swept my long, matted hair off my face and tried to look more like a woman in jeopardy than a maniac waving her arms on the highway.

"Who?"

"This man… please help me!"

"Well, get in the car!"

The woman opened the back door for me. I jumped in and ducked down as if someone were about to grab me. My entire body was shaking from the trauma.

"Are you crazy?" asked the driver, a diminutive man wearing a Fedora.

"No. I'm in terrible trouble! This boy who tried to rape me got on my train and pulled a gun on me…"

At that instant, Andronicus appeared with the gun pointed directly at the car. "Let's go!" I screamed.

The driver floored the accelerator and got back on the highway as fast as he could. I burst into tears from the ordeal.

"Now, now, tears won't help. You need to go to a safe place," said the woman.

"Could you take me to Berkeley?"

"That's too far away. We're from Richmond."

"Could I call a friend when we get there?"

167

The man and women exchanged frightened looks. The woman shook her head. "I think you need to call the police, though, no telling what they'll do!"

"Anything!" I began to sob.

The woman looked at me, now a mass of tangled dark blonde hair and tears. She tried to help me get the hair out of my face. "I don't know. I just don't know! How'd you get in this mess?"

"He pulled a gun on me on the train, so I jumped off and ran…"

The woman looked at the driver and shook her head. "Do you expect me to believe that?"

"It's the truth!"

I sobbed in the backseat of the sedan, searching for words they'd believe. "He's a maniac."

The man nodded at his wife. "We'll put you in a taxi and they'll take you to the police."

"But you saw him!"

"They won't believe us," he said. They looked at each other with varying degrees of solemn despair.

"Why not?"

"They never believe black folks." He shook his head. "No telling what they'll accuse us of, once a gun is involved."

The scenery whizzed by as we drove on the freeway. I looked at the worn-out upholstery in the car and realized these were not spoiled brats from Montecito. The man wore a very old fedora, and the woman was dressed a lot like my grandmother, plain and simple, with no frills. I began to warm to them.

"You're good Samaritans." I held my arm where it hurt most, at my elbow. I didn't think it was broken.

The woman turned her head toward me. I could see she was at least middle-aged, and that she wore her age well.

"We believe in doin' unto others as we'd have them do unto us," she said with a plain-spoken simplicity that moved my heart.

"I wish there were more people like you in the world." I fingered my elbow. I felt a sharp pain shoot up to my shoulder.

"Are you hurt?" she asked.

"Not badly. Look, just take me back to the train station. I'm trying to get home for Christmas with my family."

"Where's they from?"

"Santa Barbara." I decided not to say Montecito, for fear of sounding snobbish.

"That's pretty far from here, but we'll be happy to take you to the train."

I thanked them profusely. I was overjoyed by their kindness. I knew I could catch another train to Santa Barbara and had just enough to give them something for their time and trouble.

When I got out of their car and turned to shake their hands, they smiled at me with warmth. "It's not every day a white person is so nice," the man said.

"I love black people!" I effused. "My, um, fiancé is black!"

"You got to be kidding!" said the woman, whose name turned out to be Mabel.

"He's an English professor at Berkeley!"

The woman's smile turned to disbelief. "They ain't got no black professors at Berkeley! You telling the truth?"

"His name is Albert Curtis. You can look him up in the school's directory! It's true. I swear on a stack of Bibles."

They looked me up and down and started to laugh. "Great day in the mornin', child, you're a miracle. You got to come to our church!"

Now I was taken aback. I stepped back, clutching my purse to my side, or what was left of it, as it was as battered as me. It still had my wallet inside.

"Church?"

"The Glide Church, on Market Street, in San Francisco! It's interdenominational. You'd love it there!"

"I'll go there after I get home from Christmas, but now I have to run!" I stuck out my hand again and shook theirs with enthusiasm, eliciting huge smiles.

The train had just pulled into the station, so I turned and made a run for it, catching it just in time.

The last I saw of them was their big, warm-hearted smiles.

Chapter 18

Opening presents under the tinsel-laden Christmas tree with my parents and younger sister wasn't as much fun as last year. We were laughing and cooing over our gifts, getting ready to call Grandma, in Arlington, who would break down and bawl her head off because we were so far away. Eyeing our chintz sofa and shag rug, the large chimney that we could hear a mockingbird sing into, I felt reassured, but I was mistaken.

Nope. This year, my arm was in a sling, broken at the wrist, not the elbow, when I'd hit the ground next to the train. My mother gave me a disapproving look.

"Innocence, what have we done to deserve this? You came home looking like a ragamuffin with a broken wrist that we can't afford to pay for."

"Now, Iris," interceded my father, with little success.

"You should be married by now! We sent you to college to find a husband, and this is how you come home. And what about your nigger friend?"

"Don't you dare call Albert a nigger! He's Berkeley's first black English professor and better than all of you put together in a Christmas stocking!"

"You can't return to Berkeley!" said my mother, hitting a high C on Berkeley. She was at her white supremacist best. Her pink chenille bathrobe highlighted her brunette hair and brown eyes, her porcelain white skin and natural beauty. My sister and I hadn't come out as beautiful as she was, but we were a lot nicer.

"I have exams to take!"

The phone rang. My sister jumped up and answered it.

"It's for you, Inny!" she squealed. She was always high-spirited and fun.

I jumped up and took the pink receiver from my little sister. Albert was on the other end of the line. My mother scowled at me when I cooed, "I'm so glad to hear from you!" She knew who it was. I saw her get up and come at me like a mad cow. She grabbed the phone, but I wouldn't let her have it. As we struggled for possession, I yelled, "My mother's here!"

In his neatly arranged studio apartment living room, Albert smiled and said, "Merry Christmas, Inny!"

My injured arm gave way. My mother took the receiver and yelled, "Leave my daughter alone!" She was at her fuming best.

"Could I please speak to Inny?" asked Albert in dulcet tones.

"If you come near my daughter if she goes back to Berkeley, I'll kill you!"

Albert's eyebrows shot up in surprise. "Really? I'm not that black, Mrs. Johnson."

I heard him and started to laugh. My mother kept yelling insults into the receiver. When she wore herself out, I took it from her.

"Are you still there, Albert?"

Albert held the phone about six inches from his ear. He'd never heard such insults in his entire life.

"I am, but my ear just fell off."

"Don't listen to her. She's from the South. She doesn't know any better." I winced as my mother tried to grab the receiver again. "My grandmother loves black people!"

"She does NOT," yelled Mother. "Goodbye!" She hung up the phone.

"Grandma loves everyone except the Catholic priests who withheld absolution from dying people who wouldn't pay for it!" I yelled.

"Black people are inferior! They don't have enough brains to become a… a professor!" She walked towards my father, who was doing his best to ignore the whole scene. "Aren't they, Craig?"

My father looked up from the book he'd been reading, his gray eyes blinking as if he didn't quite understand, "If you say so, Iris."

"They're stupid and ugly! If they have any brains at all, it's because they have white blood!"

"And where did that come from?" I asked, trying to sound like my name, innocent. I knew it came from the 'massa' helping himself to black slaves' bodies while his wife slept quietly, aware or unaware, in their well-appointed plantation's master bedroom.

"I could wring your neck!" My mother's porcelain skin had turned an ugly reddish color. I thought she might have a heart attack if she kept this up.

"Sit down, Mother. You're out of your mind and it's not good for you!"

I gave my father an imploring look. He'd continued reading his book, one I'd given him for Christmas, *Light in August,* by William Faulkner. He furrowed his smooth brow and said, "Did he really win a Nobel Prize for this book?" Then, he looked at my mother. "What? What's going on?" He looked truly quizzical. He'd long ceased trying to understand the women in his family. He glanced at my little sister in her latest cashmere sweater and pleated skirt. He smiled.

At that moment, the telephone rang.

"Don't answer that! It's that nigger calling again!" My mother stood up and blocked the phone. I lunged past her and we had a brief struggle as I took it off the receiver.

"Let go!"

My mother hit me with the receiver. I shrieked and rubbed my shoulder where the receiver hit me.

"Iris, Iris…" I heard faintly.

A chagrined look came over my mother's angered face. It was her mother. She forced a smile and spoke into the receiver.

"Hello?"

"Is that you, honey? I wanted to wish you a merry Christmas!" My grandmother's sweet voice echoed from the other end of the line.

"Oh, Mother! We didn't know it was you! Merry Christmas! And thank you for all the gifts! You really shouldn't have…"

"Do the clothes fit the girls? I hope I got the right size."

My grandmother, used to my grandfather's penurious allowance, always shopped in bargain basements for our Christmas presents, and the clothes were always a size too big, but we didn't care. They were from Grandma, and we adored her.

"Some of them are a bit large, but the place mats will look nice on our kitchen table," said my mother. She'd just said the place mats were the wrong color as we ate our waffles. A honeyed tongue indeed.

"How are you and Craig? And the girls?"

"We're just fine, Mother. How are things in Lake Worth? I know we should visit there someday…"

We watched my mother expectantly, waiting to be allowed to speak to Grandma and thank her for our Christmas presents. Phone calls were expensive, so we only got to talk to her once a year, namely on Christmas Day. My sister and I waited. My mother rambled on about my father's job difficulties. He looked miserable.

"Could I speak to Inny?" asked Grandma.

I lunged at the phone. My mother gave it to me with a dirty look.

"Grandma!"

"Oh, little Inny, how good it is to hear your voice!"

"Thank you for the pretty lavender dress and the matching slip. I've tried them all on and they fit just right! You always pick the prettiest presents! We just love them!"

"Oh, Honey, I'm so happy you can wear them. I always worry that they're the wrong size…" Her voice trailed off. She started to cry. Actually, she started to bawl.

"Don't cry, Grandma! Please don't cry! We're all right here!"

Grandma dissolved into tears and could no longer speak.

"Please don't cry, Grandma!" I begged her. I was too young to understand how much she missed us. Grandpa had sold their home in Arlington – Clarendon, to be exact – and moved them to Lake Worth, Florida, to be with his family. It had nearly killed her, I imagined, but she never let on.

A stern look on her face, my mother took the phone from me. My little sister begged to talk to Grandma, too. My father looked befuddled.

"Mother, stop blubbering. You always cry and we never get to talk!"

We could hear more sobs on the other end of the line with a muffled, "I'm... sorry..."

I felt my heart sink. I wished my grandmother could be with us at Christmas. I wished she could live with us. I missed her more than I realized. I began to think of my cousin, my Aunt Edna and Uncle Jimmy, and wonderful close, lifetime friends I'd left behind in Arlington. I missed Sheila Barton's raucous clowning, Aunt Edna's dulcet voice singing out, 'Inny Ann.' Typical of the South, she used my middle name, and it was lyrical.

My mother remonstrated my grandmother for being a crybaby and hung up. I started to cry.

"Innocence, you're going to be just like Grandma! Stop it!" She only used my full name to beat me into compliance, a compliance that she never got. I always fought back.

"I can't help it! I miss her! She never gets to see us! Grandpa moved her to Florida, and I don't think she likes it there; it's too far from her friends and family. I miss Arlington, too! All my best friends are still there, and so are Aunt Edna and Uncle Jimmy and my cousins..."

I remembered feeding the goldfish in Grandma's giant sunroom, in her spacious home in Arlington, where I was brought up until my father returned from the Pacific after the Japanese surrendered in World War II. I was three years old. I also remember her telling me family stories about how she and my Great Aunt Anne had to become servants in their grandparents' home after her father died from a wound received after getting kicked in the stomach while shoeing a horse.

"We were so poor that Granny Corny, which was how we referred to our great-grandmother Cornwell, only had a few pennies to spend on us for Christmas." She looked into my eyes, by then 11 years-old, wide with expectation, for I loved to hear Grandma's stories. "She went to the five and dime store and bought some cologne. It froze overnight, because they didn't heat the quarters we lived in." My young heart lurched at the thought of my grandmother suffering at such a young age. She squeezed my little hand in hers, roughened from doing so much housework, for even though Grandpa made a lot of money, he never gave her any and expected her to do all the housework, which she did without complaint. "The next morning, we ran to see our presents under a little tree she'd chopped down, only the perfume had frozen and broken the bottle it was in during the night."

"You didn't get any Christmas presents?" My smooth young face peered into her older, wrinkled one.

"No, the bottles were broken."

I had never fathomed such sadness in our well-to-do family. My young heart foundered. I started to cry. Grandma looked at me and started crying, too. Then I looked at her. Seeing us both in tears made me start to laugh. Soon, she laughed at us both laughing-crying, and we continued laughing and crying until she ended up laughing and hugging me close. I'd never forget the day Grandma and I laughed and cried together as she revealed an anecdote from her impoverished childhood.

"Do something, Craig!" reverberated from the living room.

My father looked blankly at his wife, his two daughters, and couldn't fathom what all the fuss was about. "What do you want me to do, Iris?"

"Be a man!" My mother looked at him as if she could hit him.

My father shrank back. "Now, Iris, it's Christmas…"

The family dog wagged its tail and put its head in my mother's lap. She petted him whilst looking out the window at the garden full of chrysanthemums and lilies blooming in December. She stood up and went into the kitchen. "Let's eat breakfast."

"Can we have waffles?" My sister's face lit up at the thought of waffles and maple syrup. My father smiled at her. He loved waffles with lots of maple syrup. Daddy was easy to please.

"Yes, let's get out the waffle iron and have a nice Christmas breakfast!"

My grandmother's phone call forgotten, they went into the kitchen to fix waffles as I sat in the spacious living room on the chintz sofa in white Anglo-Saxon pain. My arm hurt and my heart ached. Those were physical and psychological pains. But, the pain of separation from my beloved grandmother for so many years and Albert, my lover, who had proposed marriage, were more than I could bear. That my mother was dead set against my having anything to do with him hurt even more, though I disguised it in anger.

Back in Berkeley, Albert Curtis shrugged his shoulders, opened his refrigerator, and took out a bottle of champagne. He'd decided to celebrate Christmas alone. Then, he heard a knock at the door. It was Maria Dolores. They could celebrate together.

A huge spruce tree sparkled with tinsel and expensive presents under it at State Senator Michael Dorland's spacious Montecito mansion. His wife, Fay – his third wife, to be exact – admired the panoramic ocean view from their large front window. She turned her carefully coiffed blonde head and opened her mouth to say something, but her husband cut her short. "Quit worrying about Andronicus. It's Christmas!" He handed her a small, oblong box, exquisitely wrapped with gold ribbons. She took it and shrugged.

"Is this a bribe?" Fay laughed. She opened it slowly, taking the diamond bracelet out with care. She smiled at her husband and kissed him. "Oh, you devil!" Then she put it on her wrist and held it up to the sparkling California morning light coming through the dormer windows. She started to look under the tree for own gift to her husband when she heard a familiar car engine pull into the semi-circular driveway in front of the tiled doorway of their home. It was a classic Spanish-style hacienda home, but Andronicus hardly cut a classic figure, disheveled with a bloodied forehead.

"Hi, Mom! Hi, Al!" he said as he threw open the door with gusto, trying to make a good show.

"Where have you been and what's that on your forehead?" asked Fay.

"Just breezed up the coast for a change of air," laughed Andronicus. He sat down heavily on the immense sofa opposite the Christmas tree. "Got any presents for me?"

"Andronicus! You're hurt!"

"Do you have any presents for us?" asked his stepfather.

"Oh, uh…" Andronicus rubbed his head, wincing as he touched the raw edge of where Crutches' metal rod had hit him.

"You certainly had the money to buy them with," he gave his wife a stern look and stood squarely in front of his stepson.

Andronicus looked like a doe caught in headlights, frozen with fright. "I don't have any money."

"We do give you spending money."

"Well, um, I spent it."

"And helped yourself to an extra thousand from the family vault." Al stepped closer to Andronicus and inspected him, his disheveled, torn shirt and pants and his head wound.

"I can explain…" Andronicus shifted his weight and attempted to stand, only to have his stepfather stand in his way. He burst into tears. "It's not my fault!"

"It never is," said Al.

"Michael, can't you leave poor Andronicus alone? It's Christmas Day, for heaven's sakes." She tugged at his new Jaeger sweater he'd just put on after opening the box under the tree.

Michael turned and glared at his wife, wondering in the back of his mind why he'd ever adopted her son. She averted her face from his cold stare, distraught.

"I don't mind dishing out endless dough to send him to fancy schools that he flunks out of, paying his endless traffic tickets, and covering up his scandals with perfectly nice girls, but when he starts stealing from me, that's where I draw the line!"

Fay tried to think fast, but Andronicus' latest misdeed took her by surprise. So she gave her son an imploring look. "Andronicus, you didn't actually take money from your father's vault, did you?" Her voice rose on the last part of the sentence. She felt her heartbeat quicken.

"Of course not! He's always treated me like a hand-me-down son. He picks on me all the time." Andronicus burst into tears. A vein in his bloodied forehead bulged. He looked like hell warmed over.

"Now see what you've done!" Fay sat down on the silken sofa made in Italy and started to sniffle. At least, she pretended to.

Michael swiveled his stout torso and stomped out of the room. "He did it, and you know he did! Some Christmas this has turned out to be!"

Andronicus and his mother stared at each other. She narrowed her eyes. "Why did you steal money from your father's vault, Andronicus?"

Andronicus touched his wounded forehead gingerly, saying "Ouch." His mother ran to the bathroom to get some water to wash it with and mercurochrome to stop any infection, plus Band-aids. She washed off the wound with care, with Andronicus pushing her away, yet letting her continue. "I just did it because of... of a woman," he said as he winced and moaned.

"The one Myrtle saw you at the Biltmore with? The older woman?"

"She's not that old... Well, maybe she is. She wanted money!"

Andronicus' mother quit mopping his wound and sucked in her breath. "What for?"

"For... for revenge! And sex!"

"Sex?"

Andronicus looked away. "She wanted to have sex with me. I took dad's money to pay for the cottage behind the Biltmore."

"Now, Andronicus, how could you get involved in a sordid affair with an old harridan? Didn't I warn you about older women? They get so desperate..." She swabbed away at his forehead with a tiny washcloth. He shouted in pain, but she put mercurochrome on it anyway. It stung, and he yelled like a stuck pig.

"Stop it, Mother! Ouch!"

"How did you get hurt? Who hit you? Tell me the truth, Andronicus," said Fay.

"Oh, just a little scuffle. Not worth talking about."

Mrs. Dorland took off her horn-rimmed glasses and frowned at her son. "Andronicus, I can tell when you're in trouble. I'm your mother. I love you and want to help you. Tell me all about it."

Andronicus scrunched his flabby features together and let out a sniff, then another. A tear slid down his puffy cheek. His mother cradled him in her arms. He began to bawl like a baby. He pressed into his mother's warm chest.

"Mom, she wanted me to… to kill…"

Fay Dorland raised her eyebrows and hugged him tighter.

"Who? That awful daughter of hers? I've heard about her."

"No, her awful daughter's black boyfriend."

Fay let go of her son, breathing deeply. "Of course, you notified the police."

Andronicus started sobbing even harder.

"You didn't kill anyone, did you?" She took a step back, her eyes opening wide in fright. She knew her son wasn't a murderer. A bit rough, sometimes, but, murder? No.

Andronicus continued to sob. "I didn't kill her boyfriend."

Fay started pacing the floor in front of their bay window with the panoramic view of the Pacific Ocean. "Where does this woman live? What's her address?"

"On Cima Linda Lane," sniffed Andronicus with a little smile, turning the corners of his mouth up ever so slightly.

His mother grabbed her pocketbook and headed for the driveway. Andronicus listened in contentment as she roared off in her El Dorado Cadillac. His mother had always protected him. He sighed and lay down on the sofa to dry his eyes.

The Johnsons were stuffing hot buttered waffles with lots of creamy syrup on them into their mouths when the doorbell rang. They looked at one another in surprise.

"It must be Monte," drawled my mother, annoyed. "She has no sense of propriety. It's Christmas morning and she wants to barge in here." She exhaled, wiped her lips with a paper napkin, stood up, and went to the door. She opened it to find a sophisticated woman wearing horn-rimmed glasses facing her.

Nonplussed, Mrs. Johnson took a step backwards, tottering a bit on the shag rug as it caught her heel.

"Who are you?"

"I'm Fay Dorland, Andronicus' mother." Fay raised a peremptory eyebrow and stared Mrs. Johnson in the eye. The latter shook her perfectly coiffed head, bewildered.

"Andronicus who?" Mother feigned ignorance as her mind cartwheeled into the Biltmore cottage with visions of Andronicus. She felt faint. "I'm not well this morning. Could you come another day?"

"You've corrupted my son! He's taken money from his father's vault because... because you wanted him to kill someone! You're... you're..." Fay ran out of words to describe her feelings for his woman. "You're going to go to jail!"

"What for?" A pallor crept over Mrs. Johnson's face.

Mr. Johnson got up and walked over to see what the matter was. I scooted past him. I'd heard 'I'm Andronicus' mother' which was enough to send chills down my spine. Andronicus Wyland? My wannabe rapist? My mother seeing him...? Anger coursed through my veins as my own mother's betrayal sunk in. How could she? I began to sputter... "Andronicus tried to rape me last summer! He's a brute!"

"With a mother like yours, do you expect anyone to believe that?" asked a determined Fay. She knew these were the kind of people who went after innocent kids like her son.

I stared at Andronicus' enraged mother; then I turned and gave my own mother a withering look. She recoiled. I intuited she had done what she'd been accused of.

"Andronicus just pulled a gun on the train I was on and tried to kill me!"

My mother stepped forward, raised her head in triumph, and said, "See? He's a killer!"

"That doesn't make you Snow White," replied Fay. "And I don't believe you, young lady!"

"He raped the president of the Theta house," I replied, standing my ground.

Fay flinched as untoward memories flowed through her brain, the bribe, the threats, what it took to get rid of that lawsuit. "How do YOU know?"

I took a deep breath, squared my shoulders, and said, "All of his friends know about it. It's no secret. Your son is a rapist and... worse!" I pulled the sash on my chenille bathrobe tighter, trying to ward off the feeling of how ugly this was. I couldn't believe my Puritanical mother had slept with Andronicus Wyland.

"He hit me and knocked me unconscious," my mother said, a bit timidly. "There was a big bruise on my jaw. My husband saw it, didn't you, Craig?" My dad flinched. "I think he had something against our family because my daughter wouldn't..." Her voice faltered.

My mother shrank into her fluffy robe, looking a bit like a lost little lamb. My father sat at the breakfast nook, dumbfounded. He'd never doubted my prudish mother's fidelity. My younger sister tugged on his sleeve. "Daddy, who's that woman? What's she talking about? Why is she here?" My father gave her an aggrieved look. He shook his head in disbelief. Then, he pushed his chair away from his syrupy waffles and walked into the bedroom.

I walked over to my mother and faced her. "How could you?"

"He... he was paying me... And he raped me!"

Fay Dorland stepped between us. "You're both lying." She looked at my mother. "People saw you with my son at the Biltmore. Tongues wagged. Yes, money was taken from my husband's vault, but you weren't raped!"

"Then where did I get that horrible bruise on my jaw...? Craig... Craig! My husband saw it. He knows something happened..."

I thought of my warm, bosomy grandmother, who loved every creature that crawled the Earth. I wished she could be here. The phone conversation still reverberated in my head; grandma's tears, the time and distance that had separated them. This never would have happened if...

"I'm ashamed of you, Mother. How could you even get near that boy after what he tried to do to me? What would you say to Grandma?"

"Grandma must never hear of this!" Mother grabbed me by my arm and started to pull it. I struggled to get free.

"What a bunch of bottom-of-the-rung Montecito people! Taking advantage of our wealth and position!" Fay thrust herself in my mother's face as I pulled free from her grip. I was near tears. My little sister looked like she was, too, as she stood in the background near the orange and yellow chintz sofa.

A shot rang out. We exchanged horrified looks and ran to the bedroom where my father had gone.

Chapter 19

Albert was puzzling over wedding rings in the window of a Berkeley jewelry store on the day before Christmas. He'd missed Inny more than he could imagine, and he wanted to have her by his side always. He knew he was more than ten years older than she was, and that she wanted to finish her degree at Berkeley. At the same time, he wanted to show how serious he was about his marriage proposal. He hoped she wouldn't turn it down. Her parents lived in a wealthy area and he knew he'd have to impress them doubly as he was black. Maybe they wouldn't allow her to marry him. That's why he bought the biggest diamond he could afford with some money he'd saved for a new car. Inny was far more important than a silly car. He fingered the box the ring was in as he walked back to his studio on Parker Avenue. He rounded the corner of the high hedges that hid the studios from public view, although people could always peek through.

He climbed the stairs to his own studio and found a present his parents had sent him, from Harlem on his doorstep, a book about slavery. He'd tried to distance himself from that hideous past, the horrid subjugation of black people to slavery, sold as chattel. Why had his parents sent him this book? To remind him of their humble beginnings or of how far they had come. After all, his father was a doctor and his mother a nurse. And here he was, the first black English professor at U. C. Berkeley.

Soon, there was a knock on his door. He recognized it as that of Maria Dolores and heaved a sigh. She could be a nuisance, but he always put up with her because that's the way he was. Kind. He opened the door and she clapped her hands together in excitement.

"Alberto!" she said in Spanish.

"Si, *señora?*" He played along.

Maria Delores gave him a look of rapt admiration. "What did your family send you for Christmas, Alberto?" she sat down on his long sofa, shifting her considerable weight, and managed to show considerable cleavage of her breasts in so doing. Albert looked at her and smiled. "It's nothing, Maria Delores. Just a book."

She scowled, her thick black eyebrows, nearly joining them, and laughed. "A book! A book for the professor!" She found this hysterically funny and laughed a high-pitched, howling laugh.

Meanwhile, Sally, still in her pajamas and bathrobe, her hair mussed and hanging in her face, as usual, made her way up the staircase to Albert's studio. She also sported a bruise on her jaw, which was darkening.

Jerry yelled something incoherent from his studio below. She knocked on Albert's door, starting to sob.

"Who's that?" said Maria Delores in her thick Spanish accent. "On Christmas Day?"

Albert gave her a wry look and got up to answer the door. He was tired of Maria Delores' possessive attitude. She didn't have a subtle bone in her body and he wanted to pack to go to Santa Barbara. He wanted to spend Christmas with Inny and her family, if they'd have him.

He opened the door to find a tearful Sally. "Merry Christmas!" he said and laughed. Sally kept on crying. Albert exchanged doleful looks with Maria Delores.

"What's he done this time?" he asked.

Sally raised her tear-streaked face to his cheery one. "He tried to strangle me."

Albert opened the door wide and she walked in. "I thought he'd given up his violent ways! Why – you're married!"

"And now I want a divorce!" Sally turned her tearful self away from Albert, saw the sofa and sank down onto it. "I'm afraid he'll kill me. He's worse than ever!"

Albert took a long look at the pitiful Sally. He took her hand in his and said, "Sally, my father is a doctor. When women were mistreated, as you have been, he'd try to get them to form a group so they could talk, help each other out." His forehead wrinkled in sympathy as he stared into her sad eyes.

"I… I need to get away from him. Where are these women?"

"That was in New York City, but they must have women who reach out and help each other here. I'll call Adrianne to see if she knows of any such group of women. Or perhaps a doctor would."

"What kind of a doctor?"

Albert averted his head and thought, *Maybe a psychologist.*

"I just want to go away." Sally pushed her hair out of her eyes and wiped her tears on the sleeve of her bathrobe.

"You can stay with me for a few nights," offered Maria Delores. Albert looked at her in surprise. He began to like her after all.

"Let me make some phone calls. Meanwhile, pack what you need and stay with Maria, and DON'T tell Jerry where you've gone."

Sally shook her head sullenly. Then, she managed a smile. "Thanks, Albert. You've helped me a lot. I don't deserve it."

"What?"

"I always flunk out, space out, get pregnant, marry the wrong man... I'm a mess."

Albert found himself without words for once, mostly because what she said was true. He took her hand in his and looked into her downcast eyes, partially hidden by her bangs, as usual. "Sally, you're dead wrong. You've just been underestimating yourself. I think I can find help for you."

"Can you?" Sally looked up with a ray of hope in her eyes. She almost smiled, though her mouth was still quivering from the punch in the jaw. It was red and would soon be black and blue.

"I'll find a place where women like you can go," Albert said. Sally looked into his eyes and he smiled a big, toothy Albert smile. Sally couldn't help but smile back. "See? You're going to be fine, Miss Sally, just fine!"

Sally snuffled through her smile. "I hope so. What will I tell my parents?" A fearful look crossed her face.

"The truth! You've got nothing to hide! They'll want to help you. I met them. They're good people."

"I guess so, but my father isn't my real father..."

"Don't you worry about who your father is," grinned Albert. "I'm going to get you together with some women who'll really help you... Who'll understand what you've been through."

A look of surprise crossed Sally's distraught, bang-in-eyes face. "How could they?"

"Because they've been through the same thing, Sally. You're not alone."

Sally heaved a sigh and lay back on Albert's comfy sofa. "That's the nicest thing anyone has said to me in a long time. You and Inny have helped me so much... I don't know what to say."

"Just relax while I make a cup of coffee and a few phone calls. Just leave this to me, you'll see." Albert grinned at her. She looked into his deep brown eyes and saw why Inny loved him so much. He was nice, really nice. He even cared about her. She wasn't used to this kind consideration of her feelings, this respect for her person. After all, she was nobody, or so she thought. Sally almost began to cry again, swallowed hard, and smiled instead. "I'm going to get a job, Albert."

"Good for you!" he said.

Albert stood up and went over to his kitchenette to make some coffee, thinking hard of a place for her to go to. He knew someone at the Bosun's Locker, a local bar, who might be able to help. He remembered hearing about how they helped beleaguered women from time to time. He stopped at the phone, picked it up, and dialed a number.

Maria Dolores stood up from where she'd been listening and went over to sit next to Sally on the sofa. "You *Americanas* have to learn to make a man respect you." She took Sally's hand in her older, calloused one. "My husband didn't respect like a proper husband in Spain, which is why I came to America."

Albert furrowed his brow as he spoke rapidly into the phone receiver. "Thanks, Eddie! I'll bring her over tomorrow." He turned and grinned at them. "It's all arranged. Sally has a place to stay."

"Not until I talk some sense into this crazy little Americana's head," said Maria Dolores, straightening her spine and holding her head high. "I know a thing or two about bad men."

Albert and Sally exchanged startled looks. Albert's face warmed like a summer's day. He started to laugh. "You never cease to amaze me, Maria!"

She stood up and hugged him, snuggling against his broad chest, which is what she'd wanted to do all along. She was in love with Albert. He gazed into her deep brown eyes and grinned at her.

"Can I trust you to take good care of Sally tonight?"

Maria slapped him on the shoulder. "Alberto, I'm going to teach this little Americana a thing or two."

She winked at Sally, who looked up from under her bangs with gratitude, mixed with apprehension. Spending the night with Maria Delores frightened her a bit. Everything seemed more sinister than it had before Jerry socked her in the jaw. She thought he'd be like her stepfather, a gentleman, respectful and kind. Of course, she'd been only four-years-old when her mother divorced her father. She had no idea what had gone on between them. That part of her life remained a blank page.

Maria walked over to where she sat on the sofa and sat next to her. "You'll be just fine. Don't worry. I don't bite." She let out a loud cackling laugh, and Sally looked at her as if she had just laid an egg. She'd always found Maria Dolores' behavior bordering on the obnoxious, but she couldn't go back to Jerry. She stood up, smoothing her pleated, plaid woolen skirt and shaking her head so that her bangs didn't fall in her face. "You need a new haircut. I can give you one. We're going to make a new Sally out of you!" Her merry smile didn't reassure Sally.

"Don't cut my bangs!" Sally said.

"They're always in your face! Let them grow out! I'll fix your hair and you'll look beautiful, you'll see."

"But I have a beaked nose! I want to cover my nose!" Albert laughed. "My nose is beaked and I'm proud of it, Sally!"

"But you're... you're a man. It looks good on you." Sally wiped her eye and pushed her bangs out of her face, but they fell right back over it. "I'll never look beautiful!" She jerked her head around so that no one could see her profile.

"Stop that silly nonsense," Albert replied in his stern, mature voice. "All women are beautiful. You just need to see your own beauty."

"I'm not going to spend the night with Maria Dolores if she's going to cut my bangs!" Sally looked defiant for the first time in her life. Her bangs were sacred.

"No, I won't touch them! You'll see!" said Maria Dolores.

Albert went to the refrigerator and took out his customary bottle of champagne. "I suggest we make a toast to Sally's new haircut!"

Sally stood up angrily. "No! I've had enough! Quit making fun of me!"

Albert closed the refrigerator door. "Nobody's making fun of you."

"Then leave my hair alone!" Sally stood firmly on her own two feet. Albert and Maria Dolores looked at her in surprise. She'd never asserted herself before.

"No haircut! I hear you!" said Maria Dolores. "Let's just have a nice little dinner and we can talk."

Sally looked around, hoping to find a way to escape Maria Dolores' unexpected and sudden generosity. Maria was grinding on her already battered nerves. She saw Albert smile tentatively at her. She knew there was no way out except to go to Maria Dolores' room. After all, she'd come here for help, and other than calling her parents, she had no place to go except back to Jerry, which she'd finally decided was a terrible idea.

Another knock at the door. There was Kathy, hoping for some champagne and sympathy. The deep vertical furrow in her brow deepened, a sort of accusation. "Oh," she said when she saw the other women. She managed a smile. "How are you, Sally and Maria Dolores?"

"Sally's going to spend the night at my house. Then, we'll find a place for her. Can't you see her chin?" Maria said.

Sally lowered her head to try to hide her bruised chin. "Get rid of that man!" Kathy said. Her face lit up in vivid anger, her furrow deepening to almost a cleft. She turned her head and began to cry. "I can't stand him."

Sally took a deep breath and said, "He has his good points. Besides, he hasn't hurt you!" She turned and faced Kathy.

"It's just that… Oh, never mind!"

"Okay, let's go." Sally lowered her head into its usual hangdog position. Maria Dolores walked up to her and put her arm around her to console her. Sally wrenched free. She didn't want to be touched. Maria Dolores understood. Albert went to the door and opened it for them. They filed out in silence. Albert had felt emotions surge in his chest during their little scene, and he knew what he had to do. He ran to a drawer and fumbled through old clipping, family photos, odd pieces of jewelry, and tie clips. Then he found it. His grandmother's engagement ring. Searching for a box, he all but emptied the drawer. Finally, he found a facsimile of a ring box and put it in. Then, he started packing an overnight bag.

Kathy had lingered behind. She watched him like a hawk, frowning. Her normally smooth brow formed an uncustomary furrow. "What are you doing?"

"Oh, Miss Kathy," laughed Albert, suddenly aware that she was still in his studio. "I've got to go to Santa Barbara to see Inny."

"Inny, Inny, Inny," laughed Kathy. "She gets all the attention, doesn't she?"

"I'm sorry, Kathy, but we are engaged, or about to be engaged…" Albert smiled a broad smile, which radiated his happiness at the thought of becoming engaged to Inny.

"What?"

Albert turned his back on Kathy to pack an Armani suit in his suitcase. "That's why I should spend Christmas with her and her family."

Kathy started to laugh. "Wait till Joe hears…" Her face turned a purplish hue as she howled with laughter, no longer a voluptuous blonde; she'd turned into a howling hyena.

Albert folded the trousers to his suit and put them neatly in his suitcase. "You can tell him whatever you like. Now I must be going. Please, forgive me for being so rude, but I'm afraid Inny might be, in trouble. Could you take Sally to the Bosun's Locker tomorrow?"

"I thought…"

"That I was gay?" Albert turned to look at Kathy's voluptuous blonde self. "I didn't know what love was until I met Inny." He looked deep into her widening eyes. "Who could resist women like you?"

"Um, yeah. I guess you're right," she laughed. "Love knows no boundaries." Kathy flicked her long hair over her shoulder with a jerk of her head. She regained her composure, smiling at her faux pas. "Let me know if I can help, Albert. I'm sorry I made that remark."

"It happens all the time." Albert grinned at her in appreciation and relief, packing as fast as his nimble fingers allowed him to. He sensed that Inny was in trouble, remembering the small but significant scratch her mother had dug into his flesh. He wondered how he could convince them that a black man would make a good husband for their daughter. He wondered if they'd chase him out of the house again, but he was determined to be there for Inny. She was having a hard time. He could feel it in his bones, which were as white as theirs.

Chapter 20

The next morning, Maria Dolores and Sally dressed, Maria in her usual, plain housecleaning dress, Sally in a wrinkled blouse and pleated skirt. They left for the Bosun's Locker, a bar Sally had never been to. It was on Shattuck Avenue, near the Berkeley campus. They took the bus, because Maria didn't have a car.

Sally watched students come and go with a dull look in her eyes. She felt that her life had ended, but she knew she had to go on. Maria Dolores watched her, remembering a time when she had felt forlorn and friendless, in Spain. Her mother had died in childbirth, so her grandmother took over, but she was aged and tired from raising five children. Maria never felt like she had a real family. After a disastrous flirtation with one of the local boys, which left her pregnant and shunned by almost all, she knew she had to leave her small town and change her life after giving the baby up for adoption. That's how she ended up in America, working as a cleaning woman. She felt better but still downtrodden. Now, she would help a downtrodden American. Not poor, as she had been, but downtrodden by her lack of will.

She brushed Sally's bangs out of her eyes as they entered the bar, which was run by black Americans. Maria smiled and greeted the bartender who owned the establishment. "*Hola*, Jackson."

Jackson was a large black man with a roundish face and a big, warm smile. It lit up the dingy interior of the bar, even though there were roses in glass bottles strategically placed to brighten things up. Jackson's smile was all Maria Dolores needed. "I've got a damsel in distress for you," she announced.

Sally shrank back, not used to being described so bluntly. "I'm not in distress!" She pivoted to face Maria Dolores and give her a dirty look.

"Okay, okay. A young lady who's been having some problems with her man."

"Oh, we can help her," laughed the bartender.

"I need a lawyer, I think," said Sally, looking furtively about at the shabby furniture, the old sofas, and cheap tables and chairs in the bar. Cheap but tasteful, with red checkered tablecloths.

A woman approached her. "You here for some lunch?"

Maria and Sally exchanged looks. Neither of them had much money on them.

"Or perhaps an eye-opener?" The waitress grinned broadly. It was infectious and Sally smiled back.

"What's an eye-opener?" Sally asked.

The waitress leaned on the bar and laughed. "Just a little something to get you going in the morning. Ya' know. Like a whisky soda."

Maria ignored her and spoke directly to Jackson. "She needs to see Sheila."

"Oh, that kind of trouble." Jackson gave Maria Dolores a knowing look. Then, he looked at Sally. "You been needing to do some soul searching, Miss Sally."

Sally started to blubber. The stress was too much for her.

The waitress put her arm around her waist and guided her to a room in the back where a white woman – gaunt and intense-looking, with a deep furrow in her forehead – sat talking to another woman, a teenaged black girl whose hair had been straightened. She reminded Sally of one of the Shirelles, a popular singing group of black women who always looked like they were on top of the world. She wondered what a girl like her was doing in the back of a bar.

"This is Sheila," said Maria Dolores. "She can help you with most anything. Now, I've got to get back to the house and start cleaning."

Sally looked from Maria to Sheila. Sheila's intense, narrow face almost frightened Sally, but Sheila smiled and said, "I go to Berkeley. I'm a French major and a straight-A student. I have a 149 I.Q. One day, let's just say I had a really terrible day, and these kind people helped me out."

"What were you doing here?" Sally couldn't help but wonder what such a smart girl would be doing in a bar run by black people. She loved Albert, but she wasn't used to being surrounded by so many black people.

"You mean in the Bosun's Locker?" Sheila laughed a shrill laugh. "It's the best place in town! Well, the Fairmont is fun, but that's for those upper-class girls who've never had... problems."

"What kind of problems?" Sally looked around the dark windowless room which had just a low-slung sofa and folding chairs and a small wooden desk for furnishings. She wondered what she meant about girls who'd never had problems. She brushed her bangs out of her face and peered into Sheila's bright blue eyes with the deep furrow intersecting them. Something was different about her.

"Why don't we all sit down? You leaving now, Maria?" Sheila asked.

Maria nodded and made for the beaded doorway. She swung her hips and laughed as she went. "Help this poor gringa. Her boyfriend... or is he your husband now? Hasn't been treating her right."

"He socked me in the jaw last night. Then he tried to strangle me," whimpered Sally as she sat on the vinyl sofa next to the black teenaged girl. Sheila stood up and dragged a folding chair over so she could face them. Maria left the room, tossing a "You've come to the right place" off as she went.

Sally heard Jackson laugh and say something to Maria as she left. Then, she turned and faced Sheila, who was examining her face and body.

"What else did he do to you?" Sheila asked.

Sally shook her unruly hair. "Everything... Well, he was nice most of the time, but he made me sleep in the hallway and took me on scary airplane flights in India..."

"So you've been to India?" Sheila brightened at the thought of travel.

"Yes. He's an engineer. He got a job over there helping build a dam. He took me with him, but he knew I was afraid of flying and made me fly with him in a small plane. I nearly died."

"He was your husband?"

"No, we just got married." Sally fidgeted on the sofa. She picked at one of the plastic buttons sewn into it. "I'd just had an abortion and he bought me flowers and promised he'd change. After a few days of living together again, he changed back to his former self."

Sheila's furrow deepened in her brow. Her stern looks were known to frighten the most composed and terrify lesser souls. After assessing Sally's distress, she stood up and started pacing the floor.

"Did your father fuck you?" she asked bluntly.

That brought Sally out of her pool of self-misery. "No! Of course not!" She looked at Sheila as if she'd just dropped a bomb.

"Then you were lucky."

Sally's jaw dropped. She was speechless. She stood up and thought of making a beeline for the beaded doorway. She turned and took a step in that direction.

"My father raped me from an early age. I don't even remember when it started." Sheila's furrow cleaved tightly on her forehead. Sally stopped in her tracks. She walked slowly over to her.

"Huh?" Her woebegone bangs splashed into her eyes.

"He was an alcoholic." Sheila looked into Sally's eyes without wavering. Sally winced.

"Oh." She sat down on the sofa and looked at the teenaged girl sitting there. "I've never heard of... that's awful!" The teenager looked up at Sheila and heaved a sigh. Sally went into shock. She couldn't talk. The room spun round her as she slumped forward into a dead faint.

Sheila walked through the beaded doorway and asked Jackson to bring some cold water. She realized this girl was another white middle or upper-class spoiled brat who'd thought she could go through life without making much of an effort. She smiled to herself, realizing how much Sally had to learn.

Jackson came running with a shot of brandy. He saw Sally's inert form, put his hand under her head, and tried to get her to drink some. She sputtered and made gurgling noises, shook her head from side to side in slow motion, and came to her senses. She stared up at Jackson without recognizing him.

"Wha… What's going on?" She blurted out a few unrecognizable sounds and struggled to sit up.

Jackson and Sheila exchanged bemused looks.

"She's going to be all right. She'd just never heard of a father like mine," said Sheila, brow furrowed.

"Young lady's got to get a grip on reality. You did. She can if she wants to," Jackson replied.

"Not all of them want to." Sheila took Jackson's outstretched hand and hung onto it tightly. "I needed lots of help."

Jackson sat down on the spongy sofa, next to Sheila, squeezing her hand. "When your biological father does something on that order to you, it's the worst. She's just been knocked around a little bit."

"Yeah, but I was tough. At least I had confidence in myself. I don't know if this one does."

Sally looked at them through dazed eyes. "I never even saw my father without pajamas and a bathrobe. How could… How could anyone do that?"

"Alcohol. Sense of entitlement. Self-loathing…" started Sheila. Jackson squeezed her hand and smiled at her.

"That's just for starters," he said in a deeply resonant voice. "Not all families are perfect."

Sheila cracked up. She couldn't help herself; she laughed until she could hardly breathe.

"What's so funny?" asked a befuddled Sally.

"Nothing! Everything! Get a grip!" yelled Sheila.

"What am I going to do?" Sally started to sniffle again.

The spongy sofa gave a bit under their weight. Jackson and Sheila looked at her. "Get a job," said Sheila. "And a divorce. Any children?"

Sally shook her head vigorously. Sheila smiled. Her furrowed forehead smoothed itself out considerably. "Lucky!"

"Lucky? Look at the bruise on my chin! You call that lucky?"

"Nah. That's just a wake-up signal. A 'time-to-pack-your-bags-and-get-on-with-your-life' signal." Sheila smiled a smug little smile.

The sofa sagged under their weight. Jackson stood up. "Gotta tend the bar," he said, walking out of the room.

"I haven't even graduated from college!" wailed Sally.

"Oh, Jesus!" Sheila gave her a furious look. "What do you want? Your diapers changed? Where's your grit, Girl?"

Sally looked away, depressed and ashamed and miserable. "What should I do?"

"That's your decision, m'dear," said Sheila. "Ever heard of working?"

"I can't even type!"

"Learn!" Sheila leaned into Sally's tear-streaked face and made a face. They both laughed. Sheila stood up, pulling Sally with her. She led her to the typewriter at the shelter and pushed her into the chair in front of it. Sally gamely tapped at the keys, but she didn't know how to type.

"There are other jobs!" Sheila said.

Sally looked up. A trace of hope crossed her face. "Like what?"

"Like working in a store or a movie theater, or cleaning houses..."

"I don't want to be like Maria Dolores. A miserable cleaning woman."

Sheila grabbed her by her shirtwaist collar. "A job is a job!"

Sally stood up slowly, pushing the chair back from the typewriter table. She looked down. Sheila walked over to the low-slung sofa and grabbed the newspaper off of it. She handed it to Sally. "You start here."

Sally looked at the classified ads dully, as if she'd been condemned to prison. Sheila looked at the ceiling. "I'm running out of patience!" She started to pace back and forth in front of Sally.

Sally looked up. "There's an ad for a receptionist at a law firm. If they'd hire me..."

"Put on a nice dress, comb your hair, and march on over there."

Sally stood up and nodded. "Okay! I'm going to get a job! I put up with an abusive... monster too long!" A look of determination came over her face. She turned and walked towards the bathroom to freshen up. Sheila smiled.

Chapter 21

Albert had driven the 450 miles between Berkeley and Montecito in record time. He'd looked in the rearview mirror the entire way to make sure he didn't get caught for speeding. As he drove into Inny's parents' driveway, he was surprised to see a late-model Mercedes Benz parked there.

He felt for the box with the engagement ring for Inny in his coat pocket. Reassured that it was there, he opened the door to get out of his car.

Then, he heard the gunshot. He bounded out of his car, ran to the front door, and started ringing the doorbell as if his life depended on it. What if someone had hurt Inny? He was terrified.

He shifted his weight from one patent leather shoe to the other, leaned on the doorbell again, and began to shout, "Inny, Inny, are you in there?" He was sure he'd heard a gunshot.

No one came to the door. Albert wedged himself between a hibiscus plant and Inny's bedroom window, tapping on it as hard as he could. He could hear voices and muffled crying. Something was wrong.

He felt along the edge of the window for an opening. Just as he was able to push the window open, a red Ferrari pulled into the driveway. Albert jumped away from the window.

Andronicus sauntered towards him with a sneer on his face. He pulled his gun out of his jacket, thinking he could get even. Albert hands shot into the air. "I'm a visitor!" he shouted.

"Sure you are, Buddy," said Andronicus. "We have lots of black guys sneaking around windows in Montecito." Albert put his hands to his heart, trying to show his innocence. "I heard a gunshot and I'm terribly afraid something has happened…"

"Yeah?" Andronicus stopped for a minute. *A gunshot?* He saw his mother's car in the driveway, next to Albert's. "Maybe someone's hurt my mother!"

"Now wait a minute! I'm Inny Johnson's friend from Berkeley…"

"And I'm a monkey's uncle," laughed Andronicus with a sarcastic sneer. He pointed his gun at Albert, who hit the ground. "Sissy!"

Voices and sobs came from one of the bedrooms. Andronicus opened the door and walked towards it, gun pointed straight ahead. Albert hoisted himself from the ground and said, "Put that thing down!" He followed Andronicus into the house.

Andronicus gave him a backward glance as he entered the bedroom, where he saw Mr. Johnson lying face up with blood coming from his head. Mrs. Johnson, Inny, and her little sister were at his side, sobbing.

"My fiancée's in there! She needs to see me!" pleaded Albert.

"Shut up!" said Andronicus. He pointed his gun at Albert.

Instinctively, Inny took the gun that lay next to her father and pointed it at Andronicus. "Drop it, Andronicus!"

Andronicus turned and squeezed the trigger.

"Andronicus!" yelled his mother.

Inny felt something graze her shoulder and fired back. Andronicus went down. His mother ran to him, screaming. She threw herself on his body.

Inny grabbed her shoulder, which had been hit and was bleeding. Albert ran to her and tore off a piece of a towel he saw in the bathroom, making a tourniquet. As he twisted it around her shoulder, above the gunshot wound, everything went blank.

Police sirens sounded outside. Two Santa Barbara police officers jumped out of their squad car and ran full-tilt towards the commotion.

Once inside, the officers pulled their guns and pointed them straight ahead with both hands holding on, as they'd been trained to do. Screams and muffled sobs issued from one of the bedrooms, so they headed for it. They found Mr. Johnson lying inert, face up, his wife leaning over him, sobbing. Blood came out of a head wound. A revolver lay nearby.

Their youngest daughter clung to him, crying. "It's not possible," she said. "He was just eating waffles!"

Fay Dorland cradled Andronicus' head in her arms. She managed to stand up and address the officers. She pointed a finger at Inny, sitting on the edge of the bed with Albert tending her wound. "That girl just killed my son!"

"It was in self-defense," said Albert. "Call an ambulance. She's been hit in the shoulder!"

"My son is innocent," continued Fay.

The officers rushed past her to see if he were still alive. One took his pulse as the other radioed in to the precinct station.

"He's a goner," said the fellow taking his pulse.

The other officer wrested the gun in his other hand free, wrapping it in a handkerchief.

Mrs. Johnson sat on one of the twin beds, sobbing. "Oh, Craig, oh, Craig," she repeated over and over. "My husband, my husband…"

Inny's sister sobbed convulsively and held her mother close. Kendra broke loose and tried to touch her father, but one of the policemen grabbed her by the arm. "Don't touch the body!" he said. She broke down and fell on the floor, rolling and tearing her hair. The policeman tried to calm her, but to no effect.

"Call another squad car and an ambulance!" he said.

Chapter 22

Back at Berkeley, the police questioned Maria Dolores about Crutches. One of them towered over her as she stood in front of the Victorian house where he'd been killed.

"Did you hear any strange noises last night?"

"No." Maria scratched her dark, unruly hair. She thought for a moment. "Maybe I heard a shot."

"When?"

"I don't remember. I was sleeping."

"Where are the other people who live here?"

"Most of them have left for the vacation. You know. The Christmas vacation."

"Was anyone else here?"

Kathy sauntered by in tight jeans and a loose blouse, her blonde hair trailing her like a flag. When she saw Maria Dolores talking to the police, she stopped. She was carrying her violin in a case, which she held onto.

They turned and looked her up and down. "Who are you?"

"I'm Kathy Stevens. I live here… in back, in one of the studios."

"Did you hear anything unusual three nights ago?"

"No, I was playing with the Berkeley Symphony." She shifted her weight and tried to get past them. She'd promised a friend she'd meet her at the UCEN for lunch, and she was late.

"Someone was killed in front of this house on December 22."

"Oh!" Kathy's hand flew to her mouth. "How horrible!"

"Who was killed here?" asked Maria Dolores. "We've had enough trouble already!"

"Yeah, we're wondering if the incidents aren't connected."

Maria Dolores leaned on the broom she'd been sweeping with and ran her hand through her hair.

"How would I know? I'm just the cleaning woman."

"Someone killed a man on metallic crutches, a cripple."

"Who would do such a thing?" Maria Dolores's forehead wrinkled in angry dismay. "So many bad things going on in this world!"

"Did either of you know this man?"

"I think I saw a man on crutches waiting by those bushes once," said Maria Dolores. "He was up to no good."

"Was he with anyone?" The officer titled his head to try to appear less intimidating.

Maria Dolores scratched her head again. She shook it. "I don't think so, but I didn't pay attention to him. There are so many strangers around this area lately."

"What do you mean?"

Kathy leaned forward to speak, but Maria Dolores interrupted her. "A man shot someone in one of the studios, about a month ago."

The shorter, stouter policeman pushed his hat back, took a pad of paper and a pen out of his jacket, and stood poised to take notes. "Tell me about this incident."

Maria Dolores cleaned her throat, pulling herself up to her full height of 5'3". Her blousy dress covered most of her body as she started talking a mile a minute about the night Jerry was shot. "It was in that psychology student's apartment; she's a slut."

The officers exchanged brief smiles. "Nothing good ever happens in the bottom studios. That night, someone fired a shot into Inny's, the one who is a slut, and nearly killed another's boyfriend. They took him to the hospital…"

"Did anyone see who fired the shot?"

"I was in the front house. I saw a fancy sport car, Italian style – I know the European cars because I'm Spanish…"

"Who was in the car?" The taller policeman stared at Maria Dolores, who began to sweat.

"I don't know. Maybe an Americano. I leaned out the window to see what model it was, and I saw a burly Americano get in. It was there, and then it was gone; and an ambulance came for Jerry. It happened very fast. I'm just the cleaning woman. I was washing the dishes…"

"But you noticed a sports car?" The policeman shifted his weight and took a deep breath.

"I always have my eyes open for anything strange in this neighborhood."

"Could you identify the owner of the car from a photograph?" He leaned over, trying to seem less intimidating.

Maria Dolores gave him a piercing look. "I could try." Then, she took a step backwards as she adjusted her bra strap. "But I can't guarantee anything."

"Will you come to the police station with us?"

Maria pulled herself up to her full height. "Of course I will. Do I have any choice?"

The taller policeman looked at Kathy, who was trying to get away to her engagement. "Do you feel safe here?"

"Yes, perfectly safe. The shooting was a terrible surprise. None of us knew who would do such a thing. Now, if you'll excuse me..."

"Just one minute, young lady. We're trying to solve a murder and your testimony could help us."

Kathy looked about, startled at the thought of a murder. "I don't know a thing, Officer. I'm a violinist in the Berkeley Symphony..." She brandished her violin case.

"Yes, that's admirable, but what about this shot out of nowhere and now a dead body?"

"I think you need to talk to the people who live downstairs," she said, taking a step backwards.

"I think it was the same sports car both times," inserted Maria Dolores.

The stout officer looked down at her again. "What makes you think that?"

"Because... Because I saw it again just before Albert and Inny left for the train station." She puffed herself up, feeling she had contributed an important piece to the puzzle of information.

Kathy pointed to her violin. "I really must go!" She gave the officers a pleading look.

"Just stick around for another minute, young lady. Who are Albert and Inny?"

"They live in the studios behind this house that I clean. He lives upstairs, next to this woman..." she gave Kathy a look. "And Inny lives downstairs, where Jerry was shot and almost died."

"When did they leave for the train station?" The officer asked with a certain amount of agitation in his voice. He felt things might start to fall together.

"It was around eight o'clock, on December 24..."

"Did you hear a gunshot?"

"I'm not sure, but I saw that Italian sports car again." The officers stared at her. Maria started to run her hands through her hair, trying to remember. "Maybe I heard something, but I'd been watching a TV show with a lot of gunshots, I think it was Bonnie and Clyde."

"And did you SEE the person the car belonged to?"

"Let me think," said Maria.

"Please let me go to rehearsal. I didn't hear any shots and I don't know anything about this," said Kathy with a pleading look in her eyes.

"OK. OK. Just give us your name and address and be on your way. Go to your symphony," said the shorter policeman. "As for you, lady, keep thinking!"

"It was bright red..." Maria Dolores ran her hand thorough her hair once again, thinking as hard as she could.

The taller policeman's eyes lit up. "Could you identify this car if you saw it again?"

Jerry was coming down the walkway. Maria let him pass with a curt, "Good day." Then, she turned to the policemen, and beaming like a beacon from a lighthouse, said, "I never forget a Ferrari!"

"A Ferrari! Can you come to the station now?" The officers exchanged looks of satisfaction.

Maria Dolores curtsied. "The pleasure will be all mine, *señores*."

The shorter police officer with the pad starting writing down information as Maria kept talking a mile a minute. She was in her element.

Chapter 23

As the funeral procession wound its way to the Montecito Cemetery, I stared at the diamond on my engagement ring. It sparkled in the sun in bright contrast to the dark dirge Albert and I followed. His mouth was resolutely firm. I put my hand on his shoulder as he followed the car with my mother, grandmother, Uncle Jimmie, Aunt Edna, and my cousin Jimmy. My father's suicide didn't seem real. I saw his body; I even tried to resuscitate him, but he'd aimed directly at his brain and had died instantly. That it happened on Christmas Day made it even worse. That the police apprehended Albert hung heavy in my heart, but he hadn't set foot in my house yet and it was a clear suicide. They couldn't accuse him of anything other than ringing our doorbell perhaps an instant too late. Who knows what might have happened if he'd come earlier? Thoughts reeled like uncoupled train wagons, jostling and banging against each other. In a few minutes, we'd put my father's body into the earth forever. I began to cry. Albert put his arm around my shoulder and I felt better.

Neither of us said a word.

The procession came to a halt at the foot of the cemetery. Everyone parked their cars as best they could and got out. Uncle Jimmy assisted my mother, who was dressed in black with a veiled hat, and my grandmother, also dressed in black, leaning on a cane. She'd been crippled ever since a car backed into her, but she pretended like it wasn't that bad. Just seeing her sent a thrill of joy through me. I wanted to help her in any way I could. Grandma kept breaking down and crying. My mother tried to quiet her and keep her own nerves calm, but Grandma always was emotional and there was no stopping her tears. "He was such a nice boy," she kept repeating. My mother and uncle stared grimly ahead. My twenty-year-old cousin whom I grew up with glanced at me and Albert. He tried to smile but fought back tears at the same time. Tears ran down my cheeks, but I tried to keep my emotions in check. The thought that we had to bury him kept running through my mind.

The oblong excavated hole in the ground, surrounded by tombstones, some quite ornate and crypt-like, didn't help. The sun shone like a beacon on the hilly Montecito Cemetery, and the ocean gleamed in front of it. If only it were raining.

It seemed so unfair that my poor father, the one who'd never harmed anyone, caved in to the horror of my mother's infidelity and took it out on himself. Why? I keep asking myself why. And why was my mother having an affair with my wannabe rapist, who nearly killed me, Andronicus Wyland? That it ended badly didn't surprise me.

Albert squeezed me to him after we descended from the car and held my hand as we walked to the oblong hole with my father's casket nearby. My cousin kept glancing at me. I'd tried to explain that Albert and I were in love, but he couldn't grasp that at age twenty coming from Arlington, Virginia, where miscegenation still ruled. It was still illegal to marry outside of your race in the South, and Virginia was very much part of the South. My mother and grandmother walked arm in arm, consoling each other as best they could.

I heard Grandma say something to the effect that she and my sister could live with her, but Kendra refused. She had to be with her friends at Santa Barbara High School. I stared at Albert, who was the only person who hadn't known my father intimately. He looked at me and smiled. "Go over to them," he said. I looked at him for a long second. Then, I bolted to where the others stood. I hugged Grandma to me. We both began to bawl our heads off, rubbing each other's backs.

"Straighten up, Inny!" commanded my mother, still composed and insistent on decorum, as usual. I found that ironic, after what she'd done with Andronicus. She'd told me it was to try to make ends meet, as Daddy was having a hard time between jobs. I'd asked her why she didn't just look for a job herself and received the backside of her hand. Sometimes, I thought she had no conscience at all. I'd studied psychopathology in one of my classes and wondered if she were one of them. I shuddered at the thought of her naked in bed with the fleshy, ghastly Andronicus, who had recently chased me alongside the railroad tracks. I'd told her, but she didn't believe me. "Inny, quit making things up," she'd said. Of course, the extent of his malfeasance was not yet known.

A minister intoned words from the Bible over my father's casket after it was lowered into his final resting place. I saw my aunt and uncle wipe tears from their eyes. Uncle Jimmy, tall, with dark, curly hair and handsome as any movie star, and my father, shorter but almost as good-looking, with his trim, slender build and well-chiseled features, used to eat themselves silly at Grandma's Sunday dinners, resplendent in Southern cooking – fried chicken, mashed potatoes, and gravy with all the trimmings. Then, they'd go off and chat for a while and end up on sofas at opposite ends of my grandparents' sumptuous living room. The sofas were inexpensive, but the house was large and welcoming, like my grandmother, whose hand I clung to for dear life right now. I looked over at Albert, standing aloof at the foot of the burial site, kissed Grandma on the cheek, and walked over to him. He took my hand and I smiled into his face.

"You can't marry a nigger!" said my mother.

Albert straightened up and said, "I am a Negro, Mrs. Johnson." He squeezed my hand. "With Egyptian blood."

My mother stared at Albert. "A nigger is a nigger. I don't care if you're related to King Tut. You're not marrying my daughter! I will not have black blood in the family."

I went over to my mother and said. "I'm sorry that you don't approve of our union, Mother, but the decision is mine, not yours. I'm an adult, and know what I'm doing. I'll continue my studies at Berkeley. After I graduate, I'll get a job and send you money from my paychecks."

Undaunted, my mother said, "I don't want his money."

Albert blinked and said, "Inny said she'd send you her money, not mine."

"Shut up, you, you…" My mother fell to the ground and started writhing around. We all tried to calm her. She shouted over and over, "My life is ruined! What will your little sister do?"

"We'll help you, Iris," said my grandmother as she leaned her shrunken, stout self over to try to embrace my mother, which was nearly impossible, as she stood up and ran. We ran after her. Albert got to her before she reached the cliff of the Montecito Cemetery, which stood some thirty feet above the ocean.

"Don't!" he said, grabbing her by the arm.

"Don't touch me, you… you nigger!" She pulled her arm away and tried to hurl herself over the cliff, but my cousin had run after Albert and grabbed her by the other arm.

"Aunt Iris," he cried, "don't do that!"

She wrested herself free and ran to the edge of the cliff, the tranquil Pacific Ocean below her. Albert and Uncle Jimmy ran after her with the rest of us holding our collective breath.

Lovely blue waves rolled onto the narrow beach below. A few sandpipers ran about, burrowing their beaks in the sand for food. *How nice my mother would look, sprawled on that beach,* ran through my churning brain after she had repudiated Albert, calling him a nigger even.

My mother sat down and started to slide over the cliff. Albert grabbed her arm as she slid. She looked down at the narrow beach below, which had some rocks on it. She looked back at Albert. Her face had changed to one of terror.

"Let me help you, Mrs. Johnson," begged Albert. "You don't want to die."

She looked at the sand, rocks, and water below. She stopped struggling and let Albert start to pull her back to the edge of the cliff. Once he had her on solid ground, she said, "Your skin isn't *that* black."

"I'm part Egyptian, Mrs. Johnson." Albert turned his aquiline profile for her to examine. She moaned and stood up, brushing herself off. "Inny, you're going to pay for this!"

A scream pierced the air. We turned to see my little sister hurl herself onto my father's coffin, which had just been lowered into his grave. "Kendra!" shrieked my mother, suicidal impulses milked from her mind in a fleeting instant.

We ran to the gravesite to extricate my sister. She was bleeding from where her head had hit the hard coffin, which was made of chrome that gleamed in the sun. Jimmy pulled her out with the help of his father. She was conscious, but she'd hurt herself. I staggered, feeling faint. I felt Albert's arm steady me. I looked up into his face, his brow furrowed, tears forming in his eyes. We were both on the brink of tears. It was then that I saw my grandmother sit down hard on the rolling hill of the Santa Barbara Cemetery.

"Grandma!" I ran to her. I sat down next to her to try to console her. Her cane had fallen with her. Our whole family was coming apart at the seams. Since I was the oldest daughter, I felt it was up to me to try to steady the ship, but I was feeling far from steady. I saw tears streaming down her face under the veil of her little black hat, no doubt bought in a bargain basement. All her years of sacrifice for her family, and now she had to witness this. It was so unfair. I held her to me as tight as I could. I could feel her old heart beating next to mine. I thought of the heart attack Grandpa had died of a few years ago. Not Grandma, too! Incongruous thoughts spun through my head. Then, I felt Albert's sure hands lift us up. Grandma looked into his dark face and began to smile. "Thank you, doll baby," she said. It was so out of context that we laughed.

Aunt Edna and Uncle Jimmy had staunched Kendra's head wound with a stocking that Aunt Edna took off. Kendra sniffled, but she stood upright and looked like she'd be okay after some medical attention. But how could she and my mother continue to live in Montecito? There was so much to be determined, way too much.

I looked at my father's gravesite out of the corner of my eye while trying to also keep an eye on my sister and mother. Overwhelmed by the enormity of my father's suicide, they'd lost their minds. I hoped they'd be able to regain their senses. My mother would have to find a job, something she hadn't done since she married Daddy. My head reeled. Albert steadied me. I reached out for my grandmother's hand, who limped over to my mother and said, "I can give you money, Iris." Grandma always gave and often got taken. My mother nodded, although I don't think she really understood that Grandma had just offered to make a tremendous sacrifice for her.

My mother walked over to us, her veiled hat askew and hair mussed up, her dark dress rumpled. "How much?" she asked, ever practical, even after a suicide attempt.

Grandma squinted up at her, the sun beaming brightly on her wizened, wrinkled old face. "As much as I can afford, Honey," she said.

My mother's face brightened. "Kendra's still in school. The house isn't paid off yet…"

"Don't worry, Iris, I've saved a lot that I intend to leave you and Edna."

My mother smiled while Aunt Edna perked her ears at the sound of her name. "You're always giving your money away!" said Aunt Edna. We knew that Aunt Edna hadn't spoken to Grandma since she found out that she was paying half of Margaret's rent in a small apartment she'd rented after Grandpa sold the family home and moved her to Lake Worth, Florida to be near his sisters. Grandma had tried to make amends by offering Aunt Edna money, but Aunt Edna was a proud woman. She tore Grandma's checks in half and mailed them back to her. When Grandma came to visit her relatives in Arlington, she no longer stayed with Aunt Edna, but rather Margaret, the country woman whom she'd rented a room to for over twenty years. Grandma rented her daughters' rooms after they left, mostly for the companionship. My grandfather already spent most of his time on a dairy farm he'd bought with mistresses although we were told he was helping the Robey's run the farm. Somehow the truth seeped out, as truth tends to do, and Grandma took in boarders out of loneliness.

The caretakers had finished covering my father's grave, but no one paid attention, though I glimpsed them put the final shovelful of dirt and sod over it. I tried to disengage myself from my grandmother's arm to place the flowers Albert and I had brought, but she held on to me for dear life.

The Methodist minister stood over it, holding the Bible, his jaw agape. He'd never seen a funeral like this before. And my father wasn't really Methodist. His father was a Mormon, so Daddy had no religion, although he'd gone to church with the rest of us.

"May Craig Grant Johnson rest in peace," the minister said.

We turned and chorused, "Rest in peace." I looked down at Grandma, who held onto her bargain basement purse with both hands, like a little bird gripping a branch for dear life, and then up at Albert, who squeezed my arm and smiled.

"It's going to be all right," he said. I nodded my head, hoping he was right.

The minister picked up his raiment and turned to leave. We continued to tend to our family members, now riven by shock and sadness. My grandmother walked over to my mother, who started mutely at the gravesite, freshly covered with sod, and said, "Iris, you know I can help you and Kendra." My mother turned her head and looked out at the ocean. She was in another world. I couldn't imagine her without my father. My sister held her head and wept next to my aunt and uncle. My cousin tried to jostle her arm to make her feel better, but she pulled away from him.

I loosened Albert's grip on my arm and ran to my little sister. I put my arm around her slender, young waist and hugged her. She resisted at first; then, she sagged into my arms. "Daddy, Daddy," she whimpered like a hurt puppy.

"It's going to be all right, Kendra," I told her, not the least bit convinced it would be, but what else could I say to my 15-year-old sister? One who had been Daddy's favorite, 'Daddy's Little Helper' as he had called her, and 'Bright Eyes,' because she could find his glasses when he lost them. "This isn't going to be easy, but life will go on. You'll go back to school and be with your friends. Mother can get a job, and Grandma can help out until things have settled."

"What about you?" she sniffed.

"I'm going to graduate from Berkeley and… and marry Albert. We'll help you, too. He's a wonderful person and would give his right arm to help us. You'll see. He's my mainstay."

Kendra looked up at me in surprise.

"You heard me," I said. "Now try to buck up. You can handle this, although we may need some counselling. We'll be all right!"

Albert walked towards me with the whole family watching. He hugged me and my sister gently. He turned to face the others and said, "I know I'm not white, but I'm a full professor at Berkeley and I'll take care of Inny and the rest of the family. I have nothing but love in my heart for you."

"You, you, you…" sputtered my mother.

"Now, Iris, give him a chance!" said Grandma, wiping her eyes with a white handkerchief.

My uncle stepped forward and shook Albert's outstretched hand. "I got nothing against black folks, and if you're a professor at that fancy university, you must have studied hard. I welcome you into our family."

Albert shook his hand and grinned his megawatt smile at Uncle Jimmy, Aunt Edna, Jimmie, and my mother, who looked down at the ground.

"Mother, what about Andronicus? How could you?" I looked my mother in the eye. I wanted answers.

She tried to push her way past me, but I grabbed her by the arm. "What were you thinking?"

"You've always had everything!" she stared at me. "Boys, boys with rich fathers, like my own, running after you, taking you to nice places… I wanted to go to the San Ysidro Ranch. I wanted to live like a rich woman…" she started to cry. I put my arm around her.

"It's okay, Mother. It's good to talk about it. You have to… We have to… We have to help each other."

She put her arm around my waist. She'd never done that before. We began to cry as she hugged me to her. I could feel her desperation like never before.

"You and Kendra can live together while she finishes high school and college," said my grandmother to my mother. I looked at my wizened, aged, and crippled grandma, squinting at us and leaning heavily on her plain black cane.

"But Grandma needs even more help. Look at her! I want you to come live with us, Grandma," came out of my mouth. It was true. She was crippled up, old, and alone. I loved her and wanted to take care of her.

Grandma and I stared into each other's eyes. She blinked hard into the bright sunlight which contrasted with this dark day. Then, she said, "I'd just be in the way, Inny honey."

"She'd be better off with us," inserted my mother, taking control. I looked at my feet, realizing she was probably right, but I still wanted Grandma to stay with me.

"You'll never be in the way. I'll take care of you and finish college. You'll love Berkeley and my friends will love you. They always have." This was true. Grandma nodded like a little hen, limping along. I kissed her on the cheek. Tears rolled down her crinkled face.

She reached out and touched my cheek. "Inny honey, I think your mother needs my help right now, though I don't want to be a burden on her. But, I can pay for all our expenses while she…" She looked into my face, unable to find the right words. I nodded my head. She was right.

"You could sleep in my old bedroom there and help Mother until she's on solid footing again. I'll graduate and get a job so I can pitch in when I can." I rubbed her gnarled hand.

She squinted up at me from her shrunken size, now less than five feet tall, for age had done her no favors. She nodded her head. "I think it's for the best, Honey," she said. She rubbed my hand and I squeezed hers. Tears sprang from my eyes. Grandma never thought of herself. "I can rent my apartment in Florida and move out here. It's for the best."

We started to walk away from the gravesite, linked arm in arm. A plaque bearing my father's name was being placed on it with the flowers we'd brought. No one looked back to see. The thought of our beloved father dead and gone staggered our minds. It was hard to believe.

Thoughts spun through my head. *What about Grandma?* I took a deep breath, resolute. I would shoulder the responsibilities and do my best to keep our family together. I knew it would be tough, because I was young and still had to graduate from Berkeley. Albert glanced at me from a distance. He smiled. I could count on him; we would pull through.

He walked over and put his arm through her other arm. She smiled up at him. "My father is a doctor. He can help you with your limp."

"Glory be!" said Grandma, beaming at him.

I felt happiness course through my veins.

I reached up, hugging Albert with all my might. He kissed me, whispering, "I love you."

Grandma grinned, and a tear trickled down her cheek.